UNINVITED GUESTS

J. Jefferson Farjeon

Spitfire Publishers

CONTENTS

ABOUT 'UNINVITED GUESTS'

To Brambles, a dilapidated yet comfortable English country house, come the uninvited guests: a motley crew, who appear at the most unexpected hours and on the most impossible errands. Singly and in procession they arrive to trouble the calm of Ambrose Blythe, sexagenarian owner of Brambles, and of Peter Haslam, his house guest. Add to these an imperturbable butler, a tragic-eyed damsel and the super-logician Detective Grant to complete the ingredients of the perfect Golden Age of Crime story.

About the Author

Joseph Jefferson Farjeon was born into a literary family in Hampstead, north west London in 1883. He was a prolific crime writer, writing over sixty novels over the course of thirty years, many published by William Collins & Sons and featuring in their hugely popular Collins Crime Club. Dorothy L. Sayers said of his work, 'every word is entertaining.' His best-known novel (and play) *Number 17*, was made into a film by Alfred Hitchcock. He died in 1955.

Praise for Uninvited Guests

'An ingenious country house mystery… absorbing'
New York Times

Praise for J. Jefferson Farjeon

CHAPTER 1

Peter Haslam paused on the side of the hill. His soul was filled with a huge satisfaction. Fifty yards away, on a little green plateau, an artist sat at her easel. Beyond, the broken forest continued on its way, slipping down gently to rustic roofs and to one particularly pleasant line of thin blue smoke. "The inn," reflected Haslam, "where there is always the best fire." Above the village, his sensitive nature glimpsed, or his imaginative nature created, an atmosphere of brooding. And he was being followed.

Nothing could have fitted better into his mood. Here were atmosphere and adventure, which he had left London to seek, and the intangible warmth of an unknown feminine presence. But Haslam was a careful man, as well as an adventurous one, and he decided that the adventure behind him must be investigated. So he stopped, and turned slowly round.

The comforting village was now behind his back. Ahead of him lay the thick wood through which he had walked. Apparently, the man who was following him decided that this was the moment to reveal himself, for he came out of the trees, and advanced with a certain air of caution. He was a tall, lantern-jawed fellow, with a long thin nose, and bright mobile eyes. Had Haslam realised what was destined to be the nature of his last meeting with this man, he would have been even more interested than he was in the first.

"Well?" queried Haslam, as the man drew near. "You evidently want to see me?"

"I have been following you, I admit," replied the lantern-jawed one.

"And I will admit that I have been perfectly aware of it," said Haslam, pleasantly. "Let me satisfy your most apparent curiosity. My name is Peter Haslam. I am sorry that does not seem to impress you. I have written several bad books, and one rather good one. From your expression, if it means anything at all, I gather you have only read the bad ones. I hope that my next, however, will be ever so much better, and I am now on the hunt for atmosphere. No, that is not quite correct. I *was* on the hunt for atmosphere." He waved his hand around. "I have found it."

The lantern-jawed man did not seem to know how to take this voluble information. He frowned at his informant, studying him.

"Perhaps," suggested Haslam, "you have never seen a real, live author before? We're quite interesting."

Then the manner of the lantern-jawed man changed. He straightened himself, and became business-like.

"You'll excuse me, sir," he announced, shortly, "but I'm looking for a lunatic."

"Indeed?" murmured Haslam.

"That's so. Well, now I've had an opportunity of studying you, I've come to the conclusion you're not the particular one I'm looking for. Good-day."

And, lifting his hat, he was gone.

Haslam smiled, and stopped to light a cigarette before descending into the village. He had to admit that the lantern-jawed man had scored. The admission did not distress him, but he hoped vaguely that he would meet the man again some day in order that he might reinstate himself.

"No, I don't like the fellow," he thought, "but I must certainly call, 'Touché.'"

He threw the match down, and resumed his way.

The artist saw him coming. She had been waiting patiently for him to move out of the way of a silver birch, in order that she might reproduce the sunlight effect upon its bark. She knew she could not reproduce it, because she knew she was a very bad artist, but she believed in trying. One soulless critic, indeed, had

4

unkindly described her pictures as studies in effort. For several seconds after Haslam had walked clear of the birch, she held her brush poised; then, suddenly, worked assiduously.

Many of Haslam's friends considered him a trifle prudish. Although he had genuinely artistic aspirations, and hoped to do big things one day, he did not live a Bohemian life or frequent studios. With marked rigidness, he refused to make his work an excuse for women—he had too much innate respect for each— and the somewhat loose habits of some of his professional acquaintances worried him considerably. Puritan blood flowed in his veins, humanised by some real understanding of human needs, and modernised by a twentieth century sense of humour.

But he was perplexed, as he strolled down the hill, to find his steps lagging, and his mind seeking an excuse to make them stop. The artist looked delicious, if absurdly prim amidst her romantic surroundings. Or did she really look prim? There was something roguish about the nose, and, although her golden hair—"really golden," reflected Haslam—was sedately coiled, it seemed to suggest that it could uncoil, if it chose, into two delightful pig-tails.

Suddenly, he found his excuse, and it was so simple that it astonished him. It was less of an excuse than a necessity.

"Excuse me," he began.

She stopped painting immediately, and regarded him with polite interest.

"The way to the village," she said, pointing with her brush, "is down that path."

"Thank you," replied Haslam, smiling, "but that wasn't the question I was going to ask you."

"No?" She regarded him for a moment, thoughtfully. Then, her instinct divining that he was harmless, she observed, "Perhaps you want to admire my picture?" Haslam's eyes became sober, as they turned towards the little canvas. Her next remark rather startled him. "Horrible, isn't it?" she said.

"Not at all," he murmured.

"It's a disappointment to hear you say that," she retorted.

"You looked truthful."

Haslam was about to laugh, but stopped himself. He was not sure whether to be amused or not. There was a humorous twist to her mouth, yet, somehow or other, she made a pathetic figure. Once more, the elusive quality about her baffled him.

"I've seen many worse pictures in shop windows——"

"I expect they were mine."

This time, he did laugh.

"I see, you object to kindness," he said, "but I am going to be kind to you, just the same. Not about your picture, though. Do you know there's a lunatic at large?"

"Is this a joke?" she answered, promptly.

"No. Or, if it is, I've no share in it. A fellow told me just now that he was looking for a madman—you may have seen us talking together up there?" He nodded towards the woods. "He imagined at first that I was his quarry, but I managed to convince him that I wasn't. Well . . . that's what I stopped to tell you. I thought you might like to know."

"It was very nice of you—really nice, you know." She looked at him musingly. "You don't think, by any chance, that *he* was the lunatic?"

Haslam smiled.

"It didn't occur to me. He might have been."

"I saw the man. He came down the hill, just before you did, while; you were lighting your cigarette——"

"Oh! You noticed that?"

"Why not? You were standing in the way of a silver birch I was waiting to mutilate. He turned off to the left there." She looked towards the thicket in which the lantern-jawed man had disappeared. Then she shook her head. "No—I don't think he was a lunatic."

"In that case," remarked Haslam, "we have no means of knowing who or where the lunatic is, or even of identifying him when we see him. So, if I were you, I would pack up my things and go home."

"Oh, but I must finish this picture," she protested.

"Couldn't you finish it tomorrow?"

"Probably not. We artists can only work when we're inspired, you know." She frowned at the canvas. "I feel that, if I don't finish this picture now, I never will. Think what that would mean! The world would lose a masterpiece, and I would lose—" She paused. "How much do you think I'd lose?"

"I'm not good at guessing."

"Prove it."

"Well—twenty guineas?"

She burst into laughter.

"You have proved it! No, not guineas—shillings—if the shopman were in a good mood."

"I wonder what it is," thought Peter Haslam, "that makes this comic creature so tragic!"

There was a silence. The comic creature began to fidget with her paint brush.

"I'm no good with audiences," she hinted, rather nervously, "unless they're quite small boys with their mouths open. I've got used to them."

"Then—you're going to finish the picture?" he asked.

"Yes. I thought I'd told you. But thank you very much."

"And you don't mind about the lunatic?"

A sudden gleam flashed into her eye.

"There are worse things than lunatics about here," she murmured.

He waited for an explanation, but she did not give it. She did vouchsafe the remark, however, as he turned to go, "I wasn't referring to you, you know."

"Thank you," said Haslam, lifting his hat gravely. "I'm glad."

He continued on his way, refusing the temptation to look back. Even had he done so, he would probably have missed the two tears which slipped from the artist's eyes, for she brushed them away quickly, and began to daub the silver birch with disfiguring yellow light.

CHAPTER 2

The pleasant line of thin blue smoke proved a true guide to the inn, and the fire came up to expectations. The afternoon had been warm, but the sun was climbing down to the tree-tops, and there was a little tang in the air that made the big burning logs very acceptable. Peter Haslam slipped his pack off his back, and sank into a faded, comfortable armchair with a sigh of content.

The maid who came for his order was not of the Mayfair breed. She would have been an amazing and distracting blot in any perfectly-equipped and smoothly-run basement. But here, amid lenient rusticity, she was a queen of her kind, a gem of unsophistication. She would have seemed positively blemished in Haslam's eyes had she appeared without a smut on her left cheek, a shoe which had the greatest difficulty in retaining its position on her foot as she slid it along, a rich accent, and a mouth ouvert.

"What will you be 'avin', zur?" she asked.

"What have you got?" replied Haslam.

She pondered, heavily.

"'Am," she said. "Or heggs."

"I'll have both," smiled Haslam, delighted in his secret heart that, even at the expense of variety, the insular tradition was upheld. "And a big pot of tea."

The maid slithered out of the room, keeping her recalcitrant shoe with a dexterity born only of long practice, and, through the half-closed door, Haslam heard the comfortable sounds of preparations. After roasting himself at the fire, he rose, and walked to the window.

The inn was on a corner. The village did not appear to boast a definite street. Long shadows licked across the lanes, and little black specks came winging from the blue uncharted heights, to drop into the trees and quarrel before settling down. A dog rushed out into the road, barked fiercely at nothing, and rushed back again.

"And yet," sighed Haslam, "I live in London, and will return to it! What fools we mortals be!"

But it was not only the rustic comfort of the place that welled into him as he returned to his armchair to await the arrival of the ham and eggs and the big pot of tea. In fact, apart from his present warm and pleasant sanctuary, there was a curious bleakness, a picturesque wildness, about the land he was in. He could not explain it. He did not try to, for a mystery explained loses its lure. Instead, he settled down into it, with a sort of literary gloating, and visualised a little room somewhere about the inn where he would be able to spread out manuscript paper and litter it with ink! Yes, the strange loneliness of the place, the sense of brooding, with a golden thread weaving through it somewhere, pleased him immensely.

The slither approached, and the meal was placed before him. The rustic Jane left him unwillingly, as though it would afford her strange pleasure to watch him eat, and twice she returned on small pretexts, once to enquire whether the "heggs were to his liking," and the second time to bring him a second, superfluous salt-cellar.

Haslam pointed to the one already there.

"Ain't I zilly, now?" exclaimed rustic Jane.

"Well, two's company," laughed Haslam; and, to his dismay, she chose to take the remark personally, and stayed.

However, he did not feel seriously compromised, and made the best of it.

"What's the name of this village?" he asked.

Astonishment spread over her features, and the mouth ouvert became more ouvert. Then,

"'Eysham," she told him.

"Heysham. Well, it's a charming place. I think I shall be staying here for a few days. Have you a vacant room here?"

The question seemed to please her.

"Yes, zur," she answered. "A nice room."

"I'll go and see it presently," he said. "And, if it's really nice, I'll book it for a week. I shall have some things sent down from London. By the way, where's the nearest station?"

"That's over at Wynton, zur."

"How far?"

"That's three or four mile."

"Excellent," exclaimed Haslam. "Then we're right off the beaten track."

This remark appeared to be too much for her. She slithered out of the room, and returned in the rear of the innkeeper.

"You're wanting a room, sir?" asked the innkeeper, civilly.

"Yes, please. For a week."

"I'll 'ave it got ready at once, sir." He turned to rustic Jane. "Go you and put No. 5 in order." He spoke as though she ought to have done it for the gentleman before. She slithered away. Suddenly the innkeeper added, "P'r'aps you'd like some 'ot water, sir, for a wash?"

Haslam nodded, the innkeeper departed with great bustle, and the meal was concluded in peace.

An hour later, Haslam descended from the room in which he was clearly going to write his best novel, clean, refreshed, and with only one serious problem troubling him.

"I'm going out," he said, as he passed the innkeeper. "I don't know when I shall be back."

"That's all right, sir," nodded the innkeeper. "It don't make no dif'rence to us. You'll be taking supper, sir?"

"Yes, I expect so. I can't say. Don't get anything ready till I return."

"Very good, sir."

Haslam hesitated, in the porch.

"Oh, by the way," he said, casually, "have you heard anything about a lunatic who's supposed to have escaped about here?"

"Lunatic, sir?" The innkeeper's brow furrowed. "No, sir. I ain't 'eard nothing."

"You haven't?"

"No, sir. Lunatic? Where from?"

"Can't say," replied Haslam. "Well—perhaps I've made a mistake."

He walked out into the lane, and turned immediately in the direction of the wooded heights through which he had walked a few hours earlier, and in which the little green plateau nestled like a bright memory, smiling amid shadows. The woods were to the east of the village, and the long shadows pointed towards them.

As he neared the plateau, he discovered that his steps were hastening, and he slackened them, with a guilty smile. The plateau itself proved empty, saving for a little dot of white at the far end. He walked across to the white dot, and picked it up. It was a lady's small handkerchief, bearing the initials "M.H."

Pocketing the handkerchief, Haslam turned his footsteps towards the thicket through which the lantern-jawed man had disappeared. He had no expectation that it would lead him to any useful discovery, nor was he even convinced that any useful discovery lay waiting anywhere for his eyes; but he had no set plan, and one way was as good as another. He walked through the thicket, and was faintly surprised to find that it did not appear to lead anywhere. In fact, the foliage soon gathered so closely around him that he returned in preference to fighting his way through and emerging with a network of scratches. Back at the plateau, with the darkness growing up around him, he quelled a foolish impulse to take out the little handkerchief and look at it, and bore to the left, down the hill, and back towards the village again.

He was deciding to return to the inn when a blackbird suddenly emitted a clear, liquid note, and altered the whole course of his life.

Had the blackbird not chosen that moment to sing, Haslam would not have looked up; and, not looking up, he would have missed the lure of a particularly charming lane. He needed just that charming vista to dissuade him from returning to the inn, and a rabbit scurrying across the lane settled the question. Obeying a faint impulse, he turned up the lane, and walked towards the heart of the mystery whose intangible, unseen fingers had already laid themselves lightly upon his imagination.

The fingers pressed upon him less lightly now. A curious activity seemed to be stirring within him. He walked forward, still without any definite purpose, but with a definite sense of expectation. This expectation often comes to us, though it does not always materialise. Maybe, at such moments, we are nearing some poignant experience, or are ready to receive it, but are diverted by some second little incident, as trivial as the first that drew us close. Another blackbird, had it sung and tempted Haslam away up another turning, would have thwarted the adventure that was now drawing him onward.

But the second blackbird did not sing. If it existed, it had no emotion to express, and merely looked down with a drowsy eye on the traveller who wended his way through the darkening country, puffing at his pipe, and divided between the familiar associations of its smoke and the unfamiliar fancies into which the smoke rose and disappeared.

Haslam could not say how long he had walked, for he lost count of time, but darkness had started in earnest when, having answered the beckoning of a narrow path through a hedge, he suddenly found himself in a wide, tree-bordered carriage-drive.

"Hallo!" he thought. "I'm trespassing!"

The gate of the drive, leading on to the lane, was a little way to his right, and he was about to make for it when he threw his eyes casually towards the left—and stopped abruptly.

At the end of the drive, a light gleamed, and the faint outline of a house was dimly revealed through the foliage. But it was not the light or the house that made Peter Haslam pause. It was a figure—a female figure—and something in its attitude arrested his attention.

Unconsciously, he stepped back into the full shadow of the

trees, watching the figure for any sign of movement. The figure did not make any movement, however, for several seconds. Its pose was one of doubt, and hesitation. Then, it turned, and walked slowly down the drive, towards Haslam and the gate. Haslam remained still, more securely hidden than he realised by the tree shadows. When the figure was abreast of him, something familiar about the lines struck him, and he advanced with a smile.

The girl looked up, startled. Haslam could not say whether she recognised him in the gloaming or not. The next moment, she was running down the drive, and was out of the gate before Haslam had recovered from his astonishment.

"Confound it!" thought Haslam, hesitating. "What did that mean?"

The idea of a chase did not appeal to him. There was no excuse for it. But a great disappointment swept over him as he looked towards the lane in which the girl had vanished—the owner of the little handkerchief bearing the initials "M.H."

Well—that was that! He supposed he had better follow her, though at a more dignified pace; for, while he had no right to chase her, neither had he any right to remain where he was. Then it occurred to him that, although she had disappeared, the house had not, and a curiosity concerning the house began to assail him. Did she live there? If not, what was the object of her visit—if she had visited it? If she had not—why had she hesitated?

"These are absurd questions," reflected Peter Haslam, "and nothing whatever to do with me. All the same, if I don't ring the bell of that house, I shall be waking up with a big query mark all night long. . . . I have lost myself. I want to know the way back to Heysham. Here goes!"

And he strode up the drive to the house, and rang the bell.

CHAPTER 3

The door was opened by a grave butler, who gave Haslam the odd impression that the door had not been opened at all; for the grave butler looked like another door, not merely made of wood, that could be hammered in, but made of flesh and blood, and possessing a mind. In the very first moment, the mind ranged itself against the idea of entrance.

Something rebellious rose in Haslam's breast. He had intended merely to ask the way back to Heysham, but now he deliberately prolonged the situation by enquiring,

"Can you tell me where I am? I've lost my way."

The butler regarded him suspiciously, while Haslam sought to gain a glimpse of the interior, blocked mainly by the butler's form. He got a vague impression of a very pleasant hall, and of a shadowy form hovering somewhere in the background. Then the butler spoke.

"There's no place nearer than Heysham," he said, shortly, and attempted to close the door.

But Peter Haslam had his foot frankly in the aperture. After all, he argued, this treatment was unnecessarily brusque. He had done nothing to deny himself the privilege owned by any traveller of enquiring the way.

"Heysham," he said, slowly, "Thank you. I've just come from there."

"That's right—there's nowhere nearer," repeated the butler, and again tried to shut the door.

Haslam felt his anger rising, but he hardly ever let his anger get the better of him.

"In that case," he said, coolly, "perhaps you will be good enough to tell me the way?"

Before the butler could reply, the voice of the shadowy form at the back of the hall made itself audible.

"Show him in, show him in!" cried the voice.

This sudden invitation surprised Haslam. It also appeared to disturb the butler. But when the order was repeated, with sharp insistence, the butler stopped hesitating, and with a hardly perceptible shrug, stood aside.

Haslam walked into the hall, and glancing round shrewdly, noticed its atmosphere of old-world comfort. Clearly, this was not the habitation of some profiteer who had bought the place and made antiquity the tortured groundwork for an ostentatious display; nor had it the preserved appearance of well-ordered and highly-polished traditions, such as one might expect to meet in a proud ancestral home. It was "comfortable-old," a place where man and ghost could meet on more or less of an equality.

"Don't keep him standing there, Pike!" cried the old man in the background. "Come in, sir, come in!"

"Very good of you," murmured Haslam, not certain that he wanted to come in, now that the invitation was so definitely extended. "I have only come to enquire the way back to Heysham."

"Well, it's complicated," snorted the old man. "Step into my library, and I'll tell you all you want to know."

Haslam advanced, and the old man's eyes burned into his as he approached. Then, without a word, he held the study door open, and Haslam passed in.

"Now, sir," exclaimed the old man, following him. "Now, sir. We can talk. You say you want to know the way to Heysham, eh? Ah! And how did you get lost?"

"It's really a perfectly simple process," replied Haslam, "in these lanes. Particularly when you're a stranger."

"Ah! You're a stranger, eh?"

"I only arrived at Heysham a few hours ago."

"And what, may I ask, are you doing in Heysham?"

This was going quite beyond the limit. Haslam decided that some definite attitude must be adopted, and he studied the old man before replying. His host was aggressive, but behind the aggression there was uneasiness, and Haslam found it difficult to be as angry as he had a right to be.

"Why are you asking me all these questions?" he enquired, quietly.

"Why do I ask them?" repeated the old man, frowning dubiously. "You don't know, eh? Is that what you're going to tell me? You don't know, eh?"

"I certainly do not know," answered Haslam.

"Then why the devil ain't you cross with me?" demanded the old man, with sudden shrewdness. "Ah, now! Explain that!"

"To be honest, I hardly know how to explain it," said Haslam, with a faint smile. "Perhaps it's because I feel sure that you are labouring under some extraordinary delusion——"

"Delusion!" The old man laughed ironically. "That's funny! Delusion! The whole thing's a delusion, is it?"

"If you will listen to me for two minutes, you will find out your mistake," Haslam assured him, patiently. "I really ought to be very angry with you. But I'm sure your explanation will be as reasonable as mine, so I'll wait for it. My name is Peter Haslam ——"

"Hi! Wait a minute!" cried the old man. "Let's prove that!"

He rose, and went to a bookcase.

"Now, then, Mr Peter Haslam," he exclaimed. "You wrote a novel called 'The Brothers.' A damned good novel, too! How does it start?"

He opened the book, and stared at the first page while Haslam regarded him smilingly.

"If I remember rightly," responded the author, "a cock crows in the very first sentence."

"Aha! He does!" A change came over the old man's face. Suddenly, in a moment, it had become friendly, and full of relief. "And how does it end?" he chuckled, turning to the last page. "Does a cow moo, hey? Or a dog bark?"

"No," laughed Haslam. "He takes her in his arms and kisses her."

The old man closed the book with a grunt of satisfaction, put it away, and came forward with outstretched hand.

"If you're Peter Haslam, the author, you need say no more, sir," he exclaimed. "I apologise. And Pike shall apologise. Gad, you must think me a queer fish! But when I've told you my story, you'll understand. You'll not be cross. You'll see that I had every *right* to cross-examine you! Yes, by Gad, you will!"

"I'm sure I shall, before you begin," said Haslam. "But let me tell you my very simple story first. I left London three days ago, hoping to find atmosphere for a new book I'm working on. I've found it at Heysham, which I reached this afternoon——"

"You'd find more here," murmured the old man, softly.

"And so I'm putting up at the inn there, and shall stay awhile."

"You're staying? Good!"

"Thank you," replied Haslam, somewhat overwhelmed by this sudden transition from enmity to friendship. "Yes, I'm staying. Before reaching the village, I met a man who said he was looking for a lunatic. Do you know anything about it?"

"Did he only say one?" cackled the old man. "My dear boy, this place is full of 'em! Full of 'em!" Suddenly he grew serious. "That's only my joke, of course. No—I don't know anything about an escaped lunatic. Well, what else?"

"There's very little else," replied Haslem, hesitating. He wondered whether to mention his two encounters with the girl, and obeyed his instinct to leave them out. "I couldn't tell the man anything, and haven't seen him since. But it did occur to me, at one moment, that you might think I was the madman."

"Couldn't have," retorted the old man, shaking his head. "Didn't know of his existence. Well, here's *my* story." He hesitated, fishing about for words. "Sounds silly, I know—but there it is. This place is—is haunted, sir, by uninvited visitors." He stared at Haslam, and Haslam suddenly read real fear in the old man's eyes. But the fear was gone again, in a flash. "Yes, sir! Did you ever hear anything like it?"

"I don't think I did," replied Haslam. "To be frank, I don't think I know what you mean. Ghosts?"

"Ghosts!" scoffed the old fellow. "Not a bit of it. I'd know what to do with ghosts. I'd say 'Shoo!' to 'em. No, sir. These are real, live, flesh-and-blood fellers. I thought you were one of them. They come here at all times, and it's getting on my nerves. I'm beginning to wonder what's at the bottom of it."

"It certainly sounds odd," admitted Haslam.

"Odd's not the word," said the old man. "It's uncanny!"

"How often do they come?"

"It varies—it varies. By the way, I've not told you my name. It's Blythe—Ambrose Blythe. Sometimes, three or four a week, perhaps. Not enough to notice. Sometimes, none at all. Sometimes, three or four an evening." He threw up his hands in an impotent gesture. "How am I to know? I made a mistake about you. Some of the others may be just harmless folk, too. They all may be! But are they? Well—that's what I'm wondering."

"This is exceedingly interesting—" said Haslam.

"For an author," interposed Ambrose Blythe, "your adjectives are ridiculously weak!"

"Well, absorbing," corrected Haslam. "I agree with you. 'Interesting' was weak. But I've still not quite got the hang of it——"

"Stay to dinner, and you will," cried the old man. "I'm expecting a crowd tonight. Maybe it's a cyclist, who wants water for a puncture, or else a traveller who's lost his way, like yourself. Or perhaps it's a passer-by who enquires whether Mr So-and-so or Mrs What's-her-name lives here. They've always got some logical pretext to give Pike—always sound quite logical and reasonable. But there's too many of 'em—too many. Do you think I'm a superstitious old fool, eh?"

"Not at all," answered Haslam, seriously. "I agree with you that there's probably something in it."

His mind went back to the scared girl in the drive; but still he did not mention her.

"Well, I didn't rush to any conclusions," resumed Mr Blythe, "and I said at first that maybe I was getting old, and too much alone—and then, you see, the quietness of the place, eh? Yes, I put it all aside at first. But now I'm sure there's something behind it, and I decided only today that I'd interview the lot myself—here, in this room." He broke off, with a laugh. "And, by Gad, Peter Haslam, the author, was the first!"

Haslam joined in the laugh. He was warming wonderfully to this queer, humorous, nervous old man. The mystery, too, fascinated him.

"Were you serious when you asked me to dine with you tonight?" he said.

"Indeed, I was!" returned Ambrose Blythe, cordially. "I'd like nothing better. Stop and interview the rascals with me, eh? Maybe you'll handle 'em better."

"I'll be delighted," answered Peter Haslam. "The way you dealt with me, you know, did rather lack finesse."

Mr Blythe stopped suddenly in the middle of a chuckle, and raised his head. Someone was ringing the front-door bell.

CHAPTER 4

Ambrose Blythe and Peter Haslam looked at each other, and neither moved until the bell had stopped ringing.

"There, you see?" muttered Mr Blythe. "Just as we were talking about it. Coincidence, eh? D'ye think so?"

Haslam shook his head, and the old man went to the door, opening it a crack.

"We'll let Pike open the door, then pounce," he whispered, listening.

"As you did with me," replied Haslam, smiling.

He smiled, but he was intensely curious, and did not feel in the least impelled to take the matter lightly. He listened, with his host, to the steps of Pike as they came along the passage from the kitchen, and then grew fainter again as they approached the front-door. The door was heard to open, and a feeble, high-pitched voice floated in from outside.

"Can you help a poor blind man, please, who's lost 'is road?" piped the voice.

Mr Blythe opened the door suddenly, and strode forward.

"Ay, that we can," he exclaimed, taking charge with an abruptness that surprised the sedate butler. "Step in, my poor fellow. I've always got a soft spot for the blind."

"Ah, it's very good of you, sir," whined the blind man, "but I'm only wanting to be put upon the road. I've lost my son——"

"Then maybe we can find him for you," interposed Mr Blythe, laying his hand upon the beggar's shoulder. "Come inside, my good fellow. And, Pike, make a cup of tea, and send it up to the library."

"The library, sir?" queried Pike, his orthodox ideas slightly ruffled.

"Yes, Pike. And be quick about it. The fellow's got the shivers!"

"You're very good to a poor man," murmured the beggar. "It's many an hour since I 'ad a cup o' something warm inside me." He shuffled along, beside Mr Blythe, and guided by him. "God's blessing be upon you, my good sir, whoever you may be."

Haslam opened the library door wide as they passed through; and, a minute later, they were all seated.

"My man'll have a cup of tea ready for you in a moment," said Mr Blythe, with a glance at Haslam, "and, while we're waiting, suppose you tell us your story, eh?"

"A poor man's story's not interesting, sir, I'm sure," mumbled the blind man.

"Nonsense! Tut, tut! Every story's interesting—eh, Mr Haslam?"

"That's quite true," responded Haslam, "though authors sometimes hash them in the telling." He addressed the blind man. "I am an author, and I should be very interested to hear something about your life. We writers live for copy, you know— and you needn't fear you'll go away empty handed."

"'Unger don't make no sort o' readin'," said the beggar. "'Unger. That's my story, sir. 'Unger—poverty—cold. That's all there is."

"He's right," admitted Mr Blythe, looking rather helpless.

"Come, there are frillings," interposed Haslam. "Your son, for instance. Where did you lose him?"

"Somewhere outside."

"Yes—but where?"

"'Ow can I say, sir, not 'avin' the use o' my eyes like you 'ave?"

"Well, when was it?"

"Hour ago. Jest about."

"I see. And what have you been doing since?"

"Walkin' about."

"The whole time?"

"Yes, sir. I ain't 'arf tired."

21

"Can you say what direction you came from?"

"Heysham way."

"From Heysham?" Haslam glanced at Mr Blythe. "Tell me, did you miss your son before you came over the little bridge?"

Mr Blythe looked up sharply, and then smiled as he turned enquiringly to the blind man. The beggar put his hand up to his dark glasses, and rubbed his forehead.

"Bridge, sir?" he quavered. "I don't know. Was there one?"

"There's not," thought Mr Blythe, "but that was a good shot of Mr Haslam's."

"How absurd of me!" exclaimed Haslam, covering his traces. "There isn't one. I'm a stranger here, too, you know, and have got this place mixed up with another. Well, we must certainly find your son. You'll wait here, won't you, till we trace him?"

The beggar protested.

"Ah, I'll be all right, sir, if you just put me on the road to Heysham. I'll go back there, and wait. I dessay I'll meet 'im on the road."

Pike entered, with a cup of tea on a glittering tray. The absurdity was so marked that Haslam concluded the butler had done it on purpose, as a sort of mute reproach. Haslam took the cup, and placed it on the table, a little way from the blind man.

"There you are," he exclaimed, "Drink it down."

The beggar felt about vaguely.

"Will you 'and it to me, sir?" he asked.

Haslam handed the cup to him with a smile. The beggar gulped it down.

"Where did you have your lunch?" demanded Mr Blythe, suddenly.

"Nowhere," replied the ragged visitor. "Didn't 'ave no lunch."

"Ah! Breakfast, then?"

"Under a 'edge."

"Yes, but where?"

"Don't know, sir. It's orl the same ter me."

"And where did you intend to sleep tonight?"

"Barn, I expeck. But, if I don't find my son, I'll go back to Heysham—if someone'll jest put me on the road—and wait for 'im there."

There was a silence. Mr Blythe glanced at Haslam, and shrugged his shoulders. The situation seemed to have beaten him. Haslam himself could not think of any more questions to ask.

"All right," said Mr Blythe. "My man shall see you to the main-road, and put you on your way. You say you'll be safe, so we take your word for it." He rang, and Pike reappeared. "Show this man to the Heysham road, will ye? And hurry back, because it's nearly time for dinner, and I'm getting peckish."

"God bless you, sirs, God bless you," mumbled the blind man, as Pike led him out, "and may 'Eaven reward you for your kindness."

Ambrose Blythe and Peter Haslam were alone again. They looked at each other, like a couple of vanquished school-boys.

"Well," barked the old man, "we didn't get much change out of that!"

"We didn't," admitted Haslam. "But I'm perfectly sure there was something fishy about him."

"Decidedly fishy! And, that being so, why did you slip a shilling into his hand before he left?"

"It was the only way to make the old rascal think we were properly duped," explained Haslam. "After all, we'll get on better acting the innocents till we've got something to go on, won't we? If we had given him nothing, and he was the wrong 'un we take him for, he'd have smelt a rat. These people mustn't know we're trying to catch them."

"You're teaching me things, young man," exclaimed Mr Blythe, admiringly. "I'm glad to have you by me."

Pike had not returned when the bell sounded again.

"Thick as berries," muttered Mr Blythe. "Who the devil will it be this time? Do you wonder this is getting on my nerves?"

He strode out into the passage, waving back a maid who had run up to answer the door in Pike's absence. He appeared to be growing warm, and Haslam hovered rather anxiously in the background. His host, as he had suggested, certainly lacked finesse. He might be useful in an emergency, but in struggling through a maze of doubt, he was hopeless.

He opened the door suddenly, and a young man almost fell into the passage.

"Hallo!" exclaimed Mr Blythe. "What's this?"

The young man regained himself.

"I—I beg your pardon," he said, in a low voice. "I——"

"Yes, what?" demanded the old man.

"Er—please could you tell me the way to Ingate?"

"Ingate? You want to go to Ingate, eh?"

"Yes. It's—it's round to the left, isn't it?"

"I believe so. But step in a moment. P'r'aps I've got a map. Hi! What's the hurry, young man?"

For the visitor was already departing.

"Thanks awfully," he mumbled. "But my bicycle's outside. I'm afraid someone may steal it. Round to the left—thanks."

And he was gone.

"Well, now, what d'you make of that?" cried the old man, angrily. "What's the meaning of it all?"

Haslam came forward.

"I'd like to have interviewed that young man," he said, quietly. "It's a pity you frightened him off."

Mr Blythe shrugged his shoulders despairingly.

"Well, you shall handle the next," he exclaimed. "I'm sick to death of them!"

A dark figure came up the drive.

"Who's that?" cried Mr Blythe, sharply.

"Me, sir," replied the voice of Pike.

CHAPTER 5

It was not until dinner was nearly over, and Peter Haslam was testing his host's excellent port, that he asked a question which might reasonably have been asked before.

"Have you any enemies, Mr Blythe?" he enquired.

"Not that I know of," replied Ambrose Blythe, promptly. "But then they say you never know your enemies, any more than you know your friends."

Haslam nodded.

"That's perfectly true. The man who makes your shoes may have a grudge against you. And the crossing-sweeper at the corner may regard you as his hero! If only you could rake up some incident which could point to the existence of a few enemies ——"

"A few!" interjected Mr Blythe. "You mean dozens! I'm sorry, sir, but I can't oblige you. I've lived a lonely life, and have made neither enemies nor friends."

"You've probably made plenty of both, without knowing it," insisted Haslam. "And here's another question I'd like to ask you. How long have you lived in this house?"

"About a year."

"Is it yours?"

"Every brick of it."

"And have these uninvited guests been coming the whole while?"

"Very likely. I can't say. The situation has only gradually dawned upon me, you see. Even now, I sometimes think I'm creating the whole thing in my mind——"

"That I'm sure you're not," interposed Haslam, definitely. "Even after my short acquaintance with the circumstances."

"No—something queer's up. That's certain. Yet not a stick of evidence that one can grasp. Theories—shadows. That's all. Otherwise, maybe, I'd have told the police."

"Well," said Haslam, slowly, "I was just coming to that. Why *haven't* you informed the police?"

"What should I tell?" retorted Mr Blythe. "You know what the local police are. They'd listen politely, and smile. I've a notion I'm thought a bit eccentric, as it is. All lonely old men are. There's a tit-bit for your literary note-book. Stick an old man in an old house by himself, and he becomes a sort of popular bogey-man." He smiled. "Well, they may be right. I dare say I've got my oddities. But I'm not going to make a laughing-stock of myself by reporting shadows to the police. Then tongues will wag, eh? Ain't I right?"

"You may be," responded Haslam, frowning. "All the same, I wouldn't let this go on too long without taking action of some sort."

The old man looked at him sharply.

"You think that, hey?" he said.

"I do, sir."

"Damme, if you're not making more of this than I am!" muttered Mr Blythe, uncomfortably.

"I don't know about that. I've not the same need to. But I believe there's a mighty serious proposition revolving round this house, all the same. Did you buy it?"

"No. It was left to me two years ago, by a cousin. I was living up in the north when he died—Newcastle—and never came near the property till a fire burnt me out of my Newcastle house. My cousin hadn't occupied it for years. Then I thought I'd come south—that was a year ago, as I say. I like this place, though it is tumbling to bits. And I mean to stay here, if the whole population of England looks me up!" He glared into his empty glass, and refilled it.

"Who was living in the house before you came here?"

"No one. It was falling to pieces. I've had it patched up here and there. It's worth saving, eh?"

"I agree with you," said Haslam, who was genuinely charmed with the place, despite its queer associations—or, perhaps, partially on account of them, so curiously are we made. There is a little morbid streak in us that takes very kindly to the eerie.

The port began to loosen Mr Blythe's tongue. He leaned forward, and tapped his guest on the sleeve.

"Yes, I like this place, Mr Haslam," he said, "and I'm hoping I shall live here during the few remaining years I have on earth. It's a pretty spot. You must see the view from the lawn, in the sunlight. Quiet, too—I like that. Just a comfortable corner to lean back in, and dream oneself out of the world, eh?" He paused; then burst out, "But I tell you, Mr Haslam, this business is getting on my nerves. They seem to be trying to drive me away. Why? Why? In the daylight, everything's splendid. Splendid. But then evening comes. I find myself—pah!" He broke off, angrily. "I'm getting old, that's what it is, Mr Haslam. I'm getting old!"

A wave of warm sympathy swept through Peter Haslam.

"What you want, sir," he exclaimed, "is a companion."

"Maybe you're right, maybe you're right," mused Mr Blythe.

Pike entered, with coffee.

"Everything all right, Pike?" asked Mr Blythe.

"Yes, sir," replied the butler.

"Cook in?" asked the old man, absently.

"Just come back, sir," said the butler.

He left the room.

"How did we come to have such an excellent dinner," enquired Haslam, "if the cook was out?"

"Rose—the housemaid—is a capital understudy," answered Mr Blythe. "She's a good girl, a good girl."

"And that comprises your entire staff?"

Mr Blythe smiled whimsically. "Yes, Sherlock Holmes. And, in these socialistic days, aren't three servants enough to look after one old man?"

"They ought to be," agreed Haslam. "Yet there's something lacking."

"Not visitors, at any rate," said Mr Blythe, grimly; and the bell rang, to corroborate his words. He gave an exasperated exclamation. "You tackle him this time," he exclaimed. "And let's get it over quickly."

"You don't want to ask him in, then?" queried Haslam, as Pike's footsteps were heard in the hall.

"Yes, yes. We'd better go on with it. But let's get rid of him as soon as we can. I'd like a game of chess."

They heard the front-door open. It was too much for Mr Blythe. He rose from his chair, and opened the door a crack.

"I beg your pardon, sir?" came the grave voice of Pike.

The visitor's voice was heard replying,

"A lunatic. You've seen no suspicious character hanging around?"

"Haven't we?" muttered Mr Blythe, and, despite his intention of keeping in the background, he opened the door, and marched out.

Haslam followed him, his mind grappling with the new turn of events. So the escaped lunatic was bound up in the mystery! Or was this merely—another coincidence?

He was not surprised to see the lantern-jawed man standing in the doorway.

"Good evening," said Haslam, smiling faintly. "Again, you see, you have struck the wrong one."

The lantern-jawed man looked up quickly, and gave a slight start.

"We seem fated to meet," he said. "I'm on my same errand."

"Had no luck?"

"None. I imagine I'm following a wrong clue altogether."

"I'm rather relieved. I feared you might retract, and come to the conclusion that I was the right one, after all. What asylum has the lunatic escaped from?"

The lantern-jawed man frowned.

"We don't give away information," he said.

"But you ask for it?" said Haslam, pleasantly.

"Yes, of course. In the public interest. Are you the owner of this house?"

"No," replied Haslam waving towards Mr Blythe. "Only a temporary guest."

The lantern-jawed man turned immediately to Mr Blythe.

"I understand no suspicious character has been seen about here during the last few hours, sir?" he said.

"Suspicious?" repeated Mr Blythe. "Depends what you call suspicious."

"It's a madman I'm looking for."

"Well, we've not seen him, or got him."

"Thank you, sir. In that case, I'll be moving."

He turned.

"I suppose you couldn't—in the public interest—tell us what asylum he has escaped from," said Peter Haslam, "so that we might report anything that comes to our knowledge?"

But, if the lantern-jawed man heard, he did not reply. He had slipped out into the enveloping darkness.

"Well?" queried Mr Blythe, back in the library. "What do you think?"

"I think," answered Haslam, "that there isn't any madman."

"Then why should he be invented?"

"I haven't the remotest notion."

"Nor have I. It's worse than chess. Shall we have a game?"

A pleasant hour passed. Then, with strange reluctance, Peter Haslam bade his host goodnight, and began his homeward journey through the dark lanes.

All the way back to the rustic inn at Heysham, he was haunted by a face. It should have been the face of the blind beggar, or the young cyclist, or the lantern-jawed man. But it was none of these. It was the face of a girl artist, painting bad pictures on a little green plateau, and though the face smiled, there was a vein of infinite sadness running through it.

But once, as he passed near an overhanging hedge, he was haunted by the face of the blind beggar. He distinctly saw the pale face and the two dark blotches made by the spectacles. But the next moment the face disappeared into the velvet of the night.

CHAPTER 6

We all of us possess true centres, from which we periodically swing away, but to which we invariably revert; and the happiest, most complete people are those who realise what their true centres are and build their lives around them. A man whose natural humour it is to be conversational may secretly admire the strong, silent individual who goes farther than he does on one-quarter of the words, but he can no more thwart his natural humour than a little mountain stream can thwart its impulse to find the sea; and the woman of few words will live a twisted existence if she attempts to emulate her brilliant, witty sister. On a hundred occasions, the conversational man will find himself silent, the silent man will burst into conversation, the quiet woman will break into astonishing laughter, and the witty one find herself pleasantly dumb; but in the end, if they are philosophic, they will respond to their particular chemical compositions, and will all realise that there is no reason why they should struggle to escape from themselves.

Peter Haslam's chemical composition was an essentially happy one. He could pass through moods of doubt, and even fear, but, as he would tell you himself, he always came up with the sun, and very often, when the sun was not there, he supplied the deficiency. Thus it happened that, when he rose next morning and looked out of his little latticed window at the picturesque village of Heysham, bathed in brilliant morning light, he found it almost impossible to take seriously the queer impressions of the night before.

"Evening can play the devil with you!" he reflected, as he

shaved in a delightfully inadequate mirror. "Particularly when you have a lonely house and an eccentric old man tacked on to it!"

He descended to breakfast, ravenously hungry, and rubbed his hands like an absurd schoolboy when he noted the generous scale upon which the breakfast had been planned.

"You will find nothing unusual about me," said the breakfast-table, "variety, in fact, being my pet aversion. But I guarantee to fill the biggest void in a wholesome and familiar way; and I am willing to wager that, although you think you can consume the whole of me, you will be beaten by at least two bits of bacon, and very likely a whole egg!"

Which prophecy was duly fulfilled.

The rustic attendant, with mouth still ouvert, and a strange indication about her hair that, later on in the day, it would burst into grace and glory (this prophecy was not fulfilled), hovered around him as she had done on the previous night. She was, though she did not know it, playing the eternal game of Eve, but she was as unsuccessful in her role as was Peter Haslam in the part of Adam.

"So you wasn't in to supper lars' night, zur," said Eve, of Heysham.

"No, I stayed out," replied Adam. "Do you know, I believe you've forgotten the pepper."

"Pepper," repeated Eve, as though she had only faintly heard of the commodity. "It's by the vinegar."

"Why, so it is," exclaimed Adam, and, as the top came off, used it with unpremeditated lavishness.

Eve ventured a little familiarity. Bees were buzzing outside, and they were quite alone.

"I do believe," she said, archly, "you're still asleep!"

"No more asleep than you are," retorted Adam, taking pity on her, "because you *have* forgotten the butter!"

"Fergot the butter, 'ave I? What's that be'ind the tea-pot, then, I'd like to know?"

Love was forgotten in laughter, and Jane, late Eve, placed her uncharming arms frankly akimbo, and roared with laughter.

But, suddenly, she stopped. A new emotion swept over her. Was it mere interest, or did it include a little twinge of jealousy as another maid, far prettier than poor Jane, passed the window, and, turning into the porch, was heard to enquire for Mr Haslam.

"He's staying here, isn't he?" asked the pretty maid.

The innkeeper's voice was heard replying that Mr Haslam was staying there, and that he was having breakfast.

"Will you give him this note?" proceeded the pretty maid.

"Certainly," said the innkeeper. "Answer?"

"Yes, please," responded the pretty maid. "I'll wait."

Poor Jane, anticipating the coming interruption and her possible eclipse, began to busy herself vaguely about the room, and a picture of a wreck off the Lizard received its first dusting for over a year. It was a wonder the ship did not sink utterly in astonishment. A moment later, the innkeeper bustled in, holding out the note.

"This 'as come, sir," he announced. "And the maid that brought it is waitin' for an answer."

"Thank you," said Haslam, taking the envelope, and wondering what on earth was in it. In this wonder, both the innkeeper and Jane participated, but the innkeeper suddenly realised that a visitor might not relish being stared at over breakfast, and shooed Jane off.

The writing was unfamiliar, and an idiotic hope that it might be the writing of the artist whose face he was striving unsuccessfully to get out of his mind, set Haslam's heart beating a trifle faster. But, even before he tore the envelope open, he decided that this hope was ridiculous. In the first place, why should she write to him? And, in the second, the writing was not that of any young artist. It was too cramped and wobbly—and then the solution dawned upon him. The note was from Ambrose Blythe, of course, and the maid who had brought it was the excellent Rose.

"Dear Mr Haslam," ran the note. "You have already discovered that I am a rather eccentric old man, so perhaps you will not be surprised at my further eccentric behaviour. Are you too attached to your present inn to consider the idea of changing your quarters? You said you intended to spend a week or two in these parts, and if you would care to spend that time as my guest, I would be very delighted for more than one reason. I may say that I have taken to you. I have always appreciated your work, and would feel it an honour if you wrote your new novel, or started it, at any rate, under my roof. You shall choose your room, fix yourself up as you like—I know you geniuses have moods!—and do as you want.

"But there's another reason why I want you here," the note continued, frankly. "I'll tell you what it is. I'm getting scared. Damn it, I am! I am not going to be driven out of this place, but things seem to be coming to a crisis, and I'd value your company and your help during the next few days more than I can write down on paper. Something else happened last night, after you left. I'll tell you about it when you come. Note the word 'when'—you see, I'll take no refusal! Rose, who will bear this note, cooks well, as you were pleased to say last night, but she was only an understudy, and the principal cooks even better. But don't think I'm running down Rose. She's as pretty as my cook is ugly, and is the one bright thing about the house. But my pen is running away with me. Trying to impress you, eh, with my literary talent!

"Well, will you come? Could you stand it? Please send a reply by Rose, and I hope you'll follow it up."

Peter Haslam read the letter through, and his mind was made up before he came to the signature.

"I'm leaving here this morning," he said, to the innkeeper; and hastened to add, as the innkeeper's face fell several inches, "Not because I'm not comfortable—it is delightful here—but I've received an invitation."

"Oh, I see, sir," replied the innkeeper, reasonable but rueful.

"Of course," continued Haslam, "you must allow me to settle with you for the full week, as I had booked the room."

The innkeeper made a gesture of joyous protest—the protest

which knows it will prove unavailing, and is careful not to disturb this security.

"Ah, that don't matter," he said.

"Well, I think it does matter," returned Haslam, pleasantly, "and I insist. Will you ask the maid who brought this to step in here a minute?"

"Yes, certainly, sir," said the innkeeper. "I can't say as I really like—well, it's very good of you, sir, I'm sure."

Later on, he told his bedridden wife that they *might* have let the room to another person the night before—you never knew —but, of course, it wasn't often that you came across quite such real gentlemen.

The pretty maid, a plump little soul with rosy cheeks, a determined chin, and bright smiling eyes, was ushered into Haslam's presence, and he took an immediate liking to her.

"Do you know what's in this note?" he asked.

"Yes, sir," replied Rose. "I've got the room all ready."

Haslam laughed.

"But I thought I was to choose the room," he objected. He added swiftly, as Rose's face fell, "That was only my joke—I know perfectly well that it will be a delightful room."

"Then you'll really come, sir?" exclaimed the maid.

"Of course, I'll come," nodded Haslam. "I'm delighted to. But —tell me—are you as anxious as the rest?"

He had noted the girl's impulsive eagerness.

"Well, sir, to be truthful, it was Mr Blythe I was thinking of," she said, rather primly. "He's always been very good to me, and I think it's a shame he's alone so much. He—oh, but there, sir, it's not my business. I beg your pardon, I'm sure."

"Don't apologise," retorted Haslam. "I'm anxious to help Mr Blythe all I can, and I shall be able to help him all the more if you speak freely to me."

"Thank you, sir," answered the maid. "Well, I'm sure you'll do him a lot of good. I was going to say that he tries to hide how nervous he is, but he can't. And he's not the only one. There's Mr Pike—the butler, sir—he's almost as bad as the rest. Frightened stiff, he is! A great coward, I call him! And then Cook's fright-ened, too, but she's old, you see, and nearly deaf, so there you are."

"And what about you?" asked Haslam. "Are you frightened, also?"

She hesitated; then lied boldly.

"No, I'm not!" she exclaimed. "There's quite enough old women in the house without me being one, too! That's what they are, sir—a lot of nervous old women!" She looked at Haslam rather anxiously, as though longing for his support. "Me frightened? What's there to be frightened about? But I'm glad you're coming, sir—I think you'll do them all good!"

"What about last night?" enquired Haslam. "Something hap-pened after I left. What was it?" The girl frowned. "Tell me, was that all nonsense, too?"

"Perhaps Mr Blythe had better tell you, sir," she replied. She felt that, although she was a friendly and talkative little soul, she had talked a little too much. "But he looks at you so kindly," she thought, in self-justification, "and sort of draws you out."

"Well, you can go back now," said Haslam. "Tell Mr Blythe I'll be along presently. Say, round about tea-time. I've just one or two little things to settle up first, but he can count on me."

"Thank you, sir," answered Rose. "He'll be very pleased, I'm sure."

She departed, and Haslam finished his interrupted breakfast. Jane reappeared once, but, finding her victim distrait, gave the wreck off the Lizard another rub, and disappeared again.

Half-an-hour later, Peter Haslam walked out of the little inn to settle up one of the matters he had hinted at to Rose. The matter rested on the little green plateau, towards which his steps were now directed.

CHAPTER 7

To his delight and surprise, he found the green plateau occupied. Apparently, time had beaten the artist, for she was sitting again at her easel, putting the finishing touches to the picture on which she had been engaged the evening before. It was, admittedly, not a great work of art, but Haslam reflected that it was considerably better than the girl's own valuation. "Or am I, already, prejudiced in its favour?" he asked himself, soberly.

She did not see him approaching, so he had a pleasant opportunity to study her. His previous impressions in regard to her attractiveness were fully confirmed, and imagination had not re-created her in a form that reality could not live up to. So absorbed was she in her work that she did not note his presence until his preceding shadow slipped up to her. Then she gave a little start, and turned.

She flushed very slightly, but otherwise she was perfectly composed, and Haslam concluded from her attitude that she had not recognised him at their last encounter in the drive.

"Hallo," she exclaimed, in a natural voice. "You again?"

"Yes," replied Haslam, "and again I've got a perfectly legitimate excuse."

"That sounds almost as bad as if you had no excuse at all," she observed. "It sounds as though you go looking about for excuses."

"Perhaps I do," smiled Haslam. "But, at least, give me the credit of admitting that I find them."

"Let me see—it was a lunatic yesterday, wasn't it?" she mused. "Yes, that was quite a good excuse—except that you didn't actually find him. What have you found today?"

"Nothing," answered Haslam. "I found it yesterday."

He held up the little handkerchief.

"Thank you," she said, taking it from him. "I wondered where it had got to. Where did you find it?"

"Here," he said.

"Here? Then why didn't you give it back to me when you found it?"

"Because you didn't happen to be by to receive it."

"Oh! I see! You came a second time." He nodded. "Why?"

"You're frowning," answered Haslam. "Please don't. I'll tell you exactly why I came, although there might have been a dozen reasons unconnected with yourself——"

"But I haven't suggested it was a reason connected with myself!" she bridled.

"Oh, yes, you have. If it were not connected with yourself, you wouldn't consider that you had any right to question me at all. But it was about yourself, and so you have the right. I came back here yesterday evening because I was worried about that lunatic, and I didn't like the idea that he might be wandering around while you were still painting."

"That was rather nice of you," she conceded, "although also quite unnecessary. I—I am quite able to look after myself."

"Even against a lunatic?"

"I suppose so."

"What would you have done if you had met him?"

"Dabbed some paint on his nose!"

Haslam burst out laughing. As Mr Blythe's maid had reflected, he had a distinct way of drawing people out, and, by his own oddly natural manner, of making them say things they had not the least intention of saying. The artist, having no love for men, was doing her level best not to enjoy this wayfarer's society, and was finding it surprisingly difficult.

"Why will I try to be funny, when I don't feel in the least funny?" she asked herself, angrily.

"Well, that would probably have settled him," remarked

Haslam. "Now I'll tell you something in return. I didn't invent that lunatic, but I believe somebody else did."

"What do you mean?" she asked.

Haslam studied her for a moment. He was trying to discover whether she were some mysterious link in the mysterious chain that wound round Mr Blythe's house—a chain that seemed to be formed of a man with a lantern-jaw, a non-existent madman, a lovely girl who painted poor pictures, a blind man, and a nervous young cyclist, not to mention countless at present unknown factors.

"I mean," he replied, slowly, "that I don't believe the fellow who told me about the escaped madman was telling the truth."

She stared at him now, and a curious look crept into her eyes.

"Why not?" she demanded. "Why should he invent a madman?"

"You've no theory?"

"Of course not!"

"Well, to be honest, nor have I. But I'll wager anything that lunatic was a myth, just the same."

There was a short silence. Haslam had been on the point of telling her about his second encounter with the lantern-jawed man, but an instinct of delicacy restrained him. He felt that, if he referred to his visit to Mr Blythe's house, it might in some way awaken unhappy memories and doubts in her mind. He did not want to appear to be trying to force any secret from her, however keen his curiosity might be.

He changed the subject abruptly. "Your picture's getting on," he said.

"Yes, it's nearly finished," she replied. "But it will never be finished if I don't stop talking to you."

"Thank you for the hint. I'm not offended. I mustn't interfere in the interests of Art."

"I may laugh at myself, but you mayn't," she frowned. "I only wish I could paint well. I told you what I expected to get for this picture yesterday."

"Yes. Twenty shillings."

"If I'm lucky."

"I hope you'll be luckier." A sudden desire to possess the picture came over him, and to ensure her luck. He wondered whether she would accept an offer from him, and decided, after a quick glance at her, that she would not. So he asked her, instead, where she sold her pictures.

"Different places," she answered, beginning to fidget once more with her brushes. "There's a kind shopman in Wynton who is putting them in his window at present. He goes in for 'lines,' and thinks he is enterprising. His last line was ladies' bags. I'm his present line. His next may be tinned salmon." What an annoying man this was! Again, he had made her say something funny. She became suddenly very stern, and toyed with her brushes more ominously than ever.

Haslam took pity on her, and prepared to depart. But he had just one more question to ask.

"I'm going now," he said, "and I hope you're not really cross with me for having wasted your time. But, before I go, may I please know what the initials 'M.H.' on your handkerchief stand for? My own initials are P.H., and they stand for Peter Haslam ——"

"The author?"

"Yes. I'm flattered that you know me."

"Why, of course, I know you. I believe *you* were once one of my shopman's lines, because he's had a copy of one of your early novels in his window for weeks—and though it's marked down to half-price, he can't sell it."

"Really!" exclaimed Haslam, smiling broadly. "Then we are brother geniuses in distress! But, you know, you still haven't told me what 'M.H.' stands for?"

She hesitated for an instant, then said, "Mary Holland," and began to paint out a cloud.

"I hope, very sincerely, that we shall meet again, Miss Holland," said Haslam; and, raising his hat, he turned and left her.

The next few hours were spent by Peter Haslam in rather an odd way. After noting a lady's bicycle in the vicinity of the easel, he climbed down to the road that ran round the base of the hill, took up a position from where he could see and not be seen, and lit a pipe. He was watching for the reappearance of the bicycle, and it reappeared, being wheeled down the hill, within twenty minutes of taking up his vigil. It reappeared with Miss Holland, a carefully packed picture, and an easel.

"Now, how is she going to ride her bicycle with all that luggage?" pondered Haslam. "It can't be done."

Miss Holland herself evidently agreed that it could not be done. She deposited her easel and painting gear at a cottage at the foot of the hill, and then, carefully strapping the picture on her back-carrier, mounted her machine and rode away.

Haslam came out of his concealment, and, walking a little way along the road after the vanished cyclist, came to a signpost which told him that he was three miles from Wynton. He covered the three miles in less than an hour.

Wynton was a small but fairly busy little town, boasting quite an appreciable High Street. There were several shops in the main thoroughfare, but only one interested him. He paused before the window, and found himself gazing once more at the familiar reproduction of silver birches. Looking carefully around him, and peeping through the window to assure himself that the artist was nowhere about, he walked boldly into the shop and addressed the shopman.

"That's rather a pretty picture you've got in the window," he remarked. "It's not sold yet, is it?"

"No, sir," replied the shopman, briskly. "But I expect it will be, before the day's out. It's not been in the shop more than fifteen minutes."

"Then I'm lucky," said Haslam, "because I want it—if I can afford it. I don't expect you're selling pictures like that for a song!"

The shopman became seriously interested in his customer. His latent commercial instinct began to devise and calculate. He had only expected to make five shillings out of the picture—twenty-five per cent of the value realised was his commission—

but it began to dawn upon him that he might make ten, or even twenty. He found himself pouring out words, while his brain worked and hoped.

"Yes, sir, it's quite a pretty picture," he said. "The artist's makin' quite a name for herself, I may say. I remember the time when she used to ask not more than thirty shillings for her pictures." His forehead perspired slightly. He had sold a picture on the previous day for fifteen, and he was not used to sharp business. However, he had to go through with it now. "Yes, sir, that's true. Thirty shillings! Think of it! But—well, of course, you can't get 'em for that now!"

"I should think not," exclaimed Haslam. "I'm afraid the price is going to beat me. I can go up to five pounds, but not a cent more."

The shopman's forehead was bathed by this time.

"That's a funny thing," he mumbled, thickly, "because that's the exact price she's asking."

"Ass and liar," thought Haslam, as he took out the money. Aloud he said, "Capital. Will you do the picture up for me? I want to take it away with me at once."

"Yes, sir," gasped the shopman.

"Oh, by the way—what's the name of the artist?" asked Haslam. "I see, she modestly refrains from any signature."

The shopman looked anxious. He put on an imposing expression, leaned forward, lowered his voice slightly, and said,

"Mary Holland."

"Thank you," answered Haslam, and the shopman breathed a sigh of relief. He had anticipated a possible protest.

Haslam lunched in the little town, and then, in the afternoon, lounged back to Heysham, with the pathetic little canvas under his arm. Commercially, it was worth the one pound the shopman had expected to get for it. But, happily, sentiment exists, to confound the financiers. Sentimentally, the picture was worth anything.

The shadows were growing long when, having collected his belongings at the inn, he completed his journey and entered the

42

driveway that led to Ambrose Blythe's lonely house. The old man met him outside the front door, and his face lit up with pleasure.

"Delighted to see you!" he cried. "Upon my soul, if you hadn't turned up, I don't believe I could have stayed the night here. Come along in, and I'll tell you what's happened."

They walked into the pleasant, sunlit study, watched with interest and some secret emotion by the rosy-cheeked Rose and the solemn, pale-faced Pike.

CHAPTER 8

"Well, what occurred last night?" asked Haslam, when they were both seated.

"Upon my soul, it sounds more like a ghost-story than reality," exclaimed old Mr Blythe, perplexedly. "The confounded mystery gets worse and worse. Not that I've anything against mysteries—but I like 'em to happen to other people, eh?"

"Yes, that's right," smiled Haslam. "I like mysteries myself—writing about them, and making other folk read about them—but when one actually encounters them——"

"Ah, there you are, you see!" interrupted his host. "That's different, isn't it? I can sit here, and read about a murder, with the utmost pleasure. But, if that door were to open at this moment, and a hand with a knife were to be thrust through——"

He stopped speaking, and gave a little gasp, as the door began to move.

"Will you have tea in the library, sir, or in the garden?" asked the voice of Pike.

"In the garden!" snapped Mr Blythe, testily, and surreptitiously wiped his forehead. "There! Now you see what a condition I'm reduced to! Even my own butler makes me jump!"

"Well, I don't wonder," commented Haslam. "This is enough to get on anybody's nerves."

"But not yours, eh?" queried the old man, a trifle anxiously.

"I don't think so," replied Haslam. "I'm fairly solid."

"That's what I felt. You're solid. Pike ought to be solid, but he's jumpy. Cook ought to be solid, but she shrieks. Rose is solid, but she's the wrong sex. Now, with you about the place, I don't mind so much. I'll wager, if you'd been here last night, we'd have found something." He jumped up, went to the whisky decanter, put his hand on the glass stopper, and thought better of it. "Last night, Mr Haslam," he said, solemnly, "I heard someone creeping about the place. Don't make any mistake about it. There was someone inside this house. Being a silly old man, who ought to know better, I popped my head under the bed-clothes, and pretended I couldn't hear anything. You know how one does it! 'This ain't true—I'm just dreaming!' you say to yourself. Then, suddenly, there was a big thud, as though someone had tripped and fallen. I hopped out of bed, rang the bell, and ran to the door. It was dark in the passage, and no one was about. But Pike soon came tumbling along, looking as frightened as a rabbit. 'Devil take you!' I exclaimed. 'What are you looking so scared for?' 'Someone's in the house, sir,' he replied. 'Well, of course, there is!' I said. 'We've got to go and find him!'"

"Your courage went up, as Pike's went down," commented Haslam.

The old man nodded. "That's the way it happens. If you hear a child howling at a ghost, you stop howling, don't you? We can't all howl at once! We searched the house from top to bottom, every nook and corner of it. Once or twice, while we were searching, I could swear I heard the dammed footsteps again, always eluding us. We didn't find anything. Not a sign! But when I got up this morning, I looked at myself in the mirror, and I said, 'Ambrose Blythe, can you stand another night like that? There'll be more uninvited guests coming along, as sure as fate, and more ghosts walking. Can you face it?' And, damme, my reflection answered, 'No.' So I sent for you. And here we are! Now, what are we to do?"

Haslam looked out of the window. Tall trees slanted their velvet shadows across the lawn. A blue-tit shot into the sunlight, spent a joyous, bright-eyed moment on the grass, and then shot away again. Horror seemed impossible.

And yet that little bright-eyed bird, Haslam reflected, stood for horror to worms and insects; and perhaps, to other comprehensions, there dwelt beauty in the very things that horrified us!

"What about putting the matter in the hands of the local police?" suggested Haslam.

"You proposed that yesterday," retorted Mr Blythe. "Maybe we'll have to presently. But not just yet. What could we tell 'em? You know what country police are——"

"They're not quite so black as they're painted," interposed Haslam. "I've had some dealings with them, and know what they're up against. All sorts of prejudices. They get too many kicks, and too little glory."

"Perhaps—perhaps. But I don't trust 'em. I'm smiled at enough, as it is. Can't you see 'em tapping their heads among themselves, and talking about my top story? No, thank you! We'll leave the police out of it for a bit—till something definite happens, or till you can back up my evidence with your own. Eh? What do you think?"

"You may be right," admitted Haslam, as Pike appeared with the announcement that tea was ready on the lawn.

Tea was a delightful meal. The sun turned all it could to gold, and left what it could not bathed in its reflection. Bees buzzed drowsily, and the wind played softly among the tree-tops like a distant sea. Pike brought the tea, but Rose produced the second supply of toast, and she threw Haslam a quiet, unabashed smile which, although not domestic etiquette, did not appear in the least forward or out of place. It merely said, "It *is* nice to have you here"; and Haslam smiled back in agreement.

"What a wonderful view you've got from this lawn," said Haslam, suddenly.

"Ah! Isn't it?" replied Ambrose Blythe. "This place would be as near perfection as one can hope for on this earth—but for the shadows!"

"The shadows are wonderful, too," observed Haslam, wilfully misunderstanding him.

"Funny, ain't you?" retorted the old man.

The day wore on. The shadows lengthened. After tea, Haslam

went to his room, and dug himself in. He unpacked his few belongings, set his five-guinea picture on the mantel-piece, delighting absurdly in his purchase, and then explored for chosen spots in which to write. He found a pleasant summer-house, a charming clearance among trees, a little beckoning lawn by a ready pool. "By Jove!" he murmured. "How I could write here! If ____"

He returned slowly to his room, ostensibly to write a letter for further belongings to be sent on to him from London; but he studied the five-guinea picture again for quite awhile before he put pen to paper. Then he ambled out into the sunshine again, and posted the letter in a "V.R." letter-box, half-hidden in an old wall some half-a-mile away.

On his way back, a curious, unsettled feeling began to creep over him. He tried hard to throw it off, but only partially, succeeded. The shadows were very long now, and had almost entirely usurped the lanes which, only a short while back, had danced with sunlight. A field here, a roof there, a hill-top in the distance, still glowed with magnificent golden optimism; but the sun was running away before the great armies of the Night, and soon only the sunshine of the spirit would be left.

Dinner was a solemn meal. Pike, silent and pale, did not add to its joyfulness. Haslam found himself wishing that the bright little maid were serving it instead, for she, at least, had sunshine in her spirit, and did her best to shoo the shadows away.

In the interval between the meat and the pudding, Mr Blythe suddenly put down the glass he had been raising to his lips.

"What was that?" he asked, sharply. "The bell?"

"I thought I heard it," replied Haslam, instantly alert. "But I wasn't quite sure."

They looked at each other, and waited. They heard Pike approach, presumably with the pudding, but the pudding did not appear immediately. It was deposited outside, and, a few moments later, an altercation was heard at the front-door.

"Here, I can't stand this!" cried Ambrose Blythe, and jumped to his feet.

He was out of the door the next moment, with Haslam at his heels. Pike turned to them, and a figure which had been standing in the porch abruptly disappeared. Pike gave an angry exclamation, veered round again, and made an ineffective snatch. He grabbed thin air.

"Well, well?" barked Mr Blythe. "What was it this time?"

"'E's gone, sir," murmured Pike, staring out into the gloaming.

"Yes! Of course! I see that! But who was he? What did he want?"

"It was that same young man who called last night, sir," explained Pike. "The cyclist."

"The one who asked the way to Ingate?" enquired Haslam.

"Yes, sir, that's 'im," answered the butler. "Said 'e'd lost 'is pocket-book, and thought p'r'aps 'e'd dropeted it in the grounds. Said 'e'd been looking for it ten minutes, and then thought 'e'd ring to see if we'd come across it."

"Quite plausible," said Haslam. "But it hardly explains the row, does it? What were you quarrelling about?"

Pike paused for a second, pulled up by Haslam's concise, determined tone. A look of half-bewildered pain and reproach came into his eyes.

"Why, sir, I told 'im flatly I didn't believe 'im," he answered. "And nor I did, sir. I don't believe any of 'em. 'E got angry, and, when you came along, 'opped it."

"Well, I don't suppose there's anything to be done, but perhaps you'd better let Mr Blythe or me do any challenging next time—what do you think?" remarked Haslam, turning to his host.

"Yes, of course, of course!" nodded Ambrose Blythe. "Don't frighten the next one off, Pike. We'll have a look at him."

"Very good, sir," said the butler.

And they returned to their pudding.

Pudding—coffee—chess. So another hour passed away. Haslam won the chess easily. His opponent played a somewhat wild game. Just as he was calling "Mate" for the third time, a knock on the front door caused Mr Blythe to spring to his feet and knock the board over.

"I'll not stand any more of this!" he shouted, beside himself with nerves and anger. "I'll have this man in, whoever he is, and lock him up. Yes, by gad, I will!"

They rushed out, reaching the door before Pike. Throwing it open, they encountered a pedlar.

"Buy a pair o' laces, sir?" whined the pedlar. "Jest to git a cup o' tea——"

He stopped abruptly, impressed with the nature of the stare he was being subjected to.

"Laces, eh?" cried Mr Blythe. "Say—have you got a hang-rope?"

The pedlar blinked, and looked alarmed.

"Wot's that, sir?" he mumbled. "A wot?"

"Come in," shouted Mr Blythe. "I want a word with you!"

The pedlar hesitated. Haslam laid a hand on his shoulder, and he began to whimper.

"Wot's the gime?" he asked. "Wot 'ave I done? I on'y wants ter sell a bit to git a cup o' tea——"

"Mr Blythe, sir! Mr Haslam! Oh, quick! Please!"

It was Rose's voice. For once, it was raised in alarm. Both men turned round swiftly.

"What's the matter?" cried Haslam.

"Mr Pike—he's being killed!"

"Good God!" screamed the old man.

The pedlar was forgotten. Rose pointed to the stairs, and a great noise was heard on the landing. In two seconds, Haslam was bounding up, with Mr Blythe at his heels.

Two figures were scuffling. One was Pike. The other was the lantern-jawed man.

Haslam threw himself forward, but the lantern-jawed man had heard them coming, and proved too quick for them. Slipping away with astonishing rapidity, he darted along the passage to the back staircase, and was down it in a trice.

"I'll follow him," shouted Haslam. "Cut him off, if you can."

The lantern-jawed man seemed to know his ground, however. He was down the stairs before Haslam had reached the top, and a shriek from the cook announced to the world that she was even less useful than ornamental. A minute later, the hares were gathered together again in the front hall, and the hound had vanished into the night.

"What about the pedlar?" demanded Haslam, suddenly.

"He tried to come in, sir," panted Rose, "but I wouldn't let him. I hit him on the nose, and he didn't want another!"

Haslam looked at her, and smiled.

"Well done, Rose," he said. "You'd better give Pike lessons. Now let's go and have a look at him."

CHAPTER 9

They found Pike in a pitiable state, though his actual body was shattered far less than his nerves. For a little while, they could get next to nothing out of him, and it was not until Haslam took the cross-examination in hand that he told a coherent story.

"Come, pull yourself together," exclaimed Haslam. "There's no danger now. What happened?"

"I don't know, sir," replied Pike, blinking. "Only that someone jumped on me from be'ind."

"What were you doing?"

"Just walking through the passage, on my way to the hall."

"And you heard nothing before you were jumped on?"

"Not a sound."

"Did you see the man?"

"Not clearly."

"Well, did you recognise him, from what you did see?"

The butler rubbed his forehead, and hesitated for a second.

"I'm—I'm not sure, sir."

"You've got some theory, though? Some idea? If you haven't, I have."

Again Pike paused. His brain seemed to be thoroughly muddled.

"Well, sir," he said, slowly, "it did seem as if he was the same fellow who asked about the madman yesterday."

Haslam nodded.

"My idea exactly, Pike. I'm sure it was. He left abruptly—as most of these queer visitors do. I don't suppose you've any idea whether he went right out?"

"No, sir," answered Pike.

"Is it possible that he slipped round to the back door, entered the house again unobserved, and produced the disturbance which woke you all up last night?"

"It might be, sir. I can't say. I wasn't near the back door at the time." He added, "We keep the back door fastened, sir."

Haslam turned to Rose.

"This man left at about five minutes past ten. I looked at my watch immediately afterwards. Do you recall whether the back door was fastened at that time?"

"No, it wasn't," replied Rose, promptly. "Cook had come in a little before, and she went out again to post a letter she'd forgot. I know she didn't close the back door properly, because when she came in she didn't have to ring, and she said she must have forgotten it."

"Yes, that's right," breathed the cook. "I'm very sorry, I'm sure. It was very careless of me."

Haslam glanced at Mr Blythe.

"Then one mystery, at any rate, seems to be cleared up," he said. "This man, who called on the pretext that he was after a lunatic, went round the front door to the back door, and it was he who disturbed you last night."

"Yes, but how did he get in this evening?" demanded Mr Blythe.

"He didn't get in at all. He was in. He's been in all day, and never left till a few minutes ago."

"Oh, lawks!" gasped the cook, and sat down rather promptly and unceremoniously on a hall chair. "P'r'aps 'e's 'ere still!"

"No, I don't think so—if the back door isn't open again."

Rose turned quickly, and ran to the back door. They waited silently till her return.

"It was unfastened, sir," she announced. "No one fastened it after he got out. But I've fastened it now."

"Then 'e may 'ave come back again!" exclaimed the cook.

"That's not likely, after this rumpus, but we'll search the house again," said Haslam. "Mr Blythe, will you have the whole place searched? I'll join you, but want a look round the grounds first."

"Oh, please be careful, sir!" cried Rose.

Haslam nodded, and slipped out of the front-door.

It was quite dark by now. He paused in the porch, in order to get his eyes used to the blackness. Then he walked out on to the drive, and explored the grounds in front and around the house carefully.

He thought his search was going to prove fruitless, but, just as he was turning back from a tour to the gate, something white attracted his attention. He stooped down, expecting to pick up a piece of crumpled paper. Instead, he picked up a lady's handkerchief.

"Good Lord!" he murmured, disturbed and bewildered.

He struck a match, and examined the handkerchief by its light. In the corner were the initials, "M.H."

He stood still for a few moments, considering. In his hand was a little clue, a little scrap of evidence. But was he anxious to produce it? Could he trust justice to see this strange episode through justly? Man is a social animal, and works, in the main, for the majority, but sometimes his communal instinct is shelved for a more personal and individual consideration; and, although Haslam knew that by all the usual laws he ought to reveal that handkerchief, he decided, before he returned to the house, that he would not.

He was convinced that there were mysteries within mysteries here, and he chose to try and unravel them in his own way.

The idea of associating Mary Holland with anything shady was too ridiculous to entertain for a moment. He was forced to admit, however, that an impartial, official mind might have drawn unpleasant conclusions from this little handkerchief, now hidden securely in his pocket, from the sudden flight down the drive on the night before, and from Mary Holland's general air of half-concealed unhappiness. They might even have drawn conclusions from her very poverty.

"Found anything?" queried Ambrose Blythe, when they were

seated again in his study.

Haslam shook his head, and wondered how far the lie removed his chances of heaven.

"Have you?" he asked.

"Not a thing. We've searched the entire place. The man seems to have been a common thief."

"You don't think that, sir," retorted Haslam.

"Why not?" demanded Mr Blythe, knowing all the time that he did not.

"Because the preparation was too elaborate, and the incident was obviously only one incident in some larger game. It must occur to you, as it has to me, that a man who calls to enquire for a non-existent lunatic, and begins his enquiries several hours beforehand, is an elaborate sort of a scamp. And, then, if he were after some haul, how does it happen that either he or one of his assumed confederates who have been visiting here for about a year, haven't landed their haul by now, or else given it up? I admit the whole thing beats me, Mr Blythe, but, clearly, it's not a case of common theft."

"Of course, it isn't," nodded Mr Blythe. "As if I didn't know that! Then I'm driven back to my original contention. They're after me."

"But Pike got hurt."

"Bah! He was in the way. If they wanted Pike, they could have landed him one on the knob any day, for he's the one who always answers the bell. And, don't forget, it wasn't until yesterday that I saw any of these people myself. Before that, Pike always dealt with them."

"And, when they have seen you, I've been with you."

"Exactly! What the devil's to be done?"

"It's obvious, sir," answered Haslam. "You must get protection."

"Ay, but not local protection. I won't have any country bobbies round the place. No—I know what I'll do. I'll engage a detective from London. I'll go up to London tomorrow. How about that, eh?" Haslam did not reply immediately, and Mr

Blythe misunderstood him. "Don't think this is any reflection on you, Mr Haslam!" he exclaimed. "Not a bit! But, since we've come to bodily violence, perhaps I ought to look after my little household more or less officially, eh? What d'ye say?"

"You're right, of course," replied Haslam, touched by the old man's thought. He had merely been wondering how he would stand if a detective were on the scene, cross-examining him; or, more important, how Mary Holland might stand. There was no denying, however, that from every other point of view, this was a case for an expert. "I expect a detective will soon get to the bottom of what, to you and me, appears a baffling mystery." Suddenly he gave an exclamation. "I have it!" he cried. "Now, here's an idea. Get your detective, by all means, but postpone it for a week——"

"Hay! I may be dead and buried in a week!" retorted Mr Blythe.

"Not if you stay the week comfortably in my rooms in London. You'll be as safe there as the King. And, while you're away, we can make an interesting little test."

"I don't quite follow you," said Mr Blythe, puckering his brow, "but, I admit, the idea sounds interesting."

"Why, don't you see," continued Haslam. "You think these people are after you. In that case, as soon as they find you've flitted—and I shall see it's known that you *have* flitted—they will cease their visits till your return——"

"Whereas, if they *do* still keep on coming, it won't be me they want!" cried Mr Blythe, thumping the table. "Bravo! I call that really brainy. Could I take Pike along with me? I'm lost without him."

"Of course. I was going to suggest it."

"Ah, but it seems unfair to leave you here to face it all alone!" exclaimed Mr Blythe, in sudden penitence. "A nice thing, inviting you to spend a week with me, and then making you spend it by yourself!"

"No need to worry about that, sir, I assure you," laughed Haslam. "I'm all for the idea. I shall have a fine chance to steep myself in my work, and, of course, I'm not in any personal danger myself. If I get scared, I assure you *I* won't hesitate to call in the local police. My only stipulation is that you give me authority to do that, in case of need."

Mr Blythe beamed. The plan appealed to him from every point of view, and perhaps, not least, because he wanted a holiday and a respite. His nerves were in a bad way. A week in London would set him on his feet. Then, with renewed energy, greater knowledge, and a detective at his back, he could return fully equipped to thrash out the perplexing problem.

"Unless I thrash it out first, all by myself," suggested Haslam.

"If you're clever enough to do that," chuckled Mr Blythe, "I'll leave the house to you when I die!" He rubbed his hands like a schoolboy, anticipating a vacation. It was quite pathetic. "And, now, what about a game of chess. And I'll beat you tonight!"

He kept his word. Haslam was thoroughly routed; and there is no need to enquire whether he assisted in his own downfall. They retired at ten. Bad dreams were the only disturbers of the night. Next morning, the sun rose gaily, driving away even the bad dreams.

The morning was spent in arrangements, and, immediately after lunch, the Ford proudly owned by the Heysham innkeeper was at the gate, ready to take Mr Blythe and Pike to Wynton station.

"You're sure you'll not be lonely?" exclaimed the old man, in a final fit of remorse as the car moved off.

"Quite sure," cried Haslam, waving his hand. "Glad to get rid of you!"

He had spoken in jest, and Mr Blythe had chuckled at the sally; but, as Haslam turned back and walked up the drive, a sense of strange peace and possession came over him. He wondered whether the coming week would be the pleasant, undisturbed period which every outward sign indicated.

Rose, he knew, would look after him, bringing a pleasant undisturbing warmth into the days. Already, under a spreading tree on the lawn, she had placed his little table for the afternoon's work, with a comfortable chair and cushions to try and tempt him into laziness. Bees buzzed everywhere, and the roses glowed transparently in the sunlight. From every side came the soft fragrance of flowers, borne on the faintly-heard breeze. Seven days of this lay before him. It was as near to perfection as he could ever hope for!

And yet, as he sat down under the tree, and began to write, there was one thing lacking. It was not Mr Blythe. Certainly, it was not Pike. It was not even the actual presence of Rose, who stood merely for a pleasant background to all this luxury. Haslam did not ask himself what it was he lacked, because he was gifted with sober sense, and he knew perfectly well what it was.

"But, of course, I'm an ass, and that's the end of it," he murmured, and, bending over his sheets, blotted out his nonsensical dreams.

He had been writing for a couple of hours when he suddenly looked up. Someone was approaching. Rose, of course, with the tea tray. But it was not Rose. His heart gave a leap, and a clever aphorism received a blot, as he saw that the girl approaching him across the lawn was Mary Holland.

CHAPTER 10

If Peter Haslam was surprised to see Mary Holland, he was no more surprised than was Mary Holland herself when she saw who it was under the spreading tree. She stopped abruptly, stared, and then came on more slowly.

"I am beginning to think Fate has a hand in this," exclaimed Haslam, rising. "We appear destined to go on meeting each other."

"It does seem so," she answered, and then hesitated, as though doubtful as to what attitude she should adopt. "I—I didn't know I'd find you here."

"It was hardly to be expected that you would," said Haslam. "The circumstances are—rather peculiar." Then he, too, hesitated, not knowing how much he ought to tell or it would be wise to reveal.

"How peculiar?" she asked, and he was quick to note that a subtle defensive quality had entered into her. Suddenly she added, "But I'm keeping you from your work?"

"And getting your own back," laughed Haslam, "for I've twice kept you from yours."

She studied him for a moment. She still seemed very undecided. Her puzzled expression contained something half-fearful in it, and Haslam decided that he would remove that fear as soon as he possibly could.

"Are you living here?" she asked. "Is this your house?"

"I am living here, for the moment, but this is not my house," he returned. It occurred to him as odd that she should not have known this for certain. It suggested that she also did not know that Ambrose Blythe lived here; yet this was the third time, within his knowledge, that she had been inside the gate. "When I arrived at Heysham two days ago—on the first afternoon I met you, you know—I put up at the inn," Haslam told her. "A chance encounter with Mr Blythe—he's the owner of this place—led to an invitation, and, as you see, I've moved over."

"Mr Blythe," she repeated.

"Yes. Did you want to see him?"

"I didn't know who owned this house, but I wanted to see the owner. I wanted to ask him whether——"

"Well?"

"Whether he'd mind my painting the wonderful view from this lawn?"

People with simple intelligence have the advantage of being invaded by only one emotion at a time. Haslam's intelligence was not simple, however, and he found himself invaded now by several new emotions. Firstly, there was the emotion of pleasure at the thought that, while he sat writing on the lawn, Mary Holland might also sit painting on it. Secondly, there was the emotion of surprise that she should ask to paint a view from a point which, ostensibly, should be quite new to her. Thirdly, there was the emotion of uneasiness that she would provide him with another proof of her active interest in unsavoury happenings. And, fourthly, there was an emotion of relief that her methods, unlike those of the lantern-jawed man, lacked the appearance of premeditation and subtlety, suggesting in fact that she was a child in the art of deception.

All these emotions passed through Peter Haslam as he replied, without giving a trace of any of them, that it certainly was a very wonderful view.

"But, unfortunately, Mr Blythe himself is away," he added. "He left only an hour or two ago, and I am in temporary charge. Will that make any difference to your request?"

"Do you mean, you can give me permission to paint the view?" she murmured.

"I can. Mr Blythe has given me carte blanche. I may do what I like, and use my own discretion, in all things. And, to save any further discussion, Miss Holland, if you still want to paint the view, of course you may do so." Something tempted him to test her a little, and he added, casually, "You know the view, then?"

"Yes—I trespassed once, by mistake," she answered, much too eagerly.

"She won't trust me," thought Haslam to himself. "Why is it that, although I know she has lied to me, I can't help trusting her? I wonder if I'm being a real fool!" Aloud, he said, "Well, that's rather funny. I trespassed here once myself, also. It was two days ago—in the evening. When I found out I was on private property, I walked boldly up to the front door and enquired where I was. That was how I met Mr Blythe."

"You didn't know him before?"

"No."

"Do you mean—you've had no connection with him at all?"

"Absolutely none! He and I were utter strangers until two evenings ago."

He forebore asking her why she put these questions, and, although she looked as though she would like to ask more, she hesitated. But suddenly, a new thought flashed into her mind, and she exclaimed, impulsively,

"Two evenings ago! What time was it?"

"Round about seven," answered Haslam, watching her quietly.

She flushed under his scrutiny, and became momentarily confused.

"Why, how funny!" she cried. "That was the time I trespassed myself. I—I'm afraid I felt rather guilty. Of course, it was very silly of me, but when I thought I heard someone, I ran. Wasn't it foolish?"

"Yes—I can't see why you did that."

She paused an instant, then plunged.

"Did you see me? Were *you* the someone?"

"I was."

"Why didn't you speak?"

"Well, I was going to, but, to tell the truth, you were too quick for me."

"I expect I surprised you rather?"

"You did. I had just had some evidence of your courage, you see——"

"My courage?"

"The madman, you remember. I couldn't frighten you over that. And it did occur to me that it must be a pretty big thing to scare you away like that. Rather bigger than trespassing, you know."

He waited, hoping. But no admission came. She merely murmured that one always felt different in the evening, didn't one? She wasn't really anything like as plucky as she had made out. Now he knew what a real little coward she was.

Haslam smiled. It was all very mystifying, and very pathetic. Noting her distress, and rejoicing at any rate in this further proof that she was a bad liar, he reverted to the ostensible object of her visit, and repeated his permission to paint the view from the lawn.

"But I do make just one stipulation," he added. "If this picture is not already commissioned, you must let me purchase it."

"But you may not like it," she objected. "You—you really mustn't go on buying pictures like this!"

"Like what?" asked Haslam, innocently.

"Oh, don't be so absurd, you nice man!" she blurted out. "I haven't many brains, but I've got a few!"

Haslam laughed, and a wave of happiness flowed through him as their conversation turned into happier channels.

"I plead guilty, Miss Holland," he said. "But, honestly, I think I got good value."

"Five pounds!" she exclaimed. "Of course, you didn't. I'll paint this picture for you, Mr Haslam and then three more—if you can stand them—and that will make the score even."

"Nonsense! I'll pay you the same price for this, or I won't have it at all."

"Well, we'll discuss the business side of it later," she conceded, a little unsteadily. "I really don't know why you should be so kind to me."

"I'm not at all kind to you," replied Haslam, "but I do want to help you, Miss Holland. That's all."

She was silent for a moment.

"Tell me," she said, in a low voice. "Are you really—only an author?"

"Of course."

"I mean, you're not a detective?"

"I assure you I'm not a detective. Why should I be?"

She seemed on the point of continuing, but either thought better of it, or a shadow on the lawn diverted her. It was the shadow of Rose, bearing a tea-tray.

Rose had many Stirling qualities, and one of these was now demonstrated. She did not drop the tray. She merely paused, noticed Mary Holland's surprising presence, and then came on again.

"I wonder what Rose is thinking?" reflected Haslam.

Rose was thinking: "Well, there's funny things about this house, but one thing I *do* know, if the whole world stops going round—Mr Haslam's all right."

For which reason, she plumped the tea-tray down without any undue raising of eyebrows, and awaited further instructions.

"Rose," said Haslam, promptly. "This is Miss Holland, an artist in the neighbourhood. I hope you don't think I've acted wrongly in giving her permission to paint the view from this lawn. I feel quite sure Mr Blythe wouldn't have minded."

"If you say so, sir, I'm sure he wouldn't," replied Rose, decisively.

"And I don't think he'd mind, either," continued Haslam, with a glance at Mary Holland, "if you brought another cup. Do you?"

Again Rose was sure he wouldn't, and marched back to the house, while Mary Holland looked after her, with a slightly puzzled expression.

"She seems a nice maid," she commented.

"Rose is a trump," exclaimed Haslam, beginning to shove his papers aside. "There's nothing wrong with Rose."

"What is Mr Blythe like?" she asked. "He sounds rather nice, too, from what you say."

"I like him immensely."

"But—you've only known him a day or two."

"That's all." A sudden thought crept into Haslam's mind, but he dismissed it at once. To doubt Mr Blythe seemed almost sacrilegious. "I think I've rather a knack for sudden friendships, and for picking out the right people. I've only known you two days, also, Miss Holland."

"And you think I'm one of the right people?"

"I do," he answered, sincerely. "And, what's more, I'm hoping that, before your next picture is finished, you'll come to the same conclusion about me."

"I think I have come to that conclusion already," she said. "Only——"

She trailed off, and Rose again interrupted an interesting moment. If Rose had not been such an estimable person, Haslam would have blessed her!

Tea was pleasant, but impersonal. Mary Holland did her best to keep it so, and Haslam considerately lent her every assistance. He noted, with concern, that the little flashes of humour were absent this afternoon, and that the cloud which appeared to be settling on the girl had descended lower. Often, as they spoke, she grew abstracted, and once when he spoke to her she did not hear him, her thoughts being elsewhere. He wondered whether she, too, were fearing the night.

After tea, she left him for a little while, to return presently with her easel. Then followed two hours of wonderful pleasure to Peter Haslam. A few feet off, while he began his novel, Mary Holland began her picture, and the pleasant proximity was a delight to him. He told himself that his work would gain warmth and humanity from this proximity, using this as a further excuse for an action concerning which he felt a trifle guilty; but he did not cover very many pages during those two hours, glancing rather too often at the graceful, slender form of the artist at her easel, and drinking in her quiet and youthful beauty.

Mary Holland, on her side, did not look at him. She worked steadily, as though her mind were resolved to risk no more conversation and the impulse to which conversation gave rise. Sometimes her glance did wander, but never in Haslam's direction. It wandered towards the house, and the gate, and her eyes at such times were full of a queer anxiety and apprehension.

"I wonder whether I have done wisely?" thought Haslam. "I can't believe that she isn't playing the game. And I can't believe either that Mr Blythe isn't playing the game. No, I'll swear they're both as innocent as I am myself. But it is odd! Confoundly odd!"

At a quarter-to-seven, Miss Holland left her easel, and walked across to Haslam.

"I think I've done enough for today," she said. "I wonder if you'd let me store my easel somewhere? It would save me taking it backwards and forwards to Wynton."

"Why, of course," replied Haslam. "Let's find some place for it."

They searched around, and discovered a little shed which would do admirably. The easel and picture were stored away, and then the girl smiled and held out her hand.

"Are you cycling back to Wynton?" he asked.

"Yes," she replied. "My bicycle is just inside the gate."

"And you'll be coming again tomorrow?"

"If I may."

"What about lunch?"

She shook her head.

"Please don't be too good to me, Mr Haslam," she said.

"As you like," he nodded, "though a lunch seemed to me such a harmless institution. But tea I can count on?"

"Oh, yes." She held out her hand. "Goodbye."

"No, au revoir," he answered, taking her hand. He dropped it rather quickly. She was too disturbing.

Just before she mounted her bicycle, he called to her, over the gate.

"I want to tell you one thing before you go, Miss Holland," he said. "I've fully made up my mind to one thing. Before your picture is painted, you will tell me your whole story, of your own accord—whatever it is."

Then he turned, and walked slowly back to the house. And Mary Holland watched him until he was out of sight.

CHAPTER 11

If Haslam imagined that the peaceful hours he had spent with Miss Holland were to form a prelude to a period of uninterrupted serenity, he was mistaken. He had hardly finished bringing his manuscript papers indoors before Rose approached him with a serious face.

"What is it, Rose?" he asked. She, he, and the cook were now alone in the house.

"Don't think I'm frightened, sir," she replied, "but I think I ought to tell you."

"I don't think you're frightened, and I'm quite sure you ought to tell me," he assured her.

"Thank you, sir. I'm sure no one ought to be frightened, not with you in the house. I tell cook so, but it's no good." Peter Haslam prayed that he might be able to maintain the reputation for courage and security which he enjoyed with the maid. "While you and the lady was at the gate, sir," Rose proceeded, "I looked out of the window, and saw a man on the lawn, bending over your papers."

"Did you?" Haslam exclaimed, frowning. "It was very rude of him. What sort of a man?"

"I couldn't see very well, sir. You see, he was under the tree. But he seemed to see me clear enough, because almost as soon as I got to the window, he hopped it. Went away, I mean."

"Hopped it will do," murmured Haslam. "It's far more expressive. Do you think he was the rascal who went for Pike yesterday?"

"No, I don't, sir. I only wish I'd had a better look at him." She paused, and then, invited by his attitude, she asked, "What do you think about it, sir?"

He looked into the honest blue eyes, and suddenly other points of view occurred to him.

"I think this, for one thing," he replied. "I'm getting so interested in this affair that I feel I've got to stay and see it through. But if you and cook have had enough of it, and want to get a room at the inn at Heysham, you have my full permission to do so. You can come over in the morning, and then go back again at night——"

"What! And leave you here all alone?" cried Rose. "A nice thing, sir! Fancy, if we came back one morning, and found you murdered!"

This frank picture of his possible fate ought to have made Haslam shudder, but it made him laugh.

"I don't think that would be likely, Rose. Anyway, I'm not going to keep you or cook here against your wills. Tell cook so, will you?"

"Yes, sir. Thank you, sir. But cook won't go, no more than I will. Dinner at half-past seven, sir."

"Oh, Rose," he called after her, as she turned to go. "You won't be on front-door duty tonight. If the bell rings, I'll answer it."

He waved her faint protest aside, and, entering the library, began to settle himself for the evening. After arranging his papers, he took a reconnoitring stroll round the grounds, peering into every shed and out-house, and looking for signs of the unknown enemy. He saw no sign. The sun sank quietly behind the trees, and a thrush suddenly startled the stillness with its sweet, loud, liquid notes. He lingered by the gate, gazing up and down the road. It was deserted. Then, returning to the house, he made sure that all the doors and windows were closed and fastened, and concluded his labours just as the steaming soup appeared.

"Are you and cook staying?" he asked Rose.

"Of course, we are," replied Rose. "Cook's more frightened than me, but she says she'd be frightened anywhere now, so she might as well be frightened here as anywhere else."

"Well, tell her not to be too frightened. I'll see no harm comes to anyone. And tell her also not to open or unfasten the back-door, on any account. If it has to be opened, I'll do it. Of course, you'll both stay in tonight."

"Very good, sir."

Over the meat, they had another little discussion.

"Do these queer visitors ever come to the back-door?" he asked, as Rose plumped a chop before him.

"No, sir," she answered.

"Isn't that rather funny?"

"Well, you see, they're never tradesmen, or anything like that."

"H'm," he observed. "Pedlars and blind men aren't exactly front-door folk."

"Blind men can't see," she pointed out, shrewdly, "and pedlars often think they'll do better if they go to the front door. I've noticed it."

"Who answers the back-door, Rose?"

"Oh, any of us. It might be cook, it might be me, or it might be Pike."

"And the front-door? Is that always Pike's job?"

"Yes, sir. Unless he's out. Then, of course, I do it."

When the pudding came on, he decided to take Rose a little into his confidence.

"You may like to know why Mr Blythe has gone away," he said. "It's to test an idea of mine. Mr Blythe thinks that all these people come to see *him*—that is, that they want to do him some injury. Now, if that's true, we ought to get a visitor tonight, and then no more until he returns. My idea is to tell the visitor that Mr Blythe is away for a week, which should put them off. But, of course, if they keep on coming, then they must have some other reason."

Rose's eyes grew big and round. Haslam could see that she thought him a very clever person. As a matter of fact, if he had wished to lower himself in Rose's estimation, he would have been hard put to it!

Dinner over, he lit a cigar, and retired to the library. At half-past eight, the front-door bell rang.

So far, Haslam had conducted himself with a certain amount of sang froid, and both his health and his nerves were in good condition. A distinctly uncanny sensation crept over him, however, when he heard that bell, and he allowed five seconds to pass before he rose to answer it. What would he find? Another blind man? The young cyclist? The lantern-jawed fellow? The pedlar? Or a totally new character? Or, perhaps, nothing!

When he reached the hall, he saw Rose's head appearing cautiously from her quarters.

"Go back!" he whispered, and the head obediently disappeared; but not, Haslam imagined, very far.

He walked across the hall, hesitated, and then opened the door. A smiling, elderly man stood on the door-step. For a second, neither spoke. Then the smiling man asked, in a benign, musical voice,

"Is Mr Ambrose Blythe at home?"

"I'm sorry, he is not," replied Haslam.

"Dear me, that's a pity," said the visitor. "This *is* the Brambles, isn't it?"

"It is," answered Haslam, concluding that it must be. It was the first time he himself had heard the name of the house.

"And—I'm not mistaken?—Mr Blythe lives here?"

"He does. But he's gone away, and won't be back for a week." Haslam studied the genial elderly gentleman, and, answering a sudden impulse, asked him to come in. "I'm a friend of Mr Blythe's, and am holding the castle for him while he's away. Haslam's my name. May I know yours?"

"Why, of course," exclaimed the visitor. "I am Professor Heath." He had followed Haslam a little way into the hall. "I knew Mr Blythe well in Newcastle, and, being in the neighbourhood, thought I would look him up."

Haslam did not reply for a moment. His keen eyes had detected a suspicious bulge in the genial visitor's hip-pocket. The bulge itself was not at all genial. Of course, it might have been a thick and bulky pocket-book. But, on the other hand, it might not.

"Do come in?" pressed Haslam. He did not wish to give any indication that he mistrusted the man. He Wanted to learn all he could from him. But the professor hesitated.

"Why should I trouble you?" he asked, pausing. "I can call on Mr Blythe some other time. By the way, how is his health?"

"His health? Oh, he's quite well, thank you," said Haslam, wondering whether it was quite usual for people to look up old acquaintances with revolvers in their pockets.

"I'm glad to hear that—very glad," pursued the professor. "He wasn't at all well when I last saw him. As a matter of fact—" He paused, and eyed Haslam speculatively. "I take it, as you're Mr Blythe's friend, you know all about him?"

"All about him?" repeated Haslam. "I don't think I quite follow you?"

"Come, come!" replied the professor, genially. "There's no need to beat about the bush. Ah! Now I think I understand. You're his—his—you look after him, eh?"

"If you mean to imply that Mr Blythe is mad, and that I am his keeper," responded Haslam, frowning, "I'm afraid you're on the wrong track, sir."

There was a short pause. Professor Heath walked close up to Haslam, and looked at him searchingly. Haslam tightened, and got ready to knock the professor down at a moment's notice. If the professor's hand had approached his hip-pocket, it would never have reached there. Perhaps the professor knew it.

"The position is not quite clear to me, I admit," murmured the professor, shaking his head suddenly. "You say you are Mr Blythe's friend, and yet you profess to be ignorant of—of—" He broke off. "Dear me, this is very painful. Perhaps I should apologise. I dare say I have said too much."

"On the contrary, professor," returned Haslam, "you have said nothing at all. It has all been implication. Tell me, when you met Mr Blythe in Newcastle, was his health poor?"

"Poor!" exclaimed the professor. "Why, he'd only just come out of—ah, well, never mind, never mind. I'll call another time. Yes, yes, I'm saying too much."

He moved towards the door, frowning heavily. He stopped, and his eyes roamed swiftly round the hall, and then back to Haslam. Suddenly he came forward again, and tapped Haslam on the shoulder.

"I am out of my depth, I can see that," he said, "but you, also, seem to be out of yours. Let me tell you one thing, my dear sir, which perhaps you would do well to note. Mr Ambrose Blythe is a good friend, and I like him—but he suffers from delusions."

"Thank you," replied Haslam, coolly. "I'll make a note of it."

He felt there was nothing more to be gained by prolonging the interview, and that a good deal might be gained by ending it. The professor's eyes were beginning to roam again, and his hand was wavering. Haslam walked to the door and opened it.

"He'll be back in a week?" muttered the professor.

"In a week," nodded Haslam.

"I hope he has not gone alone?"

"He has his servant with him."

"Ah!" The professor's back straightened. "I am relieved. Had he gone alone, I should have been seriously worried. Goodnight, Mr Haslam. Goodnight."

He strutted out, and, with a sigh of relief, Haslam closed and bolted the door after him. Then he ran to the head of the stairs, and called,

"Is the back door bolted?"

"Yes," replied Rose's not too steady voice.

Haslam returned to the library, and poured himself out a stiff whisky and soda. The tension was becoming a little greater than he had anticipated. He was perfectly convinced that Professor Heath, the pedlar, and the blind man were one and the same person.

He was about to raise the glass to his lips when he stopped. Soft footsteps were creeping by his window.

CHAPTER 12

Answering his impulse rather than his judgment, Haslam pulled up the blind, threw open the French window, and stepped out on to the lawn.

The light from the library made a bright patch upon the grass, broken by his own shadow, but beyond was utter darkness, and he questioned the wisdom of his action as he stood uncertainly for an instant, trying to pierce the blackness, and listening for a repetition of the footsteps. He could hear nothing, save the faint rustle of a bush, and see nothing, save the patch of light on the lawn, and, above the encircling bushes and trees, the faintly gleaming stars.

The advantage was all on the side of the unseen, unheard enemy, who, invisible himself, might at this moment be watching Haslam's every moment. For all he could say, a revolver might be pointing at his heart from among those silent bushes, and a finger pressed gently against the trigger. One false move

——

Haslam slipped a little to one side, till he, also, became enveloped in shadow. He could see a little better now, and the outlines of the bushes gradually grew out of the blackness. There was, however, no sign of the man or creature who had produced the footsteps.

Haslam was tolerant towards cowardice in others, but loathed it in himself. Angry at the perfectly natural chills that began to wander up his spine, he disregarded them, like a foolishly defiant schoolboy, and took a few paces forward. Perhaps, had he realised that a revolver actually was being pointed at his heart, he would have acted differently; and, even lacking that definite knowledge, he soon took counsel from wiser judgment, and possibly saved his life.

"If anything should happen to me," he reflected, swiftly, "there will be two women alone in the house. Moreover, if I move too far from the open French window, somebody may slip in without my knowing it. I'd better go back."

Keeping in the shadow as much as he could, he beat a strategic retreat, reaching the comparative safety of the library with a mixture of relief and annoyance. He fastened the window securely, pulled down the blind again, and then, with a grunt, took up the glass of whisky and soda. This time, he was not interrupted.

The evening wore on. He heard rustlings in the hall. The servants were going to bed.

"All right?" he asked, cheerfully, putting his head out of the door.

"Yes, sir," answered Rose.

"Good. I've an idea we won't be disturbed tonight, but if you want me, don't forget to shout. And, of course, you'll keep your window and door locked."

"Yes, sir."

"That's a plucky girl," thought Haslam. "Doesn't lose her head. She'll deserve the best tip I ever gave when I go!" And, aloud: "I'm just going to make a final tour of the place, to see everything's secure, and then I'll turn in myself. I wonder why Mr Blythe doesn't keep a dog?"

"He did, sir," replied Rose, "but he lost it, a month ago."

"Lost it? How?"

"I don't know, sir. It just disappeared."

"Ah," said Haslam, frowning. "Well—goodnight."

Returning to the library, he took up the lamp, and made a grand tour of the house. He was becoming familiar with it by now. The tour was satisfactory. He made no suspicious or alarming discovery. So satisfied was he that he even opened the front door when he had finished, and smoked a cigarette on the door-step in sheer bravado. Then, putting out the lights, he went to bed.

Nature, or Fate, or whatever name we may select for the silent wielder of our destinies, is full of gracious moments and redeeming qualities; otherwise, indeed, we should rebel and cease to exist. Before the storm it gives us calm, as it provides rest for us after the storm. The middle of a cyclone is a period of perfect stillness. Sunset, with all its glories and false promises, precedes the anxious night; and even death, which we fear and mistrust too much, dwelling only on its momentary agonies, is preceded by the precious gift of life.

And so it fell out that, before the big and bewildering storm descended upon the mysterious house of Ambrose Blythe in all its force, there was an interlude of almost perfect peace and delight. For six days, the rumbling in the hills receded, till one almost wondered whether the rumbling had ever been heard at all.

The night which followed the visit of Professor Heath was quiet and uneventful. If the three sleepers slept little, they were at least undisturbed. The day was full of peaceful, sunny hours, bringing with it Mary Holland and her paint brushes, and even towards evening, after Miss Holland had departed, there seemed less tension. Haslam felt convinced that they would have no visitors, and he imbued Rose and the cook with so much of his own optimism that he again failed to induce the servants to sleep at the inn. He would probably have prevailed with the cook, but Rose doggedly insisted that *she* wasn't going to let Mr Haslam spend a night in the house all by himself, and nobody need think it.

"Well, of course, if you won't go, I can't," grumbled cook, in the kitchen. "You don't get *me* sleeping in any bedroom alone, ever, after this!"

The question of the propriety of leaving Rose alone in the house with Mr Haslam did not occur to her at that moment, for she was far too much concerned with her own individual emotions; but, later on, the vision of Mrs Grundy loomed before her, contributing a further reason why she should remain in the Brambles, if Rose remained. And, as she had remarked on the day before, if one was going to be scared stiff anyhow, what did it matter where? Imagination is often worse than reality, particularly at 2 in the morning.

But nothing happened on the second night, or on the third, and Haslam concluded that his theory was correct, and that there would be no more trouble until Ambrose Blythe returned. And then he would bring a detective with him.

In these circumstances, although he had been very near it at one time, Haslam decided not to apply to the local police, and devoted his thoughts entirely to his work and to Mary Holland.

She came every day, and for a while they kept to an unspoken, tacit understanding that oppressive matters should not be referred to. As though endeavouring to deserve their good fortune, they each worked with commendable industry, and while Haslam asserted, over tea, that his novel was turning out the best he had ever written, Mary Holland proclaimed that her picture was proving the best she had ever painted. It certainly was considerably better than her previous effort, now gracing Haslam's mantelpiece, and there were many reasons why this should be. She worked more carefully and slowly, as though anxious to continue the justification of her visits. Her financial status had received a fillip. And Haslam's personal interest may also have proved an inspiration.

But the commercial value of the picture, all the same, never approached the five pounds which Haslam swore he would pay for it, and which Miss Holland swore she would not accept.

Haslam burned to ask her questions regarding herself, but he was patient because of his determination to learn her story before the week was out. This determination increased as the week drew to a close, for he noticed that her anxiety and sadness, restrained during the first days by the novelty of their friendship and by his own conscious efforts to make her cheerful, were returning to her with redoubled weight. Catching sight of her in unguarded moments, he saw that her fears were being superseded by an attitude of despair and hopelessness, which appeared to be settling upon her like a heavy, immovable cloud. On their last afternoon alone together, when Rose had brought the tea, Haslam suddenly looked the girl full in the face, and asked, bluntly,

"And now, Miss Holland—what is it?"

She did not reply, but she kept her eyes on his as he went on,

"Tomorrow morning, Mr Blythe returns, bringing a detective with him, and our pleasant tête-à-têtes will be over. Your picture is not yet finished, and I expect you will still be coming here. In fact—" He paused for a moment. "In fact, Miss Holland, I should advise it. Detectives are annoying folk, and if you have anything you want to conceal, he may think it odd you should depart the moment he comes, and rout you out. You see, I'm speaking quite frankly."

"Thank you," she answered. "I'd rather you did."

"Very good. Then I'll go on speaking frankly. That detective is coming down on a good errand, but he may prove a bit of a nuisance to you—and, therefore, to me. We shall probably both of us be cross-examined pretty cutely. I'll be asked to tell all I know, and I won't tell all I know. And you'd help me immensely by letting me know just what I can tell him, and what I cannot."

"But what is all this to do with me?" she burst out, suddenly. "You don't really think I've anything to do with it?"

"It?" asked Haslam, quietly. "What?"

"Why—all that goes on at this house."

"What *does* go on at this house, Miss Holland?"

She stared at him, and shook her head despairingly.

"I don't know," she answered.

"Is that true?"

"Of course! I wish I did! That's why I'm here—to find out." Suddenly, she challenged him. "You said just now there were some things you didn't want to tell the detective. What were they?"

A great load was being lifted off Haslam's shoulders. He had never seriously doubted Miss Holland's good faith, but this assurance that she, too, was ignorant of the mystery that enveloped them brought peace to his mind.

"I'll tell you," he said. "There's not much, but enough to interest a detective. When I saw you that first evening in the drive, you ran away as though you were frightened——"

"I was frightened," she interrupted. "I didn't know it was you."

"But would a detective believe that you were merely frightened because you were trespassing? Then, on the next evening, you came again."

"How do you know?"

"You should be more careful of your handkerchiefs," he smiled. "You dropped another, and, happily, I happened to be the one who picked it up. I kept it to myself. Then, again—your request to paint the view from this lawn. Perhaps that might get past the detective—the request was reasonable enough, on the face of it. But I'm sure you could have found plenty of other equally good views for your purposes, and I'm not vain enough to suppose that you merely wanted to improve your acquaintance with me—in fact, you did not expect to find me here at all! Now, listen, Miss Holland. Are you willing to tell your whole story to the detective?"

"No," she replied.

"Then, how can I help you to preserve it, unless you trust me with it?"

"Very well. I will," she said, and his heart gave a bound. "I believe I should have told you anyhow, you've been so good. Oh, if only you can help me!"

"I promise you I will, if I can."

"There's really not so very much to tell," she went on, staring across the lawn at her easel, and frowning at it. "It's—it's all about my brother. We live together at Wynton, and I've always tried to look after him. I promised my mother I would, just before she died—we're orphans, you know—though, of course, I'd have done my best, anyhow. He's a dear boy, but wretchedly weak, I'm afraid. Always getting into trouble—but never anything serious, till now."

She paused, and he urged her to continue.

"Remember, I'm your friend, to the last ditch," he said.

"I really don't know why you're so decent to me," she exclaimed, suddenly mopping her eyes. "But I do trust you, somehow, and I really feel I want someone's help. George—that's my brother—has been terrible lately. So depressed, and short and angry if I speak to him about it. All nerves. I haven't the least idea what it is, but at last I got so anxious that I began to watch him, and I found out that he has been coming to this house."

"And you don't know why?" demanded Haslam.

A vision of the nervous cyclist rose before him, and he looked closely at Mary Holland. He believed he detected a faint resemblance.

"I simply haven't any idea. Those times I came here, I was simply following him. That first night you saw me here, I was going to call at the house, to see if I could find out anything. I'm sure he has got in with some bad set, you see, and of course I thought the owner of the house—Mr Blythe, that is—must be one of them. But my courage failed—I really couldn't think of what questions to ask—and, when I heard a sound—that was you, you know—I got ridiculously scared, and ran. Idiot!"

"Not a bit," retorted Haslam. "I don't wonder. Did your brother know you followed him?"

"He found out once, and I never saw anyone in such a rage. He apologised afterwards, but he made me promise not to follow him again, or to say anything about it to a soul. I'm breaking that promise now," she added, slowly, "but I don't mind. You see —I really and truly trust you."

"Thank you," answered Haslam, quietly. "You may. Please go on."

"There's very little more. On the morning of the day that Mr Blythe went away, my brother disappeared. I've not seen him since. So I made my excuse about the picture, thinking that, if I were here, I might come across him. Perhaps I was silly, but I didn't know what to do. I couldn't go to the police. I was afraid of the people in the house—I didn't know then, you see, that Mr Blythe was all right. Are you sure he is?"

"Yes—quite sure," responded Haslam. "It's been suggested to me that he's mad, but I don't believe that. Tell me, does your brother cycle?"

"Yes."

"Does he know where Ingate is?"

"He could walk there blindfold!"

Haslam nodded.

"But he asked the way there the other evening, when he called," he remarked, and frowned.

Miss Holland watched him, anxiously. Now that she had told him her story, she turned instinctively to him for advice.

"What am I to do?" she asked.

"There's only one thing, at the moment," replied Haslam. "Trust me. I'm more or less pledged to help Mr Blythe all I can to clear up this mystery, and I mean to do it. But—if there are any conflicting interests—well, yours will come first, Miss Holland. That's a promise!"

Her hand went forward impulsively. He took it, and pressed it gently.

CHAPTER 13

A grey-haired, stern-visaged man in the mid-forties took up the telephone receiver at his elbow and listened to the voice at the other end.

"Detective Grant?" enquired the voice.

"Speaking," replied the detective.

"Ah! My name is Blythe—Ambrose Blythe. I don't suppose you remember me——"

"Perfectly," said Grant. "You helped me to identify a man in the Maxley case, two years ago."

"Bless my soul!" murmured the voice at the other end. "But you only saw me once or twice!"

"Once or twice is enough for me, Mr Blythe. You had come down from Newcastle, on business connected with some property that had been left you——"

"Yes, and hated London so much that I wouldn't go any farther south, but turned round as soon as I could and went back again," Mr Blythe chuckled. "What memories you detectives have, eh?"

"It's our job," replied Grant.

"Did you catch that man in the Maxley case, as you call it?"

A shadow passed across Grant's face.

"No—he gave me the slip. Everybody wasn't as helpful as you. He was caught some months later, on the continent. What can I do for you?"

"Spare me half-an-hour for a chat. Are ye free?"

"Not this morning. What about two o'clock this afternoon?"

"That will suit me. My time's my own. I'll go and look at the waxworks. I suppose everybody ought to do that once in his life, eh?" Grant smiled; an unusual thing with him. "Oh, by the way," called out Mr Blythe, before ringing off, "it's a most extraordinary case I'm going to speak to you about. From your point of view, a tip-top mystery, I should say—but, from mine, the very devil! Are you free to undertake it?"

"I'll tell you when I hear what it is, Mr Blythe."

"Then you'll undertake it," retorted Mr Blythe. "Good! That's settled!" And he put up the receiver.

A solemn clerk—almost as solemn as Grant himself, for the reason that the clerk hoped one day to reach Grant's position in the detective world, and therefore imitated him as hard as he could—entered the room, and asked, in a business, unemotional voice,

"What about the Hartshaws, sir?"

"I'm not sure yet that I shall undertake it," replied Grant.

"Not take it, sir?" exclaimed the clerk, annoyed with himself the next moment that he had shown surprise. Grant never showed surprise. He coughed slightly, and added, reverting to his unemotional tone, "They're most anxious that you should, sir."

"I know they are. I'll let you know this afternoon. Wheeler wants a chance—I may hand it over to him."

The clerk nodded, a little sadly. Wheeler wasn't a patch on Grant. Wheeler was, in his opinion, a muddler. Look at how he had muffed his last case! Why, even *he* could have handled it better than Wheeler.

Grant's voice interrupted his cogitations.

"Let me have particulars of Ambrose Blythe," he rapped out.

The clerk disappeared, and reappeared again, with a ponderous book, opened at the right page, thirty-seven seconds later. He knew it was thirty-seven seconds, because he had timed himself. Moreover, he was quite calm, and not in the least breathless. He had paused to compose himself just outside the door.

Grant was a stern man, particularly when duty called, but

he was not unkindly. He commended the clerk on his rapidity —"You were quick, Smith," he said—and Smith retired, stifling the pleasure out of his face.

Then Grant read his notes regarding Ambrose Blythe. They told him very little more than he had mentioned over the telephone. They comprised mainly a few dates, Blythe's address at Newcastle, the address of his inheritance near Heysham, a few particulars regarding his personal appearance, and a brief record of the circumstances of their previous meetings. Quite by accident, Blythe had been able to give him some slight assistance in a case which, officially, was completed and forgotten, yet which, because of a certain association, would never be forgotten by Detective Grant.

Punctually at two, Mr Ambrose Blythe turned up, and was shown at once in the detective's private sanctum by the expressionless Smith. Smith burned with curiosity about everybody and everything he saw, but he had schooled himself to disregard his emotions. Thousands of us do the same, concealing what we really feel and think, yet perhaps not with such assiduity as Smith.

"Good afternoon," said Grant, briskly, extending his strong, lean hand. "Sit down, and tell me about this extraordinary case. But, let me warn you first, it is the human habit to believe that everything surrounding us is extraordinary, or wonderful, or superlative. Even the tiniest shell-fish imagines itself the centre of all existence. So don't be too disappointed if I think your case a little less extraordinary than you do."

"Ah, but I *will* be disappointed," retorted Mr Blythe. "I'm not a shell-fish! I tell you, this is really an amazing case, and I'm not going to leave this room till I have your assurance that you'll take it up."

"Go on," said the detective. "I'm listening."

Mr Blythe told his story. He was somewhat rambling and long-winded, but Detective Grant did not interrupt him once; this was not a cross-examination, and the manner in which a story is told is often as informative, to a shrewd mind, as are the related facts themselves. The detective made notes, however, and when at last his visitor had run himself dry, he consulted them without speaking for several moments.

"Well, well!" exclaimed Mr Blythe, longing for expletives. "Now, tell me! Wasn't I right? Did you ever hear anything more extraordinary?"

"I am certainly interested," replied Grant, in the voice Smith envied, and even practiced. "Let me ask you a few questions. You say you mistook Mr Haslam for one of your uninvited guests, as you call them——"

"I did!"

"Are you quite convinced that your first impressions were not correct?"

Mr Blythe gasped. "But, my dear sir," he cried, "I tested him with passages from his own books——"

"Even a bona fide novelist may also be a bona fide crook," the detective pointed out dryly. "A duke has been known to steal a piece of cheese."

"Duke? Cheese? What the devil——"

"And you have left this Mr Haslam in sole charge of your house," pursued Grant, watching Mr Blythe narrowly. "Was that a wise thing to do?"

"Upon my soul!" cried the old man. "I've half a mind not to let you handle the case at all, Mr Grant, so I have."

"I haven't consented to handle it at all yet," Grant reminded him. "But don't get so excited. I like to put my questions in my own way, and make my discoveries in my own way. Your indignation in regard to the suggestion that Mr Haslam is a crook gives me a clearer picture of Mr Haslam than anything you have previously told me. *Now*, I'm almost inclined to believe you. But everybody's a suspect in a case of this kind, you know."

"God bless my soul!" murmured Mr Blythe. "You'll be suspecting me next."

"I suspect everybody," said Grant. "Sometimes, even, myself. There is no person in the world who will not waver under temptation, if the particular temptation to which he is most subject is placed strongly enough before him." He referred again to his notes. "What about your servants? You trust them?"

"Implicitly."

Grant was about to proceed with this point, but suddenly changed his mind.

"And you say you haven't notified the local police?" he asked.

"No, I've not told them a word. They'd have only bungled it, and I should have been a laughing-stock——"

"You ought to have notified the local police," interposed Grant. "In my opinion, it was folly not to. There might easily have been a tragedy before now, and, if there had been——" He shrugged his shoulders.

Mr Blythe began to feel a trifle uncomfortable.

"I dare say you're right, I dare say you're right," he mumbled. "But we've all got our whims, and I've got mine. I hate the local police, and I hate being laughed at. There—make what you like of that!" He rubbed his nose, and glared at Grant in amiable anger. "Of course, if you say so, we'll notify the local police at once——"

"But I don't say so," interrupted Grant. "It's not necessary at the moment."

"Why not?" demanded the old man. "You blow hot and cold!"

"Because I'm taking this case on," answered Grant quietly. "You've won, you see, Mr Blythe. You've interested me." He sounded a buzzer on his desk, and Smith appeared at the door. "Send Wheeler to me when he comes in, Smith, will you?" he said. "I'm giving him the Hartshaw case. I'm going away tomorrow, and may not be back for a few days."

"Very good, sir," replied the clerk, and evaporated.

Mr Blythe beamed. Queer though Grant's methods might be, and stern though his manner undoubtedly was, the old man felt much easier in his mind now that his responsibility was definitely handed over to a master-mind.

"Aha, but you do trip up sometimes, don't you, detective?" he exclaimed, chaffingly, when he was preparing to depart. "Fancy letting that scamp Maxley slip through your fingers, after all the help I gave ye!"

Grant did not reply at once. Then he said,

"Would you like to know how that happened? It was through my own daughter. She refused to give me the help for which I was entitled to ask. She used to work for me. But she got tired of justice, than which I contend there is no nobler master, turned against it and its methods—and quarrelled with me." He paused, and added, with a trace of bitterness, "I have not seen her for two years. After our quarrel, she disappeared. Ironic, isn't it? I can track criminals to their last lair, but my own daughter——" He shrugged his shoulders.

"Ah, but you'll find her, my friend!" cried Mr Ambrose impulsively, astonished and touched by the stern detective's sudden glimpse of feeling.

"I hope so," replied Grant, simply. "It's what I live for."

CHAPTER 14

On the morning of the day on which Ambrose Blythe was due to return, with the detective, to the Brambles, Peter Haslam received a surprise. Mr Blythe had wired that they would arrive at Wynton station on the three o'clock train, and Haslam imagined that he would have two or three more hours of solitude during which to review the strange position in which he found himself placed from all its angles. Mary Holland herself would not turn up until half-past two—he had insisted, from the point of view of policy, that she should not discontinue her visits—and thus he had anticipated a perfectly undisturbed morning. The uninvited guests had been temporarily choked off, and, in any case, they had hitherto selected the evening hours for their visits.

His calculations were upset, however, while he was pacing up and down the lawn. His eyes were bent down, and suddenly a shadow entered the little circle of sunshine on which his gaze was fixed. He looked up quickly, and found himself staring at a tall, well-built man, with a small beard, and a slightly foreign aspect.

"Good Lord!" thought Haslam. "Here's another of them! Now, what sort of a yarn is he going to put up, I wonder?"

For a few moments, neither of them spoke. Each was quietly studying the other. Haslam was trying to find some connecting link between this stranger and the previous gallery of visitors, but he could not do so, although he felt convinced that the little beard was false. The stranger, on his side, was watching Haslam with equal interest.

It was Haslam who suddenly broke the silence. There was a quality in the stranger's scrutiny which made him vaguely uncomfortable.

"Good morning," he said, a trifle brusquely. "What can I do for you?"

The stranger hesitated for an instant, then asked, in a voice which coincided with his continental aspect.

"Excuse me—but are you Mr Ernest Strangeways?"

Haslam reflected swiftly. "Now, if I deny that I am Mr Ernest Strangeways, he will depart," he thought, "and I shall learn nothing. That would be a pity!" Aloud, he temporised.

"You want to see Mr Ernest Strangeways?" he enquired, coolly.

"I do," said the stranger. "But I am not sure that he lives here?"

"Well, he does live here," answered Haslam, plunging.

"Ah—that is good. And is he at home?"

"Before I answer that question, may I ask what you want to see him about?"

The stranger raised his eyebrows.

"Of course," he murmured, "if the time is not convenient——"

"Oh, I didn't say the time wasn't convenient," interposed Haslam. "But Mr Strangeways is a very busy man, and if I could know your business, it might make a difference."

The stranger smiled.

"Ah, thank you. I think I understand. You mean that Mr Strangeways is at home to one man, but not to another. Is that so?"

"Perhaps."

"Very good. But, unfortunately, I cannot really tell my business to anyone but Mr Strangeways himself. You see, it is of a very private nature, and very important."

"Well, at least, you can tell me your name?"

The stranger shook his head, blandly. "Alas! Not even that."

Haslam found his interest growing. Obviously, this man had something to tell, and it was important to learn what that something was, if possible. He decided to plunge even more deeply.

"In that case," he said, "we will not beat about the bush any longer. I am Mr Ernest Strangeways."

"Indeed?" exclaimed the stranger, looking at Haslam hard. Haslam noticed that the man was not in the least thrown off his balance. "Perhaps you could give me some proof of what you say? You see—I have never had the pleasure of meeting Mr Strangeways before."

"That is obvious," retorted Haslam, dryly, "or you would have recognised me. You will forgive me, all the same, for refusing to supply you with any further particulars regarding myself— until, at any rate, you have supplied me with your own name, and the object of your call."

"My name is Carpentier," answered the stranger, readily. "No, I am not related to the boxer. My business is somewhat different. Tell me, sir. If you are Mr Strangeways, have you really no idea of what my business is?"

This was pretty fencing. Haslam began to enjoy himself.

"Admissions are sometimes injudicious, M. Carpentier," he returned. "An admission might be forthcoming after *you* had supplied *me* with that proof of identity you seem so anxious about. Now can I be certain that you are M. Carpentier? Can you give me no better proof than your word? A card, or a letter, or——"

"Or what?"

"Some sign?"

The stranger thought for a moment.

"A sign?" he said, softly. "Ah! But—one moment. Is not this the Brambles?"

"It is."

"And does not a Mr Blythe live here? A Mr Ambrose Blythe?"

"He does."

"Then how comes it, sir, if I may ask, that you appear to be in possession of this place?"

"Your questions are not at all clever," retorted Haslam, bluntly. "You came here knowing this was the Brambles, knowing that Mr Ambrose Blythe lived here, and expecting to meet Mr Ernest Strangeways. And now it seems to surprise you, to require some explanation from me, that your expectations are fulfilled. You must forgive me if, in the rather odd circumstances, I refuse to tell you anything further until you have explained your position a little more fully."

The stranger made a faintly protesting gesture.

"I ask your pardon, Mr Strangeways," he said, contritely. "I see I have been over-cautious. But caution is so necessary in these little matters, is it not? And, you must remember, I have never met you before. Well, I have no more doubts. I admit my foolishness. And I take it, without any more discussion, that you of course know my business."

"Very well, then, I do," answered Haslam, wondering where on earth this strange conversation was going to end. "I know your business perfectly. So let us get to it." He indicated a chair on the lawn. "Perhaps you will be seated?"

The continental gentleman walked slowly to the chair, and sat down. Haslam never took his eyes off him for an instant.

"It is good of you," murmured M. Carpentier, "but—as Mr Blythe is expected back today—I do not anticipate there will be time for a very long chat."

"Oh! You know that Mr Blythe is returning today, then?"

"Does that surprise you, Mr Strangeways?"

"Perhaps not," said Haslam. "Go on."

"I think, my dear sir, it is for you to 'go on,' as you call it," answered M. Carpentier, smiling. "You see, I have only called for information."

"Oh! You want information?"

"Yes. Or—perhaps I should say—instructions? I am entirely at your service."

Haslam frowned. He felt that he was getting a trifle out of his depth. This man was a skilful rogue, and fenced far too cleverly for him. He would give nothing away. Suddenly, it occurred to Haslam that he was remaining silent too long. M. Carpentier was eyeing him with a certain amount of doubt.

"I am glad to learn that you are at my service," said Haslam, angry with himself as he realised he was losing his grip, "and of course I have instructions for you. But, before I give them to you, kindly relate the nature of your last service to me? That we shall be quite sure of each other."

"We are not sure yet, then?" mused M. Carpentier. "That is such a pity. I dislike telling what is already known."

"In that case, sir," retorted Haslam, bluntly, "I fear I have no instructions for you."

"Very good," murmured M. Carpentier. "Then I will go."

He rose, and Haslam cursed himself more and more. If only he could detain this man till Mr Blythe returned. The detective would probably be able to handle him.

"One moment, M. Carpentier," he exclaimed. "We may be of some use to each other yet. Stay to lunch, and let us discuss business afterwards."

"But does not Mr Blythe return afterwards?" asked M. Carpentier, frowning slightly.

"Yes, but not till long afterwards. He comes—at six. We shall have plenty of time for our chat before then. And, as a matter of fact, I have quite a lot to say to you. Come, you'll stay?"

"Are you sure you can make arrangements indoors for this pleasant little lunch?" enquired M. Carpentier, nodding his head towards the house. "I confess, I am tempted. And, since Mr Blythe does not return till six, there is plenty of time."

He edged back towards his chair.

"Splendid!" cried Haslam. "I'll go and make arrangements at once!"

M. Carpentier sank back into his chair, with a sigh.

"Now, I am happy, Mr Strangeways," he sighed, with a curious accent on the name. "My doubts are dissipated. I am almost tempted to take off my beard! But I will not do that, until I learn that all is quite clear inside, and everything fixed."

"Don't worry," replied Haslam, delighted with himself. "Places shall be laid for two, and I shall return with a bottle of whisky."

He walked into the house, and summoned Rose.

"Lay places for two, Rose," he said, "don't ask questions, and keep out of the way. I've a visitor, and mean to keep him here till Mr Blythe and the detective turn up. We shall be in the library. Look out for them, and tell them to come to the library at once. You understand?"

"Yes, sir," answered Rose, hoping that her palpitations were not visible.

"And, now, bring me a small tray. I want to take the decanter out on to the lawn."

"Shall I bring it out, sir?"

"No, I'll do it. I want you to keep out of the way."

A few minutes later, Haslam emerged into the garden again. But the continental stranger had not waited. His chair was empty.

Haslam stared for several bitter seconds at the empty chair. Disappointment and self-annoyance fought for supremacy in his soul. What a chance he had let slip! What a blundering fool he was! He laid the tray down on the table, and refused to drink, as a penance.

"Idiot! Ass!" he muttered.

Then, in desperation, he threw himself into his work, and wrote the quickest—and the best—thousand words he had ever written in his life. Great work often springs from strange origins. A noble picture may be painted through a chance encounter with a bad woman, or an inspiring poem may be driven out of a poet who, with cotton-wool in his ears, is striving to forget a gramophone shrieking rag-time through a thin partition.

Haslam read his thousand words before lunch, and felt pacified. After all, he reflected, life was full of compensations. And another compensation was due at half-past two, in the form of a girl who was becoming rather significantly woven into the heroine of his new novel.

Mary Holland was a little anxious when she appeared, but Haslam reassured her. He repeated his avowal that her interests came first with him; and, since he could not see that anything would be gained by it, he did not mention his morning visitor. Deftly steering the conversation into happy channels, he contrived to make the hour a pleasant one, and at the very moment that Mr Blythe's car drove up, Mary Holland was breaking into a ripple of laughter at one of his sallies.

But the laughter stopped suddenly when she heard the gate click. She looked at Haslam with anxious eyes, and he saw that she was trembling slightly.

"Don't worry," he said, jumping up. "You've my word, remember. Whatever he has done, I'm your brother's friend!"

He felt almost guilty as he said this, but Mary's appealing eyes were too much for him. Millions of men have made worse resolutions with less provocation. Hurrying to the gate, he met the party as they were walking up the curved drive.

"Good Lord!" he exclaimed, stopping short.

Beside Mr Blythe, smiling faintly at him, was M. Carpentier. But, this time, without his beard.

CHAPTER 15

Haslam's brain began to spin. Was the world topsy-turvy? M. Carpentier had slipped away that morning to escape meeting Mr Blythe. Now, he was returning in Mr Blythe's company. The rules of logic seemed suddenly to have turned upside down.

"Well, well! What's the matter?" exclaimed Mr Blythe, astonished in his turn as he stared at Haslam. "D'ye think we're ghosts, or what?"

"Who is that man?" demanded Haslam, pointing to M. Carpentier.

"Why, our detective, of course," replied Mr Blythe. "Mr Grant. Who else would he be, now? You knew I was bringing him along ———"

"Yes, but he called on me this morning———"

"No, not on you, Mr Haslam," interposed Grant. "On Mr Strangeways, whose identity you borrowed."

"Mr Strangeways? Who's Mr Strangeways? What's the meaning of this?" cried Mr Blythe.

"Mr Strangeways is a non-existent gentleman, whom I invented for my own purposes," answered Grant, soberly. "And M. Carpentier was another creation of my own, Mr Haslam," he went on. "If you want to learn things from both friends and foes, there is no surer way of doing so than by surprising them. In fact, quite often, it is the only way of learning anything worth while at all."

"Well, I'm dashed!" murmured Haslam.

Mr Blythe was more emphatic.

"Devil take you, Grant!" he exclaimed. "What's this ye've been up to? Damme, Mr Haslam's a guest in my house, and you'll oblige me by treating him as one! What's this trick you've been playing on him?"

"I think I'm beginning to understand," answered Haslam. "It was quite a pretty idea, I've no doubt. He called here early this morning, acted very suspiciously, and was evidently testing my own good faith during your absence. Am I right, detective?"

"You are quite right," nodded Graham.

"I hope I passed the test?" asked Haslam, a little dryly. He was not sure that he quite appreciated the detective's zeal.

"Your attitude was what I expected it to be," returned Grant.

"Confound it, man—!" began Mr Blythe again, but the detective frowned on him, and he stopped.

"I go to work in my own way, Mr Blythe," he said, "and I admit only one master. That, as you know, is Justice. I am working for you in this case, but you are not my sole employer. When I once take up a case, I go right through with it to the end, and sometimes I end up facing exactly the opposite direction from that in which I started. I can never adopt the attitude of a counsel who will use all his eloquence to get the release of a man he believes to be guilty, or to convict a man whom he believes to be innocent. Facts, not arguments, are the only things that interest me."

Mr Blythe was somewhat cowed by this stern declaration.

"Oh, all right, all right," he muttered. "You must do as you like. But just be as kind to us as ye can, eh?" He turned to Haslam. "Would you believe it, he suspects the lot of us?"

"Well, so long as we know, we won't worry," replied Haslam, smiling.

It occurred to him that Grant was a rock which was not unlike that of Gibraltar, and that those who wished to travel farthest with him should adopt a good-natured and direct attitude. If only Mary Holland's brother had not been implicated in this case, Haslam would have liked nothing better than to throw himself wholeheartedly into the business of unravelling the mystery with the detective, whose brain he was already beginning to respect, and whom, despite his peculiar sternness, he was already beginning to like. But Miss Holland's brother was the one delicate factor on which he and the detective looked like splitting, and Haslam foresaw, somewhat grimly, the possibility of further fencing between them—fencing of a far more vital nature than their preliminary little skirmish that morning, and involving far greater skill.

Already, the detective's keen eyes had made out the figure of Miss Holland, sitting at her easel on the lawn, and he was asking a question about her.

"Who is that?" he enquired.

"Ah! That is our artist, I suppose," observed Mr Blythe, turning to Haslam and answering the question for him.

"Yes, that's Miss Holland," said Haslam. "You remember, I wrote to you about her. I suppose you told Mr Grant?"

"Oh, yes, of course. I've told him everything," exclaimed the old man. "It's the only way with Mr Grant. If you don't tell him, he finds out. So I thought the best thing was to show him your letters."

"Good—I'm glad to hear it," exclaimed Haslam. "That will save a lot of explanations. Then he knows about Miss Holland, and also about the mysterious Professor Heath. These have been the only two callers apart from M. Carpentier since you went away."

"And what do you think of Miss Holland?" asked the detective, transferring his gaze from her to Haslam.

"You shall have my full impressions in due course," returned Haslam. "But, perhaps, you may like to form your own first. Will you both come over and let me introduce her to you?"

He spoke easily, but his mind was anxious. This detective was the most piercing man he had ever met, and he wondered how Miss Holland would come through the interview. But there was no way of avoiding it, and the worst possible thing would have been to appear to want to avoid it. So he led them across the lawn—the butler had already preceded them to the house—and, to his relief and secret admiration, he found Miss Holland perfectly composed.

"Miss Holland, this is your real host," he said, indicating Mr Blythe. "As you know, I have merely been his proxy. And, Mr Grant." He introduced the detective, and then stepped back a little.

"Mr Haslam wrote to me about you, my dear," said Mr Blythe, promptly, "and I have already told him that he did quite right in giving you permission to paint the wonderful view from this lawn. May I look at it?"

"Why, of course," replied Miss Holland. "But I'm afraid it's not very good."

"Not good? What nonsense!" cried the old man. "Come here, Grant. Now, isn't that charming? Our friend is a genuine artist, hey?"

He glanced at the detective half-anxiously, half-defiantly. Grant examined the picture closely, and nodded.

"Very pretty, Miss Holland," he pronounced. "Have you painted many pictures in the district?"

"Yes, quite a lot," she replied. "A kind shopman in Wynton tries to sell them for me. I am afraid he has to use all his skill to do so."

"Tut, tut!" remonstrated Mr Blythe. "You paint charmingly. I don't think you need trouble your kind shopman with this one. You can sell it direct to me, and save the rascal's commission."

"I'm sorry, sir," interposed Haslam, smiling. "But she has already found a purchaser."

"Disgusting!" grumbled Mr Blythe, with a humorous twinkle. "Then, I can see, I shall have to commission another."

The detective's voice broke in upon these pleasantries.

"Do you live at Wynton, Miss Holland?" he asked.

"Yes."

"Then I expect you have some local reputation?"

"That's rather a nice way of putting it, Mr Grant," she returned. "I get a pound each for my pictures, if I'm lucky."

"And how long have you been over this one? At a pound each, you cannot find your art very remunerative."

Miss Holland glanced at Haslam as she replied,

"I am getting more than a pound for this one, and so I am taking longer over it, to try and justify the absurd price I have been offered. But, as you see, it is nearly finished. And then I won't intrude here any more."

"Bless my soul, it's no intrusion!" exclaimed Mr Blythe. "Don't forget, I've commissioned another!"

Miss Holland smiled, and began to gather up her things. She refused Mr Blythe's request to stay to tea, saying that she had an appointment in Wynton at half-past four, and must be getting back. Haslam helped her put the easel and canvas away, and five minutes later she departed. She had conducted the interview with perfect coolness and naturalness, but, as she rode away, there was a little chill in her heart; and, that night, Detective Grant ran disturbingly through her dreams.

"Well, I don't think we need trouble about Miss Holland," exclaimed Mr Blythe, when they were seated in the library after her departure. "I agree with Haslam that she's a perfectly genuine article."

"Personally, I feel sure she is," said Haslam. "What's your view, Mr Grant?"

"At the moment, if you will forgive me, I am forming opinions, not giving them," replied Grant pleasantly. "I may say, however, that Miss Holland struck me as a very interesting young lady."

"Not a bit of good, you see," remarked Mr Blythe. "You'll get nothing out of him! Now, let's forget Miss Holland for a moment. What about this other visitor? This Professor Heath?"

"Did you know anybody of that name in Newcastle?" enquired Haslam.

"Yes, I knew a man named Heath, but only slightly. Can ye describe him to me?"

Haslam did so, and Mr Blythe shook his head, perplexedly.

"It may be the same, and it may not," he declared. "I'm sure I can't say."

"He tried to make out that you were mad."

"Well, the man I'm thinking of was slightly touched himself, so that makes us quits. It's queer, though, that these confounded people stopped calling as soon as you gave it out that I'd gone away. Now, if they start coming again tonight—" He paused, and glanced at the detective. "See here, Grant. Are you going to play any more of your tricks? I'm giving you a free rein, but my nerves ain't as strong as they were, and if you're going to dodge in and out, sometimes as yourself, and sometimes as God knows who else—well, you'll have me all to bits in a couple of days, so you will!"

"Don't worry," smiled Grant. "I don't expect to play any more tricks on you."

"Well, I'm relieved to hear it. How the devil you managed this morning's trip beats me!"

"It was quite simple. One hour and forty minutes each way, by car," answered the detective. "And now, if I may, I will disappear until dinner. I want to go over the house, and make a tour of the place generally. You've no objection?"

"None in the least, none in the least," exclaimed Mr Blythe. "This is Liberty Hall."

When the detective had gone, Mr Blythe and Haslam looked at each other for a few seconds without speaking. Then Mr Blythe moved close to Haslam, and said, in a low voice,

"Upon my soul, that fellow's almost as uncanny as any of 'om! He may be outside at this moment, with his eye at the key-hole! Suspects the lot of us, he does, and as close as an oyster. But, damme, I like the chap. He's straight—like a poker. And I'll wager my last farthing that, inside a week, he'll have this puzzle solved; every tiny bit of it. Don't you agree?"

"Yes, I dare say you're right," answered Haslam, frowning slightly. "I wonder why he's so interested in the case?"

"Well, who wouldn't be?" retorted the old man. "It's unique, isn't it?"

"Yes, but he's taking it so—well, so extraordinarily seriously."

"He takes everything seriously. That's Grant's way. But I believe he's convinced there's something big behind all this. He doesn't as a rule meddle with small fry. Listen! There he goes!

He's walking across the room above this. God bless me, let's have a dose of whisky."

Haslam went to the sideboard, and officiated with the decanter and syphon.

"You know, you ought to have stayed away a little longer," he said, sympathetically.

"Damme, why?" retorted the old man, seizing the glass. "D'ye think I'm afraid?"

CHAPTER 16

It was a strange little dinner-party that sat down to the evening meal at half-past seven that evening. Detective Grant, although he was by no means surly, remained silent for the most part, and made no effort to contribute anything to the social side of the occasion. If Mr Blythe and Peter Haslam took this as a reflection upon themselves, they made a very understandable mistake, for the detective was merely being faithful to his particular methods of going to work, which, at the outset, were to receive rather than give impressions. He believed that, until cross-examination became necessary, it was apt to destroy atmosphere, and it was through atmosphere that he often laid his finger on the pulse of a case.

Others had argued that the detective himself destroyed the natural trend of atmosphere through his own solemnity. To this the Detective retorted that experience had taught him how to discriminate between the atmosphere supplied by himself and that supplied by other people; and, in justice to his view, it must be said that there were times when he did not consider his native grimness either appropriate or helpful. The present, however, was not one of those times. It rather suited his purpose and line of thought that, for the moment, everyone should remain ill at ease.

His host, from this point of view, must have yielded him infinite satisfaction. Ambrose Blythe made a valiant but quite ineffective stand against his inward depression. If he had been given the choice, he would not have selected any other detective to undertake his commission, or so he assured Haslam—"for, mind ye," he said, "I want this mystery cleared up above all things, so that I can settle down again in peace and comfort for the rest of my days." All the same, he had to add that, pro tem, he was not a whit happier with the detective in the house than he had been before the detective's arrival.

Thus it fell out that Haslam, none too happy in his own mind, was the only member of the Tittle dinner-party who brought any liveliness into it. He talked volubly. Perhaps, a little too volubly. He discussed art and politics, touched on religion, and told several funny anecdotes, at which Mr Blythe laughed heartily in mirthless defiance, while the detective smiled in a quite pleasant and polite fashion.

Not until the end of the meal, over the nuts and wine, was any reference made to the only subject which truly interested them. Then Mr Blythe burst out, suddenly,

"God bless me, we might be in a family vault! Is all your work as merry as this, Grant?"

Grant smiled, and almost relented. But he was receiving impressions too fast to risk interfering with them, sensitively accepting or rejecting them, noting details, absorbing subconscious elements, and listening to soundless voices. Some would have called Grant a super-logician, others would have called him psychic. He did not trouble to call himself either, but he knew from experience that he possessed a keen instinct for reading signs and receiving warnings, and one of the reasons why he was so particularly grave now was because he sensed, in his own being, some impending tragedy. He did not know what it was. He could not say from what direction it was coming, or who would be the victim of it. But that tragedy lurked around the house, or inside it, he would have known even had there been no definite evidence to support the theory.

"I've always understood, now," proceeded Mr Blythe, "that the modern detective was a big, jolly sort of chap, or a fellow looking like a simpleton—in fact, the last person who would really appear to be like a detective at all."

"Some are like that," answered Grant. "But, in detective work, as in everything else, you've got to find your own true centre, and work outwards from it. It's no good emulating anybody else's. A big, jolly detective might be more successful than a grave and silent one—but I'm not jolly. Genius breaks through all outward appearances. It can reside in any one of them."

"The vanity of the man!" cried Mr Blythe. "He calls himself a genius."

"In a sense, I am, but I take no credit whatever for it. I am a good detective. But I very often make mistakes."

"How often?"

"In small matters, every day. All of us do. A hundred times a day, we commit small foolish actions, receive small wrong impressions, follow small, erroneous lines of thought. The man who regards himself as perfectly accurate is perfect only in his folly. But, in big matters, too, I have made mistakes. Among a large number of successes, I could write down about a dozen very distinct failures. I spent two months once tracking an innocent man, and then another two months, proving his innocence. This game brings one too near the bone of things to allow me, personally, to be very jolly."

Mr Blythe looked uncomfortable, and cracked a nut, while Haslam reflected over the detective's words.

"There's a tremendous amount in what you say, Mr Grant," said Haslam. "I've often thought along similar lines myself. But you will be the first to admit that we must each play our part, and that, when I crack jokes, I am not disrespectful to your profession?"

Grant looked at Haslam with interest. There was a quality in Haslam's tone which commended itself to him—a quality which he might have missed had he, too, cracked jokes. Logically, the dramatis personae of this strange drama were falling into the positions he was subconsciously working for, and which can only be attained when one member is true to himself, and others follow suit.

"Of course, you are quite right to crack jokes," Grant replied. "It is your natural method of trying to equalise with Fate during an uncomfortable time like the present. You know, as well as I do—almost as well, at any rate—that we are on the edge of tragic happenings, that there is a bad shadow lurking somewhere; and, according to your custom and training, you treat the occasion socially—perhaps, even, as good copy for a novel. But I am not a social man, or a writer. I treat it professionally. Had I some other interest, it might be different."

"I wish you wouldn't talk about tragic happenings and bad shadows like that!" protested Mr Blythe. "Fiddledydee! Ain't you here to stop 'em?"

"That is my object."

"Well, then! Let's have no more ghost stories! Eh?"

"One minute, Mr Blythe," interposed Haslam. "I'd like to ask one more question. Tell me, Mr Grant. I'm a bit of a psychologist, too. That's also my profession. I read you, at this moment, as a naturally grave man, but I read also that you've something particularly grave on your mind, and that you haven't told us what it is. Am I right?"

"You are quite right," nodded the detective. "Within a very short distance of us—" He hesitated. "Shall I go on?"

"Yes, please."

"There is a potential murderer. I am quite certain of it."

"Damn it!" cried Mr Blythe, jumping up. "Now you've reduced me to a human wobble!"

The next moment, the others, also, were on their feet. The front door bell was ringing.

Grant was the first out of the room. The others heard him speaking a quick, sharp word to Pike in the hall, and, as they followed, they saw Pike standing with a pale, anxious face against the wall. Then the door was opened, a draught of air blew in, and Grant gave an exclamation.

"No one!" he barked.

Haslam hurried up, Mr Blythe hanging back safely in the rear.

"Are you sure?" he exclaimed.

"Not a soul," replied the detective, and, whipping out a flashlamp, threw the brilliant ray forward. It streaked out across the wide gravel path to the lawn. The detective played it swiftly from one side to the other. Then, suddenly, he muttered. "Ah! What was that?" and dashed out.

Haslam was about to dash after him when he felt a hand on his sleeve.

"No—you stay here!" cried Mr Blythe. "Pike's gone, by the back way. Better have one strong arm left in the house, eh?"

Haslam hesitated. He disliked staying behind. But Grant and Pike were both chasing the mysterious ringer of the bell, so perhaps his best place would be to remain on the premises, and to keep an eye on Mr Blythe and the servants. If Mr Blythe were indeed the objective of these visits, it would be folly to leave him at such a moment. The bell might have been a decoy, to get the able-bodied folk out of the way.

He recalled, too, the detective's uncanny suggestion of a potential murderer. Yes, obviously, his duty was to remain.

Closing the front door, and running to the back of the hall, Haslam called out,

"Rose! Cook! Are you all right?"

"Yes, sir," answered Rose, appearing.

"Did you lock the back-door after Pike went out?"

"Yes, sir."

"Good. See that it is kept locked. Mr Blythe and I will be in the library."

He turned to the old man, and, taking his arm, led him into the library's incongruous comfort.

"Say what you like about Grant," muttered Mr Blythe, "he's on the spot, eh?"

"Yes, he is," replied Haslam. "You did well to get hold of him."

"You think so?"

"Of course. Don't you?"

"Yes, yes, I'm sure of it. He just needs getting used to, that's all. He's a useful sort of man to have on your own side, but the very devil if he ain't! And damned uncanny, too. Damned uncanny."

"How, uncanny?" asked Haslam, wandering to the window. "Oh, you mean about that reference to a potential murderer?

He's probably a bit psychic. Feels atmosphere, you know. I've known others like him." Haslam was making conversation, partly to please Mr Blythe, and partly because, in the silences, the clock ticked too loudly. "But all these psychic people aren't right, you know. They make all sorts of wrong deductions, and you forget all about them. They make a right one—perhaps through a coincidence—and you immediately regard them with awe. It's human nature. We believe what we want to believe, and the psychic always attracts us."

Haslam felt that he was talking poorly, and inconsistently. He stopped, and Mr Blythe drummed on the table with his fingers.

"Why doesn't the fellow come back?" he exclaimed. "Devil of a time. What d'you suppose has happened?"

"Oh, he'll be back in a minute or two, I expect," answered Haslam, trying to pierce the darkness through the window. "Then we'll hear."

"H'm. See anything?"

"No. Let's have the light out—then I may."

Mr Blythe jumped up, and switched off the electric light. Then he joined Haslam at the window, and the two of them peered out into the blackness.

"So you suggest it was a coincidence, eh?" murmured Mr Blythe. "Well, it was a confoundedly queer one. That bell going, just as he spoke. And, then, nothing at the door when he opened it."

"The potential murderer evidently changed his mind, and did a prosaic bunk," remarked Haslam. "That is, if he ever existed at all." He opened the French window slightly, and listened.

"Ah! That's right! If he ever existed at all!" exclaimed the old man. "Now, I'll wager he didn't. I'll wager Grant's becoming as nervy as the rest of us, and invented him. I'll wager I've just been a silly old fool——"

He did not finish the sentence. A shot rang out crisply, followed by a cry.

CHAPTER 17

When the detective slipped out on to the lawn, it was to dash after a dim form he had spied from the porch. Grant often appeared heavy and silent, but his mind was always moving fast, and his body was ever ready to move with equal rapidity. The dim figure, however, was also fleet, and dodged swiftly into a dark thicket. Before the detective could follow, a heavy hand was laid on his shoulder.

He wheeled round sharply to face the new enemy, and found himself staring into the face of Pike. If Grant's eyes showed astonishment, Pike's eyes showed even more. They bulged with dismay.

"Mr Grant!" he gasped.

"Confound you!" muttered Grant. "What did you do that for?"

"I thought—I thought you were the man who rang the bell."

"Did you? Well, it was a bad guess. Go back to the house, and don't meddle again until you're asked."

"I'm sorry, sir," faltered Pike. "I——"

"Go back!" barked Grant.

Pike started at the detective's sharp tone. He was trembling from head to foot. For a moment, he hesitated; then he turned, and began to walk back to the house. After watching him for a second, Grant turned also, to resume his now almost hopeless chase.

There was no sign of the fugitive, so he trusted to his hunting instinct, and, running through a little wood, emerged upon the road. Here he paused, glancing to left and right. To the right, some way up the road, something was flitting. The detective sprinted for all he was worth, and faltered only once during this breathless race. This was when he passed a small clearing and saw something that caused him to waver, but he did not hesitate for more than the fraction of a second, realizing that if he stopped again he would certainly lose his quarry.

The distance between them quickly lessened. The scurrying form swerved, ducked, and dodged. He could not throw off his relentless pursuer, however, and presently Grant had the intense satisfaction of feeling a coat collar within his grasp.

"Got you!" he exclaimed.

The next moment, a shot rang out behind him, the coat collar vanished into the night, and he staggered.

The bullet had grazed and dazed the detective, but had not entered into him. He lurched forward for a step or two; then, realizing that his strength was spent, sat down rather heavily on a big stone. He took out his revolver, and waited. He felt too dizzy to move for a few minutes. He could shoot, however, if the occasion arose. And the occasion might arise at any instant.

Soon, steps sounded along the road over which he had just travelled. He straightened himself, not quite sure whether he had swooned, and his fingers tightened upon the revolver. Then, as a familiar voice sang out through the darkness, they relaxed.

"Is that you, Mr Grant?"

It was Haslam.

"Yes, it's Grant," replied the detective.

"Thank God! Are you hurt?"

"A bit dizzy, that's all. Who's with you?"

"Pike."

"And Mr Blythe?"

"No, I wouldn't let him come. That would have left the two servants alone."

"Quite right. There's too much danger abroad. The house mustn't be left, and we'd better be getting back to it."

"Yes, but what's happened?"

"I'll tell you, as we go. Help me to rise, will you? Are you sure there's no one with you, as well as Pike?"

"No! Who should there be?"

Grant did not answer. Assisted by Haslam and Pike, he rose to his feet. His hurt was not serious, but he had to confess to himself that he felt a trifle sick and muzzy.

"Back to the house, as quick as we can," he said. "I don't like the idea of Mr Blythe and the maids left there all by themselves."

"Nor do I. I told them to keep everything closed and locked, though. They ought to be all right."

"We'll hope so. It's a pity you brought Pike along, though."

"I didn't. He was already out."

The detective stopped suddenly, and stared at Pike.

"Is that true?" he demanded.

"Yes, sir," answered Pike, a little shame-facedly.

"But I told you to go back to the house. Why didn't you?"

"It seemed to me foolish, sir, begging your pardon. Mr Haslam was in the 'ouse, so I thought I'd be more use outside."

"You disobeyed my orders," frowned Grant.

"If you'd never given them, sir, p'r'aps you'd not 'ave been shot. There'd 'ave been two of us, you see."

Grant's frown deepened. He studied Pike intently, and then observed, coolly, without taking his eyes from Pike's face,

"I was shot at by someone behind me."

Pike flushed, half-scared, half-indignant.

"Are you accusing me of firing at you?" he asked. "I was behind you, sir, that's right, but if you think——"

"I haven't said what I think," retorted the detective, beginning to move on again. "I merely said that I was shot at by someone behind me."

Pike was not quite satisfied.

"P'r'aps you'd like to search me, sir?" he suggested.

"That's a silly suggestion," said the detective. "It's easy enough to throw a revolver away, isn't it? You were behind me when the shot was fired, but I haven't accused you yet. Mr Haslam may have been behind me, also."

"I wasn't, but I wish I had been," replied Haslam. "I was in the library with Mr Blythe when the shot was fired."

"I take your word for that," nodded Grant. "You're the only really useful man in this show. But, even so, the evidence doesn't point necessarily to Pike." He stopped, and peered into a little clearing on their left. "He wasn't the only person behind me. A girl was behind me. I passed her, at this spot, as I was chasing my man."

"A girl!" exclaimed Haslam, as his heart missed a beat.

"Yes—a girl."

"Do you know who she was?"

"I don't, for certain. I couldn't see her clearly. But I might hazard a guess. And it would have helped her considerably if she had appeared on the scene with you and Pike, to find out what was up, instead of joining in this universal vanishing trick. But I don't even accuse *her*. It is possible that someone else was behind me, as well. For a sparsely populated district, the population in this immediate vicinity seems to be significantly large!"

A silence followed. Grant was showing signs of fatigue. Sending Pike on ahead, Haslam took the detective's arm firmly, and helped him over the last stages of the journey. No word was spoken until the lights of the Brambles winked at them as they rounded the drive. Then Haslam asked,

"How are you feeling?"

"Better," replied the detective. "But I'm going straight to my room. I want to doctor myself up and have a think."

"Very good. I'll tell Mr Blythe what's happened, and then we'll be getting off ourselves. Ought someone to sit up all night?"

"No, I don't think so. See that everything's secure—that's all I suggest doing tonight. Tomorrow, I may have to act."

"In what way?"

"That's what I'm going to think about."

They were nearing the porch. Haslam stopped impulsively.

"Mr Grant," he said. "I want to know something. You haven't got it into your head that Miss Holland is implicated in this rotten business, have you?"

"I haven't mentioned Miss Holland," replied the detective. "But I've an idea that, if it weren't for Miss Holland, you and I would get on a great deal better."

The front door was thrown open, and Mr Blythe stood silhouetted in the bright aperture.

"Thank God, you're both standing on your two feet!" he cried. "Come in, and let's hear what's happened. Pike here is no good at all at telling stories."

"Mr Haslam will tell you," said Grant, passing in. "I'm going to my room. If I'm wanted, let me know at once."

Mr Blythe glanced at the detective, who was already mounting the stairs, and then at Haslam. Haslam nodded reassuringly, closed and bolted the front door, and walked towards the library. Mr Blythe followed him, anxiously.

"Quarrelled?" he asked.

"Good gracious, no!" replied Haslam. "Grant's tired, that's all. The bullet grazed him—nothing serious—and he decided to get to bed at once and think things over. Tomorrow he's going to take action of some sort."

"What sort?" enquired Mr Blythe, blinking.

"I don't know. But, of course, he's right. I only hope—" He paused, and did not finish the sentence.

"More riddles!" grumbled Mr Blythe. "Who was it fired the shot?"

"We don't know."

"Any suspicion?"

"Grant suggested it might have been Pike——"

"Pike!" exclaimed the old man, incredulously.

"Yes. Or a girl whom he dimly saw by the roadside. Or 'some other person or persons unknown.' I expect that's what he's thinking about at this moment. And the rest of us have done as much thinking as is good for us, so I vote for bed. What about it?"

"Yes, bed's the place—with our heads under our pillows! I've already sent the servants up. God bless me, didn't some fool say that an Englishman's home was his castle? Rum sort of castle, eh?" He glanced ruefully towards the chess-board. "No, not tonight," he murmured. "Every time you said 'Check,' I believe I'd

110

jump. Well, come along."

They put out the lights, and mounted to their respective rooms. Mr Blythe wisely went straight to bed, but Haslam felt too disturbed to do so, and, lighting a cigarette, threw open his window, and smoked.

The detective's remark about Miss Holland worried him. It was obvious that he mistrusted her, and that, because of this mistrust, and of his insight into Haslam's own mental attitude, Haslam would not be taken wholly into the detective's confidence. This, Haslam had to admit, was perfectly reasonable and logical, but it was none the less disturbing. Of Mary Holland's innocence, Haslam was assured. He was not assured, however, that Mary Holland might not get into serious trouble through her attempts to shield her brother.

Then, again, what had Mary Holland been doing in the road, when Grant had come upon her? Haslam had no more doubt than had Grant himself that it was Mary Holland. And why had she not proclaimed herself? These questions rose to perplex Haslam's mind, and caused him to light a cigarette.

He decided to interview Miss Holland on the morrow, and to endeavour to persuade her to change her attitude. If harm had already come to her brother, she might be denying him protection as well as herself by continuing to hide such meagre facts as she possessed. Having reached this decision, Haslam was about to close and leave the window when something shot through it.

He started back, in astonishment. It was a little piece of twisted paper. Picking it up, he unfolded it, and read:

"Please meet me at the gate. Very urgent. M.H."

CHAPTER 18

Haslam stared at the little piece of paper for a moment, then ran to the window. It was a front window, and he could make out the driveway below him. He saw no figure, however, and he did not like to risk calling, lest someone else in the house heard him. Closing the window, softly, he returned to the centre of the room, and thought.

It did not occur to him not to answer Mary Holland's request. He was thinking how to get out of the house with the least possibility of detection, for if he were discovered he would find himself in an exceedingly embarrassing position. He decided on the back door. Probably, everyone was settling down to sleep by now, and if he were detected before he actually left the house, he could say that he had heard noises and was making a tour of the place. Happily, Detective Grant's room was not next to his own. His neighbour was Mr Blythe, whose head he hoped was under his pillow. He tip-toed softly to his door.

"So this night of adventure is not yet over," he thought, grimly. Had he realised it, the night of adventure had barely begun.

Turning the door handle carefully, he opened the door, and stepped out into the passage. It was dark and deserted. He stood still for a moment, glancing apprehensively at Mr Blythe's door, and then, farther along the passage, at the detective's. Neither door opened, and he heard no movement behind either. Closing his own door, he crept cautiously to the head of the wide stairs that led down into the main hall, and, once on the stairs, he felt more secure, for they were thickly carpeted. A vision of Miss

Holland anxiously waiting for him at the gate made him hasten. In ten seconds he was at the back door, and in another five he had unbolted and opened it. The cool night air stole in upon his temples.

Once more, he paused, examining the door's latch. Fortunately, he could re-open it from outside, so it was unnecessary to leave it ajar; all the same, he did not like the sensation that he had to leave an unlocked door behind him.

However, it could not be helped. Keeping close against the side of the house, lest he should be seen from any of the windows, he made his way towards the gate. He found a secluded path between high hedges which emerged in the driveway at a point beyond the view of the house. Once here, he hurried forward with less caution. Just inside the gate a figure was standing.

"Who is that?" he whispered softly.

"Is that Mr Haslam?" came a somewhat trembling reply.

"Yes," he answered, recognising Miss Holland's voice, and now making out her figure. "Are you all right—I mean, in danger at this moment?"

"No."

"Good. Then let us walk a little way along the road, so we can talk undisturbed. This is a little too close to the house for my liking."

He pulled the gate open a short way, and they slipped out. Not a word was spoken until, some fifty yards up the road, they found a well-sheltered spot. Then Haslam stopped, and, drawing his companion out of the road, asked,

"Well? What's happened?" He saw that Miss Holland was trembling, and patted her sleeve reassuringly. "Try and keep up your courage," he said. "We'll work through this, whatever it is. Have you heard from your brother?"

"I'd better tell you the whole story, Mr Haslam," she replied. "And then you will let me know whether I did rightly to come to you——"

"I know that already, Miss Holland," he interposed. "You will

113

always do rightly to come to me, in any trouble."

"You are awfully good! I don't know what I should do at this moment, if it weren't for you. When I left you this afternoon, I really had an excuse to go early, although I wouldn't have stayed to tea, in any case. I had to go to Ingate, to get some materials I ordered—Ingate is bigger than Wynton, you know, and I do most of my shopping there. Well, this took me a good deal out of my way, and as I got a puncture and had to have it mended, it took me all the longer. It was half-past six before I could leave Ingate, so I decided to stay and have dinner there, and cycle home afterwards."

"Have you a house at Wynton?" enquired Haslam.

"No—only rooms. We haven't been there awfully long, but I'll tell you all about that in a minute. Over dinner, I found a London newspaper on my table. It had been left there by some-one who had come from London, I expect, because it was an afternoon edition. As I was turning over the pages, I came upon —well, this." She drew a torn sheet from her pocket. "Perhaps you'd better read it. I'll explain about it afterwards."

Haslam took the bit of newspaper, and, with the aid of his flash lamp, read the report to which she pointed.

"Burglars appear to have made a big haul at Mrs Eltham Smith's house in Arundel," it ran, "and a valuable necklace, worth many thousands of pounds, has disappeared. An odd fea-ture of the case is that there is no evidence of thieves having en-tered the house, or of the date on which the necklace was taken from the safe in which it had been deposited. The safe had not been opened for some time previous to the discovery that the necklace was missing.

"The local police are reticent in the matter, but enquiries have elicited the fact that a maid, who was under notice to go, was dismissed a couple of days before the theft was known, and that, since this date, no trace of her has been found."

Haslam snapped off his light, and handed the report back to her.

"How does this affect you?" he asked. "Have you some reason

to suppose that your brother is involved in it?"

"Yes—every reason," faltered Miss Holland. "It's too awful! I was only suspicious before. Now, I feel sure that George is a—a thief." She covered her face with her hands, but suddenly removed them, and Haslam found her eyes fixed upon him in the dimness. "Are you still interested in me?" she asked. "Do you still want to help me—after this?"

"Of course!" he retorted. "You are not your brother! Besides, you haven't told me yet why you suspect him of being mixed up in this affair. At the moment, I can't see any remotest connection."

"Well—we used to live at Arundel," said Miss Holland. "My brother is an artist, too—a much better one, really, than I am. He's studied properly. While we were at Arundel, he received a commission from Mrs Eltham Smith to paint her house—that's the house from which the necklace has been stolen, you know. I think I told you that my brother was very weak. I've always known that, but I never knew he was quite as bad as he's turned out. While he was painting the picture, he grew much too friendly with one of Mrs Smith's maids. The one, I feel sure, who has been dismissed. That was really why we left Arundel. I insisted on it—and he was so weak that he even obeyed me. I felt sure that something bad would happen if we stayed, so we came to Wynton and tucked ourselves away there."

She paused, and Haslam regarded her sympathetically. He had become so engrossed in her story that he had forgotten the possibility of immediate danger; but suddenly he left their little sheltered spot, and peered out on to the road. He saw nothing, and returned to her.

"Just for safety's sake," he remarked. "This locality's none too healthy at the moment." He returned to their subject. "Is this all the evidence you have to suggest that your brother has had anything to do with the theft?"

"No. There's something more. But, even so, I'm not certain, you know. After reading that report, I couldn't help worrying, and I worried all the way to Wynton. When I got home, I found a note there. It was from George. It told me that he had been there and had waited for me, but that he dared not wait any longer. 'Dared not'—those were his words. Then he begged me to bring some money to him. I would find him at an old disused mill, ten miles away from here. We both know it well. We've painted it. He said he couldn't explain anything—he'd do so later—but it was a matter of life and death, and he must have at least twenty pounds, and more if possible."

Haslam looked grave. This certainly sounded a very bad business.

"Well, and what did you do then?" he asked. "Did you want to go to him?"

"Yes—of course."

"But you didn't?"

"No. You see—" She suddenly flushed, and hung her head.

"Poor child!" thought Haslam, as he realised the situation. "Good Lord, what a scamp that George must be!" Aloud he said, "I think I understand, Miss Holland. You haven't got twenty pounds?" She shook her head. "I wonder—may I know how much you have?"

"Just thirty shillings."

"Why, that's ridiculous! Surely you can save a little more than that out of your pictures!"

"You forget, I'm a rotten artist. I only took it up when—when ____"

"When you found that your brother's pictures didn't quite cover expenses?"

"Yes. That's it."

"But he's a good artist, you say. He ought to have earned enough for both of you." With sudden intuition, he exclaimed,

"Has your brother any debts?"

"I'm afraid so."

"And did you take up painting to try and help him pay them off?"

"Yes. It became absolutely necessary, at last. Things got very pressing. And, anyway, it was quite natural, I wanted to feel that

I was doing my bit."

"I imagine you've done your bit all right," muttered Haslam. "George has better friends at his back than he deserves. But we'll stick to him, Miss Holland. You did perfectly right to come to me. Will you stay here, while I return to the house, and get the money?"

Her eyes filled with sudden tears.

"He'll pay it back to you—I promise you!" she said, tremulously.

"I'm quite sure he won't," answered Haslam, grimly, "and I'm also sure that I don't lend it to him with that idea."

"Then, I'll pay it back."

"Well, we'll talk about that later. Good heavens, Miss Holland, if a selfish author who's piled up a bit more money than he can spend on himself can't help one of the few real friends he's ever made in his life without thinking in terms of capital and interest—Oh, well, I'll say all that another time. We must get busy. Will you be all right here?"

"Yes. Quite."

"I don't like leaving you," frowned Haslam. "I suppose you were somewhere near by when that shot was fired?"

"Yes. I was on my way here when two men ran by. I don't believe they saw me. I went farther into the wood—my nerves are all going to pieces—and presently I heard voices. Yours among them, and the detective's. So I decided to stay hidden. You see, I didn't think I could be of any use, and I didn't want to be seen, naturally."

"Yes, naturally," nodded Haslam, thoughtfully. He wondered whether, if it ever came to an issue, Grant would be as willing as he was to accept this explanation. "Creep under that clump of bushes, and stay there till I return. I'll not be gone more than five minutes. But, look here, how are you going to get to that mill? It must be over thirteen miles from this spot."

"It's just about that. I've got my bicycle."

"You cycled here, then?"

"Yes. I've hidden the machine in a hedge."

"Well, I don't like the idea of your going to that deserted mill all by yourself. This is a rotten job your brother has set you. Anyway, I'll get the money, and then we'll talk about it."

He gave her a reassuring smile, and stepped out on to the road. It was still deserted. He kept his eyes skinned, but saw nothing as he retraced his way to the gate, and everything was still as he swung it open and stepped inside. As before he took the little, hedge-protected path that led to the back of the house, thus avoiding the open drive and the possibility of being seen from one of the front windows. The only incident he encountered on his way to the back door was supplied by a large toad, which suddenly jumped across his path and would have been justly proud could it have divined the disturbance it caused in the breast of a creature so much bigger than itself.

The back door was reached. Haslam gave a sigh of relief. When he turned the handle, he discovered that it was locked.

CHAPTER 19

"Now what?" muttered Haslam, making a brave stand against an uncanny, clammy sensation that was trying to paralyse his thought and action.

It was a wretched, perplexing position to find himself in. He could, of course, adopt the simple expedient of ringing the bell, but this, for sufficiently obvious reasons, did not appeal to him. He did not want any light thrown upon his present adventure. However, although he deduced that the back door had been re-fastened by either Grant or Mr Blythe, or possibly Pike, it was also possible that it had been bolted by some other individual who had got into the house during his absence. He was in a dilemma, and no mistake about it.

"Well, the only certain thing," he pondered, "is that I've got to get inside somehow or other. If I wake the household, I shall have the devil's own time to get out again. I must get in quietly, if it's humanly possible."

He groped his way round to the front of the house, picked out his bedroom window, and studied the wall. A convenient pipe ran up the wall, and he recalled, with a pang of relief, that, although he had closed his window before leaving the room, he had not fastened it. "Thank heaven for my carelessness!" he murmured, and began to climb.

A less determined man would never have attempted to swarm up that water-pipe, and a less athletic man would never have succeeded in doing it. The pipe was not thick, and there were many impeding creepers. The creepers were deceptive as well as impeding, and once, when he trusted to a vine, he slipped and nearly fell down to the bottom again. It was only by suddenly grasping the protruding window-ledge that he saved himself from catastrophe. After this, it was comparatively easy to raise himself on to the ledge and work the window open. With a grunt of relief, he dropped into the security of his room.

"Another stage over!" he murmured. "What will be the next obstacle, I wonder?"

Closing the window, and this time fastening it, he hurriedly collected twenty-five pounds, and stuffed the notes into his pocket-book. Then, with a queer feeling that history was repeating itself, he opened his bedroom door, and listened, and crept out into the passage. He went through almost the identical performance that he had gone through half-an-hour earlier. He ascertained that no one was stirring. He tip-toed to the head of the broad, soft-carpeted stairs, and increased his pace down them. And, as before, he did not attempt to leave the house until he had made another thorough and satisfactory investigation of all the unoccupied rooms.

One thing surprised him. When he reached the back door, he found that it was not bolted. At first, he believed that someone had got into the house, after all, and had now left it again while he had been climbing up the water-pipe; but then a simpler solution occurred to him, and, perhaps because the wish was father to the thought, he accepted it. He discovered that the handle of the back door was apt to stick, even when it could be opened from the outside. Probably it had stuck when he had tried it, he concluded, recalling that he had not tried to force it but had taken it for granted at once that he was locked out. He called himself a fool for not having made certain of the necessity for that unpleasant climb up the water-pipe.

Now, all was clear sailing. He hurried through the familiar path to the drive, slipped out of the gate, and ran along the short stretch of road that led to the spot where Mary Holland was waiting for him. He found her there, to his relief, and she told him that she had not moved since he had left her.

"But, oh! you were a time!" she exclaimed. "I thought you

were never coming."

"Yes, I made a silly muff of it," he replied, "and had to climb in through the window. Anyhow, that doesn't matter now. I've got the money—I made it twenty-five, to be on the safe side—and, now, let's get back to your bicycle. I wonder if you'd better let me ride to the mill, instead of you? I hate to think of you making that trip tonight."

But she shook her head.

"You've done quite enough, Mr Haslam," she answered. "You've done too much. Please don't make me feel too ashamed of myself by doing any more."

Perhaps, he reflected, she wanted to make that journey. After all, it was natural. She would wish to speak to her brother, and to hear his story from his own lips. He followed her silently, till he heard her give a little gasp.

"What's the matter?" he asked. "Lost the spot?"

"No—no!" she exclaimed. "The bicycle!"

"Do you mean, it's gone?"

"Yes!"

Haslam very nearly swore. Everything was going wrong. This made him all the more determined that, in the end, everything should go right.

"That's a real nuisance," he said, "but we won't waste time crying about it. I'll get you another. Meanwhile, you must let me walk back with you to Wynton."

"Oh, I couldn't——"

"Miss Holland, forgive me, but I'm going to take command. You haven't told me that you're nearly done up, but I can see you are, and I've just one job on—to get you back to your room—and, I think, to leave you there. Don't worry about your brother. I'll find some way of reaching him. Honestly, I don't think you've got the strength."

He took her arm, and, for a moment, she leaned upon it heavily. By asserting his will, he had provided her with the sudden luxury of being able to relinquish hers, and, even in the midst of her doubts and troubles, a momentary sensation of peace pervaded her.

"Yes, I am tired," she said. "I think—if you don't mind—I would like you to walk back with me."

"I'm glad you want me to, because I should have done it anyhow," answered Haslam, cheerfully. "Let's have one more good hunt for your machine, and then, if we don't find it, we'll be off."

They searched for five minutes, despite Miss Holland's assertion that she knew that she had not mistaken the spot. There was no trace of the missing bicycle. It appeared to have vanished into thin air, which habit, as Haslam observed, did not appear to be confined to bicycles in this district. Having satisfied themselves that further search was useless, they turned their faces towards Wynton, and began to walk the three miles that separated them from the little town.

For a while, they were silent. Only the sounds of their footsteps scrunching on the road mingled with the rustlings of the night. Occasionally, some small animal scurried through a hedge, or an owl hooted in the distance. Apart from themselves, there was no evidence of human presence.

To Haslam, it was a wonderful walk, with something magic in it. It was like an oasis in a desert, or a sanctuary accidently discovered amid stormy times, and in the consoling warmth of Mary Holland's companionship, the nightmares behind and ahead of them seemed impossible, unreal things. He hated to think that the walk would presently end. He felt that he could have walked so, happily, throughout the night, speaking no word, hearing scarcely a sound, feeling the cool air on his face and the touch of human warmth on his arm, and moved by a sense of companionship which, often as he had written about it, he had never before personally experienced.

Haslam loved silence, but hitherto he had only loved it alone. In company, he was communicative, almost voluble. Now, though he was not alone, he felt no need of words, regarding speech almost as an intrusion. He wondered whether his companion felt as he did, or whether her silence were merely a reflection of her fatigue.

Presently, however, the silence had to be broken, and purely practical considerations forced their way into his mind.

"Has your brother a bicycle?" he asked, as they neared the end of their journey.

"Yes," she answered. "But I'm afraid he's taken it. It was in the shed where I keep mine until this evening."

"That's a pity. I expect he rode it to the mill."

"He must have."

"Do you know of any other bicycle I could get hold of?"

"There's one belonging to my landlady's son. It's a terrible old thing."

"That doesn't matter. Where does he keep it?"

"In the same shed."

"Capital! I'll take the liberty of borrowing it."

"Mr Haslam," said Miss Holland, "I think you're the biggest brick a girl ever had for a friend. Are you really going to see my brother?"

"Of course, I am!" he answered, briskly. "Somebody must. And, even if you were in a condition to yourself, how could you manage it on a man's bicycle?"

She was silent for a few moments. Then she asked, abruptly,

"What will you do when you see him?"

"I shall do exactly what I think you would want me to do. I'll hand him twenty-five pound notes, get as much of his story from him as I can, and give him all the advice I can."

"But suppose he really has stolen the necklace—won't you be doing something illegal to help him get away?"

"No more illegal than you would have done."

"But that is different. I'm his sister."

"And I'm your friend. Don't worry about that, Miss Holland. I'll try and adjust matters, if I can, and perhaps I'll be able to administer to your brother a useful little lecture at the same time. The ideal thing would be to find out what's happened to the necklace—always assuming he has really had anything to do with it, which isn't proved—and to secure your brother's safety at the same time. That will be my object. But, however I stand in the matter, your brother's safety will be my first consideration, if that is your wish. Is it?"

"Yes," she answered, in a low voice. "It may be wrong of me, but I can't help it. The thought of my brother going to prison is too terrible."

"Very well. He shan't go to prison, if I can keep him out of it. And you needn't fear for me, because I don't intend to go to prison, either!"

He spoke lightly, but in his heart he was by no means as confident as he sounded. Morally, he was acting for the best, according to his lights; but, legally, he was not on such secure ground, and he was quite aware of this fact.

They passed the first cottages on the outskirts of Wynton hardly noticing them. The little buildings loomed up suddenly, appearing unnaturally big in the darkness. Almost before they knew it, they were winding into the high street, and passing the shop in the window of which reclined one of Miss Holland's unsold pictures—and also, Haslam recollected with a smile, a novel by himself, unsalable at half its original price.

Presently, they stopped before a small house up a by-street. The house was in darkness, and, taking out a key, Miss Holland said that this was where she lived. A wave of indignation passed through Haslam as he noted the humble nature of the house. It was not at all the sort of place in which a person like Miss Holland ought to be doomed to spend her days. Probably it was presided over by some ignorant, greasy landlady . . .

"And that is the shed," said Miss Holland, breaking in on his indignant thoughts. "I'll open it first." She produced a second key, and, hastening to the little wooden building, gave a sigh of relief as she threw the door open. "Yes, it's there," she whispered. "I had a horrible fear that the bicycle would be gone."

Haslam entered the shed, and brought the bicycle out. It was, as Miss Holland had warned him, a pretty dilapidated affair, but the tyres were inflated, and it appeared to be in working order.

"This is all right," he pronounced. "And, now, will you go in to bed?"

"I'll go in, but not to bed. I couldn't sleep till I know what's happened."

Haslam frowned, and shook his head.

"Must I again take matters into my own hand?" he asked. "I have a twenty-mile ride before me, and it may be hours before I get back. There's no knowing how long your brother may keep me. I insist that, when you go up to your room, you go straight to bed and try to get some sleep. Otherwise, I'll throw up the case!"

He spoke gently, but firmly. Miss Holland smiled a pathetic little smile, and promised. Her eyes were heavy with fatigue. She gave him directions for reaching the mill, and then held out her hand.

"I'm not going to try to thank you," she said. "I can't."

"I don't want you to thank me," he replied, pressing her hand warmly. "I want you to trust me."

"I do," she answered, and, opening the door of her house, slipped in.

Haslam waited a moment, till a light appeared in a window. Then he wheeled the bicycle into the road, and began his strange journey.

CHAPTER 20

There is a quality investing the hours after midnight in the open country which is peculiarly its own. These hours are totally different from the same hours in a sleeping city, while they are divided from the hours before midnight by as wide a gulf as is the period before midnight from the period before sunset.

Between nine and twelve, the darkness is merely gathering force. Man is gradually and contentedly relinquishing his grip, and as the little yellow lights blink themselves out, one by one, his dominance decreases. Then, when midnight strikes, such lights as still remain—if all is not utter darkness—become mere feeble ghosts or reminders of human activity, glimmering with bravado or timidity amid a nocturnal atmosphere which reigns supreme.

Swing by a silent village church at one a.m., and a light in the upper window of a cottage will look unnatural and strange. You will notice it, and speculate about it. "Someone is ill," you will think. Or perhaps the someone has lit a candle to try and trace the source of some disturbing noise. No perfectly happy explanation will occur to you, for this is not man's natural time, and only some urgent circumstances could explain that light.

Meet a pedestrian, and a query will again be raised in your mind. Who is he? You will be curious, very likely suspicious. It is too late for any man on natural business to be abroad. But when a small animal darts across the road, or a shadowy owl flops and hoots over your head, or a bat causes you to duck anxiously as it dashes in its queer, rudderless fashion through the air, you do not question it. It forms a natural part of the night's great army that has crept up silently to take possession.

And what are you yourself doing abroad at this hour? It must be some unusual enterprise, even if only an enterprise of sheer adventure. You may not be afraid, but your courage will not be at its highest point, and the perfect comfort of your journey will be strangely disturbed by an odd sensation of indefinable guilt.

Peter Haslam, an optimist by nature, and with his full share of human courage, was not immune from these eerie influences as he began to cycle through the dark, strange country. They might have existed, in any case; but now they were enhanced by the very nature of his journey. The road was unknown to him. He was "seeing the unseen country" for the first time, dependent only upon careful directions and the small shaft of light from his lamp. He might go wrong at any moment with wonderful ease, to encounter some quite unforeseen adventure, and, even if he did not go wrong but found the old deserted mill without mishap, he would be faced with an adventure of the most uncertain description.

Added to this were two very disturbing reflections. The first, and least disturbing, was that his protracted absence from his bedroom at the Brambles might be discovered. If the night passed peacefully at Mr Blythe's house, no one would be likely to know of his adventure; but suppose there were some disturbance to arouse the inmates, all of whom would doubtless be sleeping lightly? Then his absence would become known for certain, and he might find himself in a most delicate position when he got back.

The second disturbing reflection was of a more immediate character. He felt convinced that he was being followed.

Now, this sensation is quite common at night-time, and as a rule can be traced directly to nerves or to the strange accoustics of the night. A rustle that would not be heard in the day-time sounds loud and significant at night, and its significance is exaggerated by the subconscious idea that only guilt itself could stalk amidst night's enmity. Haslam, who was quite a sane man, and more logical than most, fought for a long while against his unpleasant suspicion, but at last he was compelled to believe that his nerves were not the defaulters, and he decided to apply a test.

Ahead, a tall, black steeple rose dimly into the sky, blotting out a little space of stars. A feeble yellow light twinkled somewhere, and a dog suddenly barked. Concluding that he was approaching a village, he put on a spurt, till he estimated that his pace had increased to about sixteen miles an hour. This was ridiculous, because a chance stone or brick in the road would have concluded his journey. He did not think of that, however, but threw himself unreservedly, as we sometimes do, into the lap of Fate—and, happily, the lap was kindly. There were no bricks or stones, though a sudden little rise and fall over a small bridge that spanned a stream gave him a nasty momentary sensation that his back was rearing up to heaven, leaving his head behind; and, just beyond the bridge, a big rat, too wily to be caught by trap or poison, had the narrowest squeak of its life.

He was in the village now. The tall spire reared up abruptly and enormously, and a bent shadow loomed grotesquely against the little illuminated window-blind. Haslam swerved round a sharp curve in the road, then darted up a little by-lane on the right. Here he dismounted, and, seeking the sanctuary of a hedge, quickly put out his lamp.

He was now in the position of being able to see without being seen. The main road (not so designated on the ordnance maps) could easily be seen from the spot where he crouched, and a faint glow from the illuminated window, itself out of sight, assisted his vision. He kept his eyes glued on the little stretch of road out of which he had turned abruptly, hardly daring to wink lest, in that instant, his pursuer would flash by.

The moments ticked away. Suddenly, the church clock clanged the quarter-hour—two queer, jangling notes, quaintly defiant of harmony. Annoyance and perplexity flitted across Haslam's face as no sign of his pursuer rewarded his little ruse.

"Either I'm mistaken," he reflected, "or he's too clever for me.

Confound it!"

The idea of returning to the main road did not appeal to him in the least. He felt that, by doing so, he would be throwing himself into the very limelight designed for his pursuer, who, even at that moment, might be watching the same stretch from another quarter. Haslam decided, rashly, to continue along the little lane he was now in, till he could swing round into the main road again at a point farther on.

Wheeling his machine away from the hedge, he walked it along for two or three minutes without relighting the lamp. A spasm of uneasiness came over him when he realised that he was as dependent upon matches as a man thrown up on a Pacific island is on water; happily, however, he found his box more than half-full, and, presently applying a match to the wick, he watched with satisfaction a round patch of lane grow into comprehensibility, and remounted his machine.

The lane evidently resented Haslam's presence upon it at this hour, and did its best to render his visit uncomfortable. It was all on the side of the enemy. It turned and twisted, provided him with confusing problems, stunned his bump of locality, and played havoc with the compass. Haslam soon regretted that he had not returned to the main road, for he did not know where he was. North might be south, or east west. He was just deciding that he was riding in the wrong direction, with his back to the old mill instead of his face towards it, when history repeated itself in bewildering fashion. Ahead of him loomed the tall spire, the little light glowed, and, to complete the illusion that Time had stood still, the dog neatly and obligingly barked.

Only the church clock, twanging the half-hour as Haslam bumped over the small bridge, told him that time was behaving in a perfectly orthodox fashion, and that he had wasted fifteen valuable minutes.

For the second time, he rode through the village. He felt almost as familiar with it as though he had been born there, though it is doubtful whether he would have recognised it by daylight. Beyond, on the silent high road again, he tried to make up pace.

"If that fellow's still following me," he thought, grimly, "well, he must, that's all. But I would like to know who the devil he is?"

Was he the lantern-jawed man? Or the blind man? Or Professor Heath? Or George Holland himself? Or some totally new character? It occurred to Haslam, suddenly, that he had twenty-five pound notes on his person, and if anyone had overheard his conversation with Mary Holland, that someone might have considered him a prize worth waylaying. But, if so, why had he not made his attack earlier? What possible object could there be in waiting....

"Hallo!" he cried, pulling up sharply, as a tall figure lurched round a corner.

The only way to save an accident was to ride into a hedge. This Haslam obligingly did, but he was on his feet the next moment, and he swung towards the stranger with a very useful punch ready.

The stranger, however, did not seem anxious to invite the punch.

"Evenin', gen'l'men," he gurgled, in a high treble.

Haslam stared at him, and noticed that he was an exceedingly old man. He kept his punch ready, all the same.

"A fine night, gen'l'men," continued the old man, wagging his head foolishly. "Ay, 'tis a fine—hic—night—as one'd 'speck arter a fine day. Hic!"

"Well, is that all you've got to say?" demanded Haslam.

"All I've gotter say? My, my! She was dressed just like 'er old gra'ma, ay, so she was—hic—but I mind 'er gra'ma 'ad more orange-blossom. Ay, so she did! And that—hic—gen'l'men, was nigh sixty year ago!"

"I say, don't you think you'd better be going home?" asked Haslam.

"Eh? Wha's that? Eh?" quavered the old man, lurching closer.

"I said, don't you think you'd better get home?" repeated Haslam, eyeing him warily.

"'Ome? Oh! I see. Hic! Well, gen'l'men, p'r'aps if ye'd take one

130

of me arms——"

He lurched against Haslam, but Haslam swiftly pushed him away.

"Be off!" he cried.

"Lard'sakes, it's a nellyfunt!" hiccoughed the old man, and staggered away in brisk terror.

Haslam resumed his bicycle, happily none the worse for the encounter with the hedge, with a guilty feeling that he had been unkind to an old veteran whose granddaughter had been married that morning. But he couldn't help that. Not for all the grandfathers and granddaughters in Sussex was he going to relinquish his caution!

"He imagined he saw two of us," thought Haslam, smiling grimly, as he began to work up his pace again. "I only hope he wasn't right!"

Ordinarily, he would never have left an old man in such a condition to grope his way home alone, but he was needed more urgently elsewhere; moreover, there was always the odd chance, on such a mysterious adventure as this, that the old man may not have been quite as harmless as he looked.

The surface of the road improved, and it grew straighter. Somewhere in the distance, the Sussex Downs loomed, shutting off the sea, but Haslam could not see them. The stretch he was passing over was flat and marshy, and soon he noticed that dikes ran alongside the road. "Windmill country," he reflected. "We are getting to it."

A sign-post rose up at a corner. He put on his brake, and dismounted. It was one of the land-marks which had been mentioned by Miss Holland. The old mill could be seen, in daylight, from this point, and stood only a mile away. Half-a-mile along the road, and then up a lane on the right. Haslam strained his eyes, but, as yet, could see nothing.

He went a little more slowly and cautiously now. He was on the last lap, within a few minutes of the next mysterious stage of his adventure. He wondered whether George would be meeting him alone, or whether he would find him among a collection of doubtful associates. It seemed possible that he might meet many old friends here—all the uninvited guests, in fact, who showed such baffling interest in the Brambles. In this case, he would certainly have to go warily, and keep his wits about him!

But, surely, George Holland would not have subjected his sister to the insult of a nocturnal visit to this gang? Weak though George clearly was, there must be some point of common decency below which he would not drop. No, Haslam inclined on the whole towards the theory that he would find George waiting at the mill alone—a theory which proved to be wrong.

He was cycling slowly up the lane now, and had left the straight wide road that led southwards into the heart of the Downs. The lane was not very narrow, but it was badly rutted, and showed little sign of use. Towards the end, it curved, and, standing some little way back from the point where it curved, a dark, squat shape stood glumly, like a battered, stunted giant, or one that had had its head cut off.

The mill was a dilapidated ruin. It was of use, by day, to artists, and, by night, to bats. Half-a-dozen bats slanted about it now, like escaped liver-symptoms.

Haslam got off his bicycle. No sign came from the deserted mill. He listened, but could hear nothing. He stared at it, till its shape became solid velvet, but could see no sign of any human being.

"Well, now I'm for it!" he muttered; and, putting his bicycle in the most secure place he could find, he walked gingerly across the ground that lay between the road and the mill.

CHAPTER 21

Haslam approached the old mill quietly, as well as slowly. If there was going to be any surprise, he preferred to be the one to give it. Of course, since George Holland expected his sister, and not a total stranger, it was reasonable to suppose that Haslam's appearance would create some astonishment; but, in view of the incidents of the journey, Haslam considered it very possible that his coming might be anticipated, and that George Holland would not be alone to receive him.

It even occurred to him that the whole thing might be a deliberately planned trap, in which Miss Holland's brother had been used as a bait to capture her—though for what possible object, he had not the remotest idea.

He was now up to the mill. Still, no sign from within. He put his hand forward, and felt the cold stone. Then, creeping round to a doorless opening, he stood for a moment on the threshold, and called, softly,

"Hallo! Anyone there?"

Something rustled instantly, in response. The next moment, a figure appeared. But it was not the figure of George Holland. It was the figure of a girl.

Haslam stared at her in astonishment, but his astonishment was no greater than her own. Her eyes grew big and startled, and she retreated almost immediately. Haslam, after a moment's hesitation, followed her.

He found himself in the lower chamber of the mill. The structure was a mere ruin, and was open to the skies. Another doorless aperture on the other side of the chamber let in more faint light, and in the dimness Haslam was able to make out the form of the frightened girl quite distinctly. It was a pretty, rounded form, with something very alluring about it. The girl's eyes, too, looked curiously bright. But Haslam's main interest was centred in the fact that she remained silent, as though struck dumb with terror, and that her whole pose betokened fear.

Fear—of what? Merely of a stranger suddenly walking in upon her? Or something more definite than that?

Haslam glanced round the chamber quickly, satisfied himself that they were alone, and then said,

"Don't be afraid. I won't harm you. I'm not a ghost."

"Who are you?" replied the girl, in a scarcely audible voice.

"Who did you expect me to be?" he parried.

"Expect you to be?" she repeated, dully. And then, suddenly, she flashed out, "Why should I expect you to be anybody?"

"She expected me to be George Holland," Haslam thought, but, for the moment, kept the thought to himself. Aloud, he said, "Well, weren't you expecting somebody?"

"No," she answered. Never had a girl lied more obviously.

"Then may I ask," continued Haslam, pleasantly, "what you are doing here?"

"Is that any business of yours?" she retorted, frowning.

"No. Only a very natural curiosity."

"If it comes to that, I might ask what *you* are doing here?"

"And perhaps I'll tell you. But I'd rather hear your story first, if you don't mind."

She looked at him hard, drawing a little closer to do so. It occurred to Haslam, as he watched her, that an old deserted mill possessed dangers of a kind he had not visualised during his ride thither.

"Well, suppose I tell you," said the girl, after the scrutiny. "Will you go away then?"

Her voice was pretty, and Haslam was surprised to find that the common streak in it was very slight. Since he was beginning to guess who the young lady was, he was a little puzzled over her refinement. But a dark night and an old deserted mill, he decided, can cloud the judgment astonishingly.

"You want me to go away?" he asked.

"Well—I don't suppose you want to stay?" she bridled.

"Would it be quite gallant to admit that?" remarked Haslam.

He was not quite sure what attitude to adopt, and his remark was an attempt to propitiate her. As soon as he had made it, he realised his mistake. She shot an angry glance at him, for which he awarded her a good mark. And it came to him that she probably needed a number of good marks, to make the score even.

"Let's cut that out," she said, frowning hard.

"Very well. Agreed. I don't want to leave this spot for a little while, and I have no intention of leaving it. But, rest assured, my reasons are not in the least romantic."

Now she began to look frightened again.

"What do you mean?" she whispered.

"Look here, I think the best thing you and I can do is to stop playing at cross-purposes," said Haslam. "Let's try seeing how frank we can be. You say you didn't expect me to be someone else. Am I to believe that?"

"No, she answered. "I did expect someone else."

"Ah! Why didn't you say that before?"

"Why should I have said it? Do you suppose a girl likes to have her private affairs gone into by total strangers? I'm here to meet my sweetheart. There! And, now you know, will you please go?" Haslam shook his head, and she stamped her foot. "Why won't you go? He might be here any minute!"

"I suppose you won't tell me who he is?"

"Why should I, when I don't know who *you* are?"

"Perhaps I'm more of a friend than an enemy."

"Enemy? Why should you be an enemy? I haven't got any enemies!" It occurred to Haslam that she was curiously emphatic on this point. "Oh, you fool!" she burst out. "I beg your pardon! No, I don't. You are a fool! If I told you who my sweetheart was, you wouldn't know him. It wouldn't help any! Really, you're ridiculous!" She looked charming in her anger. Haslam wondered whether Mary Holland's brother had seen her so, and fallen in love with her, perhaps, after a quarrel; for Haslam was now convinced in his mind that this girl was the maid who had disappeared from Mrs Eltham Smith's house at Arundel, from which the valuable necklace had been stolen. If this were so, it supplied a connecting link, and proved almost beyond doubt that George Holland had had some hand in the wretched affair. "You don't seem able to understand anything," the girl ran on, in a complaining tone. "Why, even a blind man could see what a position you're putting me in! What'll my sweetheart say when he *does* turn up, and finds you here with me?"

"That's true," nodded Haslam. "I never thought of that. But, somehow or other, I don't believe he'll worry about me. Particularly if he's Mr George Holland, as I expect."

The girl's hand went up to her breast, and she gave a little gasp. But she recovered herself, almost at once.

"I don't know who Mr George Holland is," she said, doggedly.

"I wish you'd be truthful!" exclaimed Haslam. "I tell you, I'm Mr George Holland's friend—and, therefore, yours."

"It's no good," she retorted. "I don't know who you're talking about."

"Of course, you're hopeless!"

"So are you! If you were a friend, as you say, you'd go."

"Since your sweetheart isn't George Holland, who is he?"

"There you go, again! Asking impertinent questions! His name's Henry Dence, if you must know. And now, perhaps——"

"That's a pity," interrupted Haslam. "You see, I've no interest in Henry Dence. If you're his friend, I've no interest in you. But, if you'd been George Holland's friend—well, then, I might have helped you. You see, I've come here to meet George Holland, and I don't mean to leave this spot till I've done it, or, at any rate, know where he is. That will upset you, of course, but I'm afraid you and Henry Dence will have to find some other place——"

"Oh, do stop!" she cried, passionately. "You're awful!" She stepped close to him, and laying her hand on his coat, looked at him hard again. Her eyes were suspiciously bright, and Haslam assigned the fact to the imminence of tears. "Do you want to drive me crazy?" she asked. "Suppose I *did* know George Holland? What then?"

"I am a friend of his sister's."

"Of his sister's? Is that true?"

"Of course."

"Well, go on. Why have you come here?"

"Why should I tell Henry Dence's friend that?"

She stamped her foot again. "Perhaps I do know George Holland," she burst out. "Well—what if I do?"

"Why, if you do, you can tell me where to find him, because I want to assist him."

"How? How should you assist him? Why should you want to?"

"I've told you. It is because of his sister. I've twenty-five pounds in my pocket I want to give to him—or, to someone who I know will pass it on to him."

Unconsciously, she had kept her hand on his coat all this time. Now, Haslam suddenly felt the grip tighten. Several seconds passed in silence.

"Do you mean that? Really? Do you mean you've got twenty-five pounds for us—I mean, for—for—" She trailed off, and, falling away from him, passed her hand before her eyes.

Haslam took out his letter-case and opened it. Extracting the twenty-five pound notes, he held them out to her.

"Here they are," he said, simply. "Don't be afraid to take them." She made no movement. "Still suspicious of me?" he asked. She put out her hand then, and took the notes. "Good! And, now I've proved my good faith, please prove yours, and let me know where George Holland is. Is he hiding somewhere about here?"

"I don't understand this at all," she murmured. "Is it a trap?"

"No. Perhaps it ought to be, but it isn't. To tell you the truth, I hardly understand it myself. It's all wrong. But there it is, and *you* needn't worry about that."

"Are you fond of George Holland's sister?"

"Ridiculously. But you've not told me yet, you know, where George Holland is?"

"He's—he's not here."

"So I gather."

"He came here, but he went away again."

"Where?"

"To—to that house."

"What house?"

"No—I didn't mean that. I don't know where he is. I don't know what he's done."

She was suddenly frightened and desperate again. She kept on glancing furtively about and Haslam saw that she was torn with doubts.

"You oughtn't to be afraid of me now, you know," he said, gently. "Haven't I proved that I'm trying to help you? Why did George Holland go back to the Brambles?"

"The Brambles? I never mentioned——"

"Why did he go back?"

"I don't know! I don't know anything! If you want it, perhaps you'd better take your money back——"

"Don't be absurd."

"I'm not absurd! But I'm afraid! Can't you hear something?" Haslam raised his head, and listened, and, at that instant, she tried to dart by him. But he was too quick for her, and caught hold of her firmly. "Let me go, let me go!" she almost sobbed.

"Not till you've looked at me in the face, and read from my eyes what my lips seem unable to tell you!" replied Haslam. "Look at me! Now, then! I love George Holland's sister, and, for her sake, I'm going through with this. Do you *still* disbelieve me?"

She stopped struggling, arrested by the note in his voice. Once more, they looked into each other's eyes, and, even while he was telling her of his love for another, Haslam suddenly felt the terrible spell that all women possess when they are young and beautiful, and are held close. He let her go quickly.

"Well?" he asked, "Are you satisfied?"

"Yes—I trust you now," she whispered, a little breathlessly.

"Then why has George Holland gone to the Brambles?"

"One moment. Sh!"

She put her fingers to her lips, and stole to the aperture. He followed her, making no effort now to detain her. For a moment, they stood outside, listening. Then, suddenly, Haslam felt himself seized by her strong, trembling fingers.

"Oh—you brute!" she murmured. "You brute!"

And, before he had recovered from his astonishment, she had slipped away from him and was lost in the shadows.

CHAPTER 22

The girl's departure had been so sudden and unexpected that Haslam did not even make any effort to stop her. By the time he had pulled himself together, it was too late. He searched around vaguely for a few moments, but soon realised that his chances of finding her again were negligible, and gave the hunt up.

What had caused her sudden change of attitude? Was the whole thing an elaborate ruse, and, mistrusting him still, had she merely feigned confidence to throw him off his guard? He could hardly believe that, for both her voice and her eyes, at one moment, had been very sincere, in response to his own sincerity. The only alternative, however, was that something had occurred while they were standing outside the mill to bring back her suspicions. What?

He hastened, suddenly, to the spot where he had left his bicycle. With a sigh of relief, he found that the machine was still there. He relit the lamp, which he had put out before entering the mill, and spent two or three minutes in a further search, flashing the lamp over the desolate land. This time, he was not looking for the girl, but for some sign of the mysterious cause of her flight. As before, his search proved fruitless. Frowning, he replaced the lamp on the machine.

There was only one thing to do. He must return to the Brambles as fast as he could, endeavouring to overtake George Holland, and, if necessary, to warn him. The boy was heading straight for the lion's mouth, and if he attempted to enter, and Detective Grant discovered him, there would be very little that Haslam could do to help him. What would become of the strange girl with whom he had spent the last ten minutes, he could not say.

"Well, she's evidently chosen the crooked path," reflected Haslam, sadly, "and, I dare say, she deserves whatever fate will come to her."

But few men—and Haslam was not one of them—can bear the thought of a hunted girl being caught, whatever her offence, and however necessary her capture may be for the safety of the community, or of a principle. Haslam would have given a good deal, as he started on his return journey, if the girl had only trusted him wholly. His one consolation was that, at any rate, she had in her possession twenty-five pounds.

"If she is caught, and they are found on her, I wonder how she will explain them?" he thought.

Once more, he found himself on the open road. His back, now, was to the invisible Downs, and before him, through ten miles of darkness, was the too-magnetic house of Mr Blythe.

He looked at his watch. Twenty-five minutes to three. Had he really been sitting in the dining-room of the Brambles, with Mr Blythe and Mr Grant, six hours ago? It seemed more like six days. He calculated that, with good luck, he ought to be back again by twenty-five to four. What would have happened at the Brambles in the meantime?

"Confound it!" he suddenly muttered.

He recalled that he had, of necessity, left the back door unsecured. This meant that, if George Holland intended to try and enter the house, he would have no difficulty in doing so. He visualised the foolish boy's entry, and Grant, waiting and listening in his room. He heard, in his mind, a trip on the boy's part, a swift, almost soundless journey on the detective's followed by the boy's miserable consternation, and the detective's triumph—and then, heaven knew what tragic, sordid business! The picture was so vivid that, as he went through the outskirts of the village at which he had encountered the festive and hiccoughing old fellow who had unwisely celebrated the prospect of great-grandchildren, he seemed actually to hear the panting of the captured prisoner, and the heavy breathing of. . .

"Good Lord! That's not imagination!" he thought, abruptly. "It's that damned rascal following me again. By heaven, I'll come to grips with him this time."

He pulled up sharply, feeling the sort of anger that a teased bull feels in a ring, jumped off his machine, swung it round, and jumped on again. It was a clever manoeuvre, smartly done, but the mysterious pursuer, if he existed outside Haslam's imagination, was smarter still. A shadow that might have been illusion, and a sound that might have had one of a dozen origins, were all that rewarded Haslam's enterprise. Disgusted, finding nothing, he turned round again, and resumed his way.

"This is ridiculous!" he fumed, in a very bad temper. It must be remembered that he was also very fatigued. "I feel like a blessed human sandwich—something in front that I'm trying to catch, and something behind that refuses to catch me. Oh, Hades!"

And he gave way, an unusual thing with him, to the less happy phrases of vocabulary.

After this, he felt a little better, and found it possible to increase his speed. He increased it to such effect that, just beyond the village at which he had wasted a quarter-of-an hour on the outward journey, he definitely spied a cyclist some way ahead of him.

"At last!" he thought. "George Holland, I'll wager."

Whether it was George Holland, or whether it was not, he never found out. At that moment, Fate played its last unkind trick of the journey, and led his back tyre over a tack that had been dropped by a small boy some dozen hours earlier. There was a sudden, dismal swish, and the tyre gasped itself flat.

Haslam did not use bad language this time. He did not use any language at all. It came over him that Fate did not mean him to interfere with its programme that night, that whatever tragedy lay ahead had been written down in its book too long and too indelibly for any effort of his to wipe out. In a new spirit of passive, fatigued acceptance, Haslam dismounted from his machine, lit a cigarette, and proceeded with the business of mending the puncture.

There was no difficulty in locating the damage. The tack remained in the tyre until he pulled it out. Behind him, as he began to take off the tyre, the familiar clock struck a-quarter-past-three. The sound aroused his curiosity, causing him to turn and glance back in the direction of the village to see whether the little light was still glimmering. This abrupt action, though he did not know it, very nearly provided him with the proof he had so often sought that he was being followed; very nearly, but not quite; as he glanced along the road, he found it deserted, and the little light was still glimmering.

This light, to him, was a mere incident, scarcely to be remembered in a journey full of more important happenings. In the course of time, Haslam would forget it altogether. Yet, to a silent old man, who sat through the night hours and watched a companion slip away, it marked a spot and an occasion that blotted out all other things, till he too should slip away, unwatched, in the silence of another night.

As the church clock struck half-past-three, the old man bent suddenly over the still form he was watching, and Haslam completed the mending of his tyre and rode away.

He decided that the longest way back, through Wynton, would be the quickest, for he did not know the route across country to Heysham, and the sign-posts were few and far between. He reached Wynton without further incident, and made a short detour in order to pass Mary Holland's house. This took him only two minutes out of his way, and the temptation proved too strong for him to resist. Her window was in darkness. He prayed that she was sleeping soundly. Then, turning off into the three-mile stretch to Heysham, he began the last lap of the journey.

A vague, uneasy greyness began to mingle with the utter blackness of the night. Haslam shivered suddenly. When one has ridden through hours of darkness, the beginnings of the cold grey dawn react on one as though a cloak were being lifted from one's person. One forgets the night's own tremors, and rebels instinctively against the changing condition. The sun will be good, but the approach to it is dismal.

Haslam watched the gradual thinning out of the darkness anxiously. He wished to get back before the dawn, realising that the lighter it grew, the greater would be the prospects of his discovery. A great weariness, also, was overcoming him, and twice he nearly went to sleep in his saddle. He felt that his mind was growing clouded, and that it was refusing to respond—that if he suddenly came face to face with Grant, he would not be in a condition to think of anything to say, or of anything to do beyond staring at him foolishly.

"Yes, there's no mistake about it," he reflected, as he jerked himself out of another dangerous lethargy. "I'm tired."

He hardly remembered the last part of the journey. Suddenly, he found himself outside the gate of the Brambles. "By Jove—I'm here," he thought, in a sort of surprise. He opened the gate. Bed became a wonderful thing. It seemed impossible that he would really soon be in bed. But—would he? He tried to remember. Oh, yes. George Holland. He would have to find out about George Holland . . .

He found himself outside the back door. He did not remember getting there. He put his hand on the handle. It turned easily. Good. It occurred to him, muddily, that the last time he had tried it, it was locked. When was that?

He was inside now. All was still and quiet. Bed—that was the thing. Lord, how tired he was! No—George Holland first. He kept on forgetting George Holland. This wouldn't do! "Buck up, man!" he muttered. He would just go over the house, and then . . .

"My God!" he murmured.

His sleepiness disappeared. He was glaringly awake now. A sharp shot had resounded from somewhere upstairs.

"What's that?" he cried, and bounded up, with a fast-beating heart. He heard movements inside rooms, and voices. Others, too were being roused by the shot, and were hurrying out to discover its cause. But Haslam encountered no one.

"Hallo! Anybody hurt?" he shouted, again.

There was no response. Racing at full speed, he reached at last the spot from which the shot had resounded, and nearly tripped over something as he did so.

A slim shape lay on the ground. He pulled out his matches, and struck one.

On the ground, with a revolver at his side, lay Pike.

CHAPTER 23

Haslam dropped swiftly on his knees beside the butler's prostrate form, and, before the match had spent itself, he discovered that Pike was dead. Dropping the match, and striking another, he ran along the passage in the hope of finding some sign of the man who had fired the shot, if it had not been fired by Pike himself, but his investigations were cut short by a sharp word behind him.

"Come back!"

He turned, and saw Detective Grant standing beside Pike with a lighted candle in his hand.

"Pike's dead," replied Haslam, shortly.

"So I see," remarked Grant.

"Well, I want to find out who did it."

"So do I. Stay here. I'll go." Haslam hesitated for a moment. "Do you hear?" snapped the detective, sharply.

"Oh, as you like," murmured Haslam, returning. "I suppose this is your job now."

"It is my job," retorted Grant, looking at Haslam steadily for an instant. "I want you to remember that."

Haslam shrugged his shoulders, and, taking up his position by the body, watched Grant run along the passage to carry out the investigations he had himself been about to make. He felt very much at a disadvantage, both by his position and his fatigue. Events were toppling one upon another with too dizzy a speed, and, in his tired state, he found them too difficult to consider and sort out. He did not even know exactly what point he was making for. To shield a thief was one thing. To shield a murderer was quite another. But, as yet, there was no evidence as to who the murderer was, or even if a murder had been committed at all. Oh, for two hours' sleep! He felt he was on the verge of making some foolish blunder.

He wondered whether Mary Holland were asleep at this moment. She was, at any rate, blissfully unconscious of these tragic developments. He wondered, also, where the girl at the old mill was, and what she was doing. Was she still waiting in the gruesome place for George Holland to return? How long would she wait, if he never returned? And where would despair drive her?

Someone came along the passage towards him. Instinctively, he altered his position, till he was between Pike and the approaching person.

"Oh, sir! What is it?" came the voice of Rose.

She had thrown on an old dressing-gown, and, despite her prettiness, would have looked comically humorous in other circumstances. On the stage, for instance, she might have aroused a laugh. But neither she nor Haslam felt in the least inclined to laugh.

"Is that you, Rose?" asked Haslam, vapidly.

"Yes, sir."

"You'd better go back to your room."

"I couldn't. Cook's there." Anything, apparently, was preferable to the cook's company at this moment. "What's happened."

"You're a brave girl. Don't scream. It's Pike."

"Is he shot, sir?" she whispered.

"Yes. Poor old Pike won't have any more troubles. His term's over." There was a short silence. Suddenly, his inactivity became too much for him. "Look here, Rose—I must go and see what's up. I can't stand this."

"I'll wait here, sir, if you like," answered the girl, pluckily.

"Do you mind? Grant told me to stay, but I can't help that. Tell him, if he comes, that I've gone to look for Mr Blythe. I can't understand why he isn't here!"

Grant reappeared at that instant. He was alone.

"I'd rather you stayed where you are for just a few moments

longer, if you don't mind, Mr Haslam," he said, quietly.

"Why the deuce should I?" cried Haslam. "Are you accusing me of this damnable affair?"

A shout from below interrupted further discussion.

"Hi!" screamed the voice of Ambrose Blythe. "Help me, some-one! I've got him!"

Rose clasped her hands, while the two living men suddenly disappeared from her side, leaving her alone with the dead one. She drew away from the body with a shudder, then suddenly approached it again.

"Poor Mr Pike!" she said. "You're not dead, are you? P'r'aps they're wrong!" She knelt down by his side, and, though he was undeniably dead, tried to staunch his wound.

Meanwhile, Grant was assisting Mr Blythe to complete his capture in the hall below. Haslam stood by, having no relish for the job, and realising that his help was not necessary. The captive seemed too weak and dazed to offer any resistance, and one glance at his face proved Haslam's worst doubts. It was George Holland.

"Found him trying to sneak out of the back door!" panted Mr Blythe. "Tripped him up from behind. Now, then, my lad, what have ye got to say for yourself?"

The boy made no reply, and Grant frowned warningly.

"I'll do the questioning, if you don't mind," he said. Then, turning to the prisoner, he asked,

"Well—what's your explanation?"

The prisoner shook his head.

"Come, silence won't help you. Let me hear your story."

But the prisoner remained dull and obdurate. He seemed to have made up his mind to say nothing.

"You know what's happened?" rapped out the detective.

Silence.

"You know that one of the maids in this house has just been murdered?"

"What's that?" cried Mr Blythe, and Haslam also stared at the detective. But Grant's eyes were fixed on the prisoner's face, and the prisoner alone showed no surprise at the news.

"It's not a maid—it's Pike," Haslam whispered to Mr Blythe, suddenly realising that this was merely the detective's ruse, designed to obtain some confirmation that the prisoner had personal knowledge of the precise nature of the tragedy. But either the prisoner did not have that personal knowledge, or he was a good actor.

Mr Blythe was not so shrewd as Haslam.

"But it's not one of the maids!" he exclaimed. "Good God! It's Pike, Grant—so Haslam says."

"Oh—the butler?" replied Grant coolly. "I see. Well, whoever it is, it's murder, so I take it you fully understand your position, my man. You're not obliged to answer my questions. At the same time, if you've any explanation you want to give of your presence here, it might be just as well to give it."

"I've got nothing to say," said the prisoner, in a low voice, speaking for the first time.

"But, damme that won't do!" burst out Mr Blythe. "I should think you'd have the devil of a lot to say! Ain't you the fellow who's been coming round here with a bicycle, asking the way to God knows where, and losing a pocket-book ye never had in the grounds——?"

"Steady, Mr Blythe," murmured the detective.

"Not a bit!" retorted Mr Blythe. "Pike's dead, and if you or I ask questions, it can't bring the poor fellow back to life again. But all this means more to me, Grant, than it means to you—yes, damme, it does—and I've got one or two questions I mean to ask while I've got the chance. I'm not going to wait weeks and months while you detectives and lawyers haggle over it! So, now!" Grant shrugged his shoulders, and realized that, at this moment, Mr Blythe might prove more of a success at cross-examination than he himself. "You've been here before, haven't you?" rapped out Mr Blythe, turning again to the boy.

"I—yes," answered the prisoner.

"Ah! Now, then. Why?"

Silence.

"Come, come! Why?" insisted the old man.

"Is this any good?" asked the boy, wearily, and turned to the detective. "Please tell me what you're going to do with me. I've got nothing to say at this moment."

"Of course, you haven't," cried Mr Blythe. "You've not had time yet to invent one of your pretty stories. You see, one doesn't break into a house at four in the morning to ask the way to Ingate, or search for a lost pocket-book! You belong to that pack of rascals who keep on calling at this house. Bah! I know that! Well, the game seems to be up now, whatever it is. Damned old fool that I am, I feel like a murderer myself, for having let it go on so long! You've killed my butler——"

"Better not make statements," interposed Grant, frowning.

"Oh, I beg your pardon," retorted Mr Blythe. "P'r'aps he didn't ____"

"No, I didn't," said the boy.

"Why, there you are, you see!" cried Mr Blythe, with an almost hysterical laugh. "Then it must have been Mr Haslam, who hasn't been to bed, I see, and has evidently sat up all night in his clothes with a revolver in his pocket, or me, p'r'aps, in my sleep, or even you, Detective——"

"Or even me," nodded Grant, sternly. "We're all under suspicion."

Mr Blythe paused. Grant was looking at him disapprovingly, and his tone had been harsh. Having subdued Mr Blythe, Grant turned his eyes upon Haslam, and studied him thoughtfully. On the point of asking him a question, he suddenly changed his mind, and turned once more to the prisoner.

"You asked me what I was going to do with you," he said, and everyone noted that there was now a new tone in his voice. It was the tone of one who had decided on a plan, and meant to brook no interference; from this moment, Grant took full control of the situation. "Well, I'll tell you," he continued. "I'm going to lock you up here. You couldn't expect anything else. But, before doing so, I'm going to ask you one or two questions to which you need not reply. What's your name?"

"I won't tell you," said the boy. "But I didn't fire that shot."

"What shot?"

"You know!"

"Yes, I know. You were in the house when it was fired, then? You heard it?"

"Yes."

"But you didn't fire it?"

"No."

"Or see it fired?"

"No."

"Or come upon anybody who *did* fire it?"

"No."

"In fact, although you say you did not fire the shot yourself, you have no knowledge of who did fire it?"

"None."

"Very well. Did you come here to steal anything?"

"If you like."

"You will give no other reason?"

"No."

"How did you get in?"

"Through the back door."

"Wasn't it locked?"

"No."

"Not locked!" cried Mr Blythe, but the detective checked him with a look.

"Have you any suggestion to make about that?"

"I tell you, I don't know anything about anything!" the boy burst out. "All I've got to say is that I didn't shoot anybody. If the back door wasn't locked, then somebody else could have got in and done it."

"But nobody else has been found here."

"Well, I can't help that. I can't help anything. And I'm not going to answer any more questions."

"Just one more, please, if you will. You say you didn't shoot Pike. But did you come here tonight to see him?"

Silence.

"Have you ever had any dealings with Pike?"

Silence. The boy had shut his mouth again. He looked dazed and weary. At one moment, he tried to assert himself, while at the next he sank back into an atmosphere of confused and dogged sullenness.

"Very well. That will do for the moment." Grant put his hand on the boy's shoulder to lead him away, then turned to the others. "No one, of course, is to leave this house," he said. "Technically speaking, we are all under suspicion. Please go to the library and wait for me there. I shall send the maids down, also, with your permission. When I have locked this man away, I am going to ask each one of you to give me an exact account of your actions tonight, from the moment we last separated to the moment the shot was fired."

He led his prisoner away, and Mr Blythe turned to Haslam.

"Well, let's do as he says, and go to the library," he muttered. "This is a bad business, Haslam, and I'm afraid I behaved like an old fool. I wish you'd pull me up when my silly tongue begins to run away with me. I'd rather you did it than Grant. But, of course, he's right, he's right. He's always right. He won't learn much from our stories, though, will he?" he added. "Seems waste of time to cross-examine the lot of us. Wonder what his idea is?" Suddenly he clapped his hands. "Ah—that back door, of course! It was unlocked. That wants a bit of explaining, eh?"

CHAPTER 24

The scene which was enacted, a few minutes later, in the library was rich in both tragedy and comedy, and Haslam, with his trained literary instinct, went through the painful agony of realising each aspect. There are times when our perceptions are too keen. The humorist, at a serious Board Meeting, is at a disadvantage, while the grave, analytical mind finds a modern revue difficult to laugh at. But when the mind has been trained to perceive both the grave and the gay sides of life, and has become immediately responsive to each, occasions often become twisted into grotesque and ironical shape, and a tired brain loses itself in its own mazes of intelligence. The man who stands for one thing, or one purpose, is rarely troubled in this way.

In thinking back over the strange mystery of the Brambles and the bewildering days into which its crises were crowded, Haslam always found that this queer little meeting in the library, beginning precisely at 4.10 a.m., stood out with absurd clearness, and the exceedingly uncomfortable sensations through which he personally passed were almost forgotten in his memory of other quite superficial aspects of the drama.

Rose, wonderfully wide-eyed and solemn, seemed quite unconscious of her curl-papers. Probably, she was. The strange intimacy of their presence in the stately library impressed itself on Haslam's mind as immensely comic, particularly as one of the papers, half-uncurled, revealed itself as a portion of a newspaper advertisement of an Aid to Beauty. The Cook was even more comic. She was old and ample, and, possibly because—unlike Rose—she found it difficult to appear charming even at normal times, she made extra efforts during an emergency, and had now seized a very inappropriate boudoir cap to conceal her tangled grey hairs, and wore a pair of bedroom slippers of startlingly gay green wool.

Even Mr Blythe himself looked comic in his anxious frailty to cynical analytical eyes. From the detective alone emanated no single gleam of humour.

The tales that were told, also, possessed their moments of incongruous entertainment.

"Me?" exclaimed Cook, the first tackled by Detective Grant. "I went straight into my bed, and stayed in it."

"You didn't leave your room from the moment you entered it to the moment you heard the shot?" asked Grant.

"Not likely!" replied Cook. "I put me 'ead under the piller, and kep' it there."

"Did you go to sleep?"

"On and hoff."

"Were you disturbed?"

"Yes, sir."

"By what?"

"Dreamt I was bein' chased across the roof!"

"I don't suppose the detective wants to hear about your dreams," snapped Mr Blythe.

"On the contrary, dreams are often instructive," replied Grant. "What else did you dream?"

"Oh, them dreams!" gasped Cook. "I 'ad another that someone was climbin' up the wall and gettin' in at the winder."

"You're sure this was a dream?"

"Lawks, I 'ope so, sir!"

"Well—and what did you do when you heard the shot? Were you awake at the time?"

"No, sir. It woke me up. I sits up in bed, sir, and Rose she ses, 'What's that?' and then I ses, 'Gawd knows,' and flops down again. I was all tremblin', sir. I think I must 'ave gone off pop, becos' when I opens my eyes again Rose was out of the room, and all the hollerin' in the world wouldn't bring 'er back. So I waited, and presently Rose came in and said we was wanted, and that's all I know, except that she told me about poor Mr Pike." She shivered, and her boudoir cap slipped a little to one side. "It ain't really true, sir, is it?" she whispered. "He ain't really—he ain't——"

"I'm afraid it is true," answered Grant. "Thank you, that's all I want to ask you. You can go back to your room now, if you want to."

"What, alone?" she gasped. "Not me!"

Rose's turn came next. Her story, on the face of it, did not provide any more information, though there were one or two points which appeared to interest the detective.

"Did you, also, get straight to bed when you went up to your room last night?" he asked her.

"Yes, sir," replied Rose.

"And did you, also, stay in your room?"

"Yes, sir."

"And did you go to sleep at once?"

"No, sir. I lay awake some time. Then I went to sleep, but I kept on waking up again."

"Did anything special wake you up?"

"No—not till the pistol shot, that is."

"Did anything disturb you while you *were* awake?"

Rose hesitated for an instant, and stared hard at the ground. Then she answered, "No, sir," and looked up again.

"You didn't seem quite sure of that answer," commented Grant. "Think again."

"Well, sir, I had fancies sometimes, but I don't think there was anything more than that."

"What sort of fancies?"

"Oh, just all sorts of noises, like one would."

"Can you name any particular one?"

Rose thought again, then shook her head. "No, sir," she said. "Just creaks, and things like that."

"But nothing special?"

"No, sir."

Grant frowned thoughtfully, then switched on to another point.

"What did you do exactly when you heard the shot?"

"I jumped up and spoke to Cook, as she said. Then I got out of bed——"

"Did you hear anything in the passage? Any scurrying, or anything?"

"No, sir. I put on one or two things—what I've got on now—and went out of the room. I think Cook had hysterics, but I couldn't stop and listen to her. When I came upon poor Mr Pike, Mr Haslam was standing by him—as you told him to—well, you know the rest, because you came almost at once after that."

"And you met no one between the time of leaving your room and seeing Mr Haslam?"

"No, sir."

"And heard no one?"

"No, sir."

"Thank you. That will do. You and Cook can now both go back to your room together. Perhaps you can get another couple of hours' sleep. You'd better try. And I advise you to lock your door."

The advice was somewhat superfluous. Cook cast up her eyes, and, in response to Rose's, "Come along," allowed herself to be led from the room. The door closed behind the two maids. Haslam wondered whether his turn would be next, and prepared for the encounter, but Grant turned to Mr Blythe, leaving Haslam to the last.

"Can you tell me anything useful?" he asked.

"Damme, yes," replied Mr Blythe. "I can tell you how to add up two and two to make four."

"Meaning——?"

"That the fellow I caught killed Pike, and there's no two ways of thinking about it."

"There are always two ways of thinking about everything until one way is proved correct, and since nothing in this world has even been proved correct, there must always be two ways of thinking. We are guided through life by a series of strong impressions, and as we must always *act* one way or the other, even if it is only negatively, we allow the strongest impressions to sway us. You could find a flaw in every conviction that has ever been made, if you dived deep enough."

"I don't see what all this has to do with it," remarked Mr Blythe.

"It just means that you must let me go to work in my own way, and work out my own sums as best I can. Two and two, to your mind, means that the young man you caught has murdered Pike. Another arithmetician might say it meant suicide. Have you thought of that? Then there are other explanations worth considering, in the light of other events. The previous attack on Pike, for instance, does not seem to have been launched by our present prisoner. There, at once, is one unknown quantity. And, in addition, up to the present moment, we have not the slightest clue as to motive. We merely have a series of odd incidents, which appear to be connected. But we have not connected them. If we simply assume that our prisoner murdered Pike, does that clear up the mystery of this house? If not, and they are not separate propositions, how can we possibly be reasonably sure of anything until we *have* connected all our pieces up? I have various theories in my mind, and only by close questioning can I find out which of my ideas fit into facts, and which do not."

"That sounds quite reasonable, I admit," said the old man. "But I may take it that *one* of your theories is that our prisoner killed Pike, and that none of the rest of us have had any hand in it?"

"Why, of course. But our prisoner says that he walked in through an unfastened back door."

"Pike might have let him in," suggested Mr Blythe, shrewdly.

"Yes, he might. But, if he did, Pike's own mental attitude is difficult to follow, and the tragedy would more logically—not necessarily, but certainly more logically—have occurred at a spot nearer the back door than it actually did. I do not think myself," he added, slowly, "that Pike let anyone into the house last night. It is, however, a theory we must not ignore."

"Well, if Pike didn't let the fellow in, someone inside the house must have opened the door first from the inside."

"Ah, now you begin to see the reason why I am asking all these questions. Obviously, I have got to cross-examine everyone who *was* inside—or whom we know to have been inside."

"One moment, one moment!" exclaimed the old man, suddenly. "We've only the rascal's word for it that the door *wasn't* locked."

"It was unlocked at the time of his capture, anyway," replied Grant. "I ascertained that. He may have broken in by some as yet unknown method, and then have unfastened the back door to expedite his flight when it should become necessary. But, again, I don't believe *that*."

"Someone ought to have gone over the grounds," muttered Mr Blythe.

"I went over them as soon as I could," answered Grant. "It was, necessarily, a brief survey, and I shall probably go out again. I had a look round after locking up our young friend, while you were waiting in the library. But I didn't find anyone. And now, Mr Blythe, will you give me the account I've asked for of your movements?"

"Right," responded Mr Blythe. "I can tell 'em in a nutshell. My story is something like Cook's. I went straight to bed, and I stayed there. I didn't put me head under me pillow, but I had the nastiest dreams I've ever had in me life. And it won't help you if I relate 'em, because in one I was being chased by a tiger with an elephant's trunk, and in another I was drowning in treacle—and if ye can make anything out of that, ye can have it. God bless me, Grant, I know that every word ye say is sound sense, but for the Lord's sake let me get back to bed now, or I'll go pop like Cook did or bite your head off. There's a statute of limitations to what an old man like me can stand!"

Grant smiled, and nodded.

"In just one minute, Mr Blythe. I've only to hear Mr Haslam's story now, and that will conclude matters for the moment." He turned to Haslam. "Did you leave your room last night? I see you're fully dressed?"

"I decided not to undress, in case I was wanted," replied Haslam, coolly.

"I see. Then you didn't leave your room?"

"As a matter of fact, I did. Twice I heard noises, and twice I went over the house to see if I could find anything. I wonder I wasn't heard. But I found nothing."

"I see," repeated Grant. "You found nothing." He paused, considering. Haslam wondered what his next question would be. It occurred to him that he was putting up a losing fight, but if only he could evade a direct issue until he had retired to his room and had had an hour's quiet reflection, he might find the happiest way of meeting the situation, and of preserving, to the best of his ability, the interests of two women, one of whom he knew deserved no shadow of guilt upon her name, and the other of whom, though less deserving, had curiously awakened his sympathy.

Then Grant shot a surprise on Haslam. He suddenly nodded, and opened the library door.

"Well, let us leave it at that," he said. "I dare say the best thing we can all of us do is to try and steal a couple more hours of rest. Naturally, I rely upon your honour not to attempt to leave this house until I give you permission."

"As ye like," answered Mr Blythe. "It's your house, not mine. Give me a hand to my room, Haslam, will ye?"

Haslam took the old man's arm, wondering why on earth the detective had switched off his questions so suddenly. Was Haslam merely suffering the self-conscious torment of a man with an uneasy conscience? Was it possible that, after all, the detective was so convinced of Haslam's innocence that he did not think it necessary to cross-examine him more fully? This theory did not fit into the picture at all, but Haslam was too tired to try and solve any more problems. He helped Mr Blythe up to his room, and then sought his own.

"Thank the Lord!" he murmured, and wiped his forehead. "A few minutes to myself at last!"

He sponged his face with cold water, and sat down on the side of his bed. The next moment, he heard a knock on his door.

"Who's there?" he asked.

"Grant," came the reply. "May I come in?"

CHAPTER 25

"More questions?" demanded Haslam, wearily, as the detective entered the room.

"You can't complain that I've asked you many as yet," replied Grant.

"That's true," admitted Haslam. "Sit down."

Before doing so, Grant brought out his cigarette-case, and offered a cigarette to Haslam. Haslam accepted it, returned the compliment with a match, and then again invited the detective to make himself comfortable.

"Thank you," said Grant. "I meant to. You and I are in for a bit of a chat."

"Splendid," murmured Haslam, without any enthusiasm.

"I mentioned just now that I hadn't asked you many questions," commenced Grant, after his preliminary puffs. "That fact probably raised a question in your own mind. Why hadn't I? Well, I didn't think the moment opportune. It was a postponement. Those unasked questions, of course, have got to come."

"Well, fire ahead," said Haslem. "What's the first?"

"The first is a very broad one. Have you anything you feel disposed to say to me?"

"No, nothing," replied Haslam. "The only thing I feel at all disposed to at the moment is sleep, and that you won't allow."

"You yourself will determine the length of your Chinese torture," returned Grant, smiling grimly. "I am not going to leave this room until I have certain information, and it depends upon you, rather than upon me, how long you take to give me that information."

"Oh—that's interesting," commented Haslam.

"I'll begin by giving *you* some information which, apparently, you don't possess," proceeded Grant. "Being a detective, I am safeguarded to some extent from other people's curiosity. It does not seem to have occurred to any of you, for instance, to enquire how *I* spent my time between going up to my room and the firing of the fatal shot. No one thought of questioning me. Well, I'll volunteer the information."

"Just a minute, before you begin," said Haslam. "This question may not be quite orthodox, but I'm not exactly an orthodox person—and, as you say to your own victims, you needn't answer it unless you want to. Officially, you suspect the lot of us. That's all right. But, actually, do you suspect me?"

"Suspect you of what?"

"Of killing Pike?"

Grant pondered over the question.

"I don't see what possible object you could have in killing Pike," he conceded.

"Ah! That's awfully nice of you!"

"No, not so very nice. I haven't said that I see yet what possible reason anybody could have in killing Pike. But he's killed. Sometimes the motive appears after the suspicion."

"I see," nodded Haslam. "Then, with your permission, I'll withdraw my thanks."

"Certainly. I'm not sure that I'm entitled to them. When I went up to my room, I decided—as you did—not to get to bed. I wanted to be ready for any emergency, and, as events proved, my decision was a wise one.

"It wasn't long before I heard noises about the place. Very soft noises—but not quite soft enough. My ears are very alert. I made investigations..."

"And found?" queried Haslam, for the detective paused.

"I found that someone had left the house. This, naturally, aroused my curiosity. I decided to lock the back door, in the hope that, by so doing, I should put the deserter in the awkward position of having to proclaim himself, or herself, on his or her return."

"Wouldn't a simpler method have been to make a tour of the occupied rooms?" suggested Haslam, in order to find out whether the detective had done so.

"In a sense, I did. I listened at the doors, and heard breathing behind all but one of them."

"Which one was that?"

"I'll tell you in a minute. I spent quite a little time waiting by the back door, and at last, since nothing happened, I decided to enter the room behind the door of which I had heard no breathing. I found it empty."

"Really?" exclaimed Haslam. "What did you do then?"

"I returned to the back door, and went out," proceeded the detective.

Haslam thought, "That must have been while I was climbing in. Evidently, when I tried the back door, he was in my room, or he'd have heard me."

"Certain signs led me to follow a certain route—it's remarkable what a lot of clues exist for a trained mind to observe. This route led me to the gate, and out on to the road, and towards a spot where a certain young lady was hiding. I decided to hide, also, and to wait. And, presently, I saw someone coming along the road——"

"Yes, that was I," nodded Haslam. "Go ahead."

"Yes, it was you. And, since it was you, can't you guess the rest?"

"No, not quite. You saw me meet the certain young lady, of course. Then what did you do?"

"I followed you, on a lady's bicycle I borrowed, to Wynton. And, after that, I followed you—you alone this time—to a ruined mill. You did your best to trip me up, but you didn't quite succeed. The only person who saw me was the girl you met at the mill, and who disappeared with wonderful rapidity just as I was beginning to grow seriously interested in her. I had to follow her or you, and you interested me most. I didn't want to let you out of my sight. So I kept behind you all the way back to

Heysham, saw you enter this house, heard a shot, and then entered myself."

Haslam did not know whether to despair or laugh. The whole thing was like some absurd comic opera. So it was Detective Grant who had been on his heels all the while, and Detective Grant who had frightened the girl at the mill away, causing her to believe that Haslam was consciously leading her into a trap.

"Now, the shot occurred some fifteen seconds after you entered the back door," Grant went on. "You had just enough time to reach Pike, to find yourself suddenly accosted by him, and to shoot him. Do you realise that possible sequence of events?"

Haslam could contain himself no longer. This time, he laughed aloud.

"Forgive me," he exclaimed, "but I'm very tired, and somehow it does strike me as funny that I should be accused of Pike's murder."

"I'm not accusing you," retorted Grant. "I'm merely pointing out that the circumstances are suspicious. Doesn't this give you any impulse to be more frank with me?"

"I'm dashed if it does," responded Haslam. "The whole thing's too ridiculous. And, anyway, it's not likely I'd go back on my word, just because——"

He stopped suddenly, and Grant eyed him almost amusedly.

"My dear Haslam," he murmured, "there are moments when you're not at all clever! What word have you given that you don't want to go back on?" Haslam was silent. "Your word to Miss Holland? Well, we have our different codes, and I'm not your moral judge. But my own idea is that no word should ever be given to anybody which may involve a concealment of the truth, and that to seek to protect a possible murderer from the punishment devised by Society to prevent a repetition of his crime——"

"Oh, I dare say you're right," burst out Haslam. "To tell you the truth, I'm not too clear about all this myself, but the devil of it is that you've pounced upon me before I've had time to think things out. There—that's frank enough for a start, isn't it?"

164

Grant held out his hand, and his attitude changed.

"Come, that's much better!" he exclaimed. "I hate dragging facts out of honest people, and I know you're honest, although we may not see eye to eye in this matter. Can't we work together, instead of against each other?"

"I assure you, I'd much rather work with you than against you," answered Haslam. "The only thing is, I'm not quite such a machine as you are. The personal element has always meant a lot with me."

"Too much, it seems. But without going into ethics, it's the machine that will win, you know."

"Well, that's to be proved."

"Believe me, it will be proved," insisted Grant, earnestly. "I'm not going to let this case go till I've got to the bottom of it—to the bottom of this foul murder and all it involves. You can help me, if you will. You're the only person who can. But. whether you help me or not, it will make no difference in the end. I'm simply advocating a short route against a long route."

"What do you want to know, then?" asked Haslam. "If you've followed my movements so closely, you must know a good deal."

"I've inferred a certain amount, and am gradually fitting the pieces into my theories. But, because I followed you, it does not imply that I know everything. I did not hear your conversations. A word here and there, perhaps. I am still a good deal in the dark."

Haslam thought for a moment. It seemed to him that the time had come to make a confidant of Grant, or, at least, a partial confidant. Certain matters that were not immediately relevant, such as the supposition that George Holland was implicated in the Arundel theft, need not be touched upon. Grant could ferret those out for himself, if he wished. But George Holland was in such a serious position already that little Haslam could say would be likely to make it worse, while a little light thrown on Mary Holland's attitude would effectively clear her personally of suspicion.

"Of course," Grant was saying, "until you are wholly frank with me, I shall not be wholly frank with you. That, you must realise, is reasonable. I could only share certain things I have discovered and suspect with someone who gave me his entire confidence. But I'll tell you this. I did suspect you, just for a moment —or, at least, I thought it possible you had shot Pike. Recall the circumstances. They were highly suspicious. Many people, knowing no more than I do, might suspect you still. But I don't suspect you now. And I don't even suspect George Holland——"

"What!" cried Haslam, a terrific load lifting from his mind at the detective's words.

"Don't be too hasty," said Grant. "He may have done it. I'll certainly have to keep him under lock and key until I can lay my hand definitely on anyone else. But—well, come out into the garden with me. I want to show you something."

Haslam jumped up, and wondered whether the gathering light of day might be regarded as symbolic. He followed the detective through the house, now gradually awakening with light, till they reached the back door. Grant unfastened it, and walked a little way along the borders of a hedge. Then he pointed to two bicycles.

"Good Lord!" thought Haslam, as his mind groped back to the moment when he had leaned one of the bicycles against the hedge. He had been so tired that he hardly remembered it. Aloud he said, "Yes—there's the one I rode. And the other is Miss Holland's—the one you rode. Well—what of it?"

"Two bicycles, you note," commented Grant. "If my ideas are right, shouldn't there be three?"

"Why, of course!" thought Haslam. "Where's the one that George Holland rode?"

"As a matter of fact," continued Grant, "I happen to know that there *were* three bicycles here a little while ago. I placed my own bicycle—or rather, Miss Holland's—behind yours, just where it is now. Over there was another bicycle. It's gone. Now you see why I am by no means sure that Holland killed Pike. Someone else was assumedly in the house, when we entered it.

Assumedly, that someone else left the house, and rode away on the missing bicycle. He left in the devil of a hurry. Why?"

"You mean——"

"I mean that the sudden disappearance of Bicycle No. 3 is a very distinct point in Master Holland's favour."

CHAPTER 26

In the short silence that followed Detective Grant's remark, Peter Haslam caught himself in the absurd psychological process of blessing a murderer. That the man who had ridden away on Bicycle No. 3 had murdered Pike seemed highly probable, and, since the theory removed or lessened suspicion against George Holland, it was difficult not to feel a certain strange sense of gratitude towards the cause of the new theory. Then normal reaction set in, and logic reasserted itself. If the rider of Bicycle No. 3 had not committed the murder, George Holland could not have been suspected of it; and, now that this suspicion was removed, Haslam found himself thinking rationally again, and began to experience a sane man's loathing for the detestable crime.

Grant watched him, and noted with satisfaction the transition. Once he had Haslam wholly on his side, he felt that the mystery of the Brambles would be swiftly cleared, for he was formulating certain ideas and plans, and needed intelligent assistance. Had Haslam persisted in his attitude, Grant might have summoned that assistance from outside; but the author's antagonism was thawing rapidly, and the detective believed now that they might be able to carry matters through between them.

"The disappearance of the third bicycle, of course, only gives us very circumstantial evidence," said Grant, breaking the silence, "and I am not going to pretend that it by any means clears up George Holland's position, or yours."

"Or mine?" exclaimed Haslam.

"Or yours," nodded Grant, smiling. "As matters stand, a certain amount of suspicion, in the strictly legal sense, obviously attaches to you, while a considerable amount still attaches to George Holland. Come, you must see that? Have you definitely proved yet that you and Holland are not accomplices, or is it proved that the unknown person who rode away on the third bicycle is not an accomplice of both of you, or one of you?—that he is not the man, let us suggest, who saw the murder committed, but who did not actually commit it?"

"That's quite true," admitted Haslam. "But, surely, you don't think——"

"I have shaken your hand, Mr Haslam," replied Grant, gravely, "and you may take it from that that I am quite convinced in my mind that yours is a worthy hand to shake. If I had the least suspicion that you had committed this crime, I could never shake hands with you. Your ideas and personal feelings are a confounded nuisance, but even a white man may make mistakes, and I know you are white. In regard to Master Holland, I am sure he is *not* white, but I shall be very much astonished if he turns out to be the real blackguard of this tragedy. Now you know my position. Surely you can give me your whole confidence?"

"Most of it, anyway," responded Haslam.

"But not all?" demanded Grant, looking disappointed.

"Perhaps—I dare say. What about getting inside again? This garden doesn't seem exactly a healthy spot at the moment."

"It isn't," agreed the detective. "We'll go into the library."

They went indoors, locking the back door again after them. Grant sat down without a word, and waited patiently for Haslam to begin. After a moment's hesitation, Haslam started, with a question.

"Tell me this, Mr Grant," he said. "Do you think you know who committed the murder?"

"I am not going to answer that," replied Grant. "How much I tell you—and maybe I have more to tell you than you conceive —will depend very largely upon how much you tell me."

"All right—have it your own way," answered Haslam, with a

grimace. "I wish you weren't quite so confoundedly logical! But I'm afraid you'll be disappointed. I haven't a great deal to tell. I expect you know that George Holland has been paying visits to this place, along with the rest?"

"Oh, yes. I know that," said Grant.

"What the object of these visits is I haven't any more idea than you have——"

"Perhaps you have less."

"Less?" exclaimed Haslam.

"I merely offer the suggestion. Go on."

"Of course, you're uncanny," complained Haslam. "If I didn't have the same sneaking respect for you that you seem to have for me, I should begin to wonder whether *you* had a hand in this game yourself!"

"You ought to wonder it," returned Grant, with his odd, inscrutable smile. "I may have a hand in it. Go on."

"Oh, don't be an ass!" retorted Haslam. "I wish you'd be human, for a bit. Anyway, whatever *you* know, *I* know nothing whatever about the mysterious game that's being played here. All Mr Blythe has told you about me is true. Miss Holland knows nothing about the affair, either, and only came here because she found that her scamp of a brother was doing it, and she wanted to know what it was all about."

"Why didn't she ask him?" enquired the detective.

"She did," answered Grant, slowly.

"With what result?"

"He got angry. She could get nothing out of him. And, at last, he disappeared."

"One minute," interposed Grant. "What is your opinion of young Holland? Does he strike you as a straight sort of a chap?"

Haslam hesitated; then, suddenly, he exclaimed,

"Confound it, Grant, why are you cross-examining me like this? You can read George Holland as well as I can! You know perfectly well he isn't a straight sort of a chap!"

"Of course, I know he isn't," nodded Grant, quietly, "but it helps me to know where I stand when I hear you pronouncing the same opinion. If you had told me you believed he was straight, it would have weakened my expectation that we may be able to work together. I should have sought the reason for an obvious lie. Well—so Holland disappeared. When was this?"

"Just after Mr Blythe went up to London, I believe," answered Haslam, somewhat oppressed by the detective's frank and ruthless logic. "Miss Holland thought the best place to look for him was round about here, so she invented the pretext of wanting to paint the view from the lawn in the hope that she might learn something."

"That was quite understandable," said Grant. "But why did she confide in you?"

"I practically forced her to."

"By what means?"

Haslam frowned, and then looked squarely at the detective.

"By my genuine interest in her," he exclaimed. "Is that clear enough, or do you want further particulars?"

His tone was slightly ironical, but Grant ignored it.

"No, the position is quite plain," he responded. "She needed advice, and read you, correctly, as an ally. She thought you would be wholly on her side, even if it came to shielding her brother from the penalty of any unknown sins he might have committed. When did he turn up again, after his disappearance?"

"Last night," said Haslam. "She was on her way to tell me about it when you passed her, just before you were shot at. And, by the way, that explains her presence by the roadside. You can understand, now, why she did not want to be seen. I believe you had the idea once that it was she who fired at you."

"I included the possibility among my theories, as I included the possibility that Pike had shot at me, or some unknown person."

"Or me," added Haslam.

"Or you," corroborated the detective. "But you were ready to prove an alibi. What did Miss Holland tell you when you met her by the roadside?"

Haslam's brain worked furiously. Should he tell Grant everything, even to the suggestion that Holland was mixed up in the Arundel necklace theft?

"She told me that, when she arrived home late, she found a note from her brother, asking her for money. The note was very urgent, and explained nothing. He had evidently waited for her as long as he dared, and had then gone off to an old mill that they used to paint—the mill you tracked me to, in fact. He asked her to bring him twenty pounds there, and—she hadn't twenty pounds." Haslam paused, then plunged on, with a slightly heightened complexion. "Of course, you'll call me a fool, but we've already agreed to differ on certain points. I'm not a machine. I can't help that. I saw her back to her rooms at Wynton——"

"Returning first for the money?" asked Grant.

"Yes, while you marched off with Miss Holland's bicycle! You gave us a nice walk!" His colour suddenly went a shade deeper still, as he recalled how peculiarly nice the walk had been. Grant, considerately, was looking out of the window. "After leaving her at Wynton, I rode to the mill, and—and found a girl there."

"But not George Holland?"

"No. I think you know that. I'd never seen the girl before, and she wouldn't tell me who she was, but I got it out of her that Holland had suddenly started off for the Brambles from the mill, and I decided to try and catch him up."

"But you didn't catch him up," nodded Grant. "A puncture prevented you. Tell me, why did the girl disappear so suddenly, when you both came out of the mill?"

"At the time, I couldn't make out. But, when you told me that you were also on the spot, I took it that her eyes must have been sharper than mine, and that she didn't like the look of you."

"Did she say why Holland had returned to the Brambles?"

"No."

"Have you any idea why he came back?"

"Not the remotest."

Grant studied Haslam, and nodded slowly.

"Well," he commented, "you saved your twenty pounds, anyway."

"Ah," murmured Haslam.

"Ah," replied Grant.

The situation suddenly beat Haslam. He found himself laughing.

"Look here, Grant," he cried. "You and I are as opposite as the two poles. What do you think? I gave that twenty pounds—as a matter of fact, it was twenty-five pounds—to the girl, not knowing who she was, and not believing her honest, but just because, somehow or other, I couldn't help myself. She was in trouble. Awful trouble. Upon my soul, when I think of her now, and wonder what she's doing, I almost want to go back to the mill at this minute—and not because I'm in love with her, you inscrutable Sphinx, but just because she's a girl in distress, and that sort of thing always upsets me." He broke off abruptly. "I wonder what you really think of me, Grant?"

"Perhaps I should be happier if I were more like you," answered the detective, reflectively. "Yes—it is very possible. But I am not like you. My God is not a flesh and blood one, because I do not believe a flesh and blood God can protect us from ourselves. You excuse yourself for small omissions when you look into a tragic girl's eyes. Yet, Mr Haslam, there are certain omissions which you would not excuse yourself. Murder, for instance. Our difference therefore, is in degree rather than in nature. I will excuse myself for no omissions, and if I commit them, I blame myself. Truth, whether it be glorious or hideous, is man's only salvation. I do not believe in any other road. But if, one day, I am tempted too sorely—well, who shall say?" He stopped, and reflected heavily for a moment. Then, suddenly, he changed his tone. "Have you anything more to tell me?" he asked.

"I have told you very nearly everything," answered Haslam, "but not quite all. The little I am keeping back has no stain of blood upon it, and I do not think it would help you to clear up the mystery of the Brambles, or of Pike's murder."

"That little," replied Grant, patiently, "might be the very connecting link for which I am waiting."

"It might be, but you must forgive me for believing that it isn't," said Haslam. "Anyway, I'm not in the witness-box yet. I suppose you've no objection to my going to see Miss Holland? I'm anxious to let her know what has happened."

"I think you ought to go," agreed Grant. "But please tell her that, in her brother's interests, she must not breathe a single word about this affair just yet to anybody."

"It's hardly likely that she would," observed Haslam. "But what is your own reason for this secrecy?"

"I have a very good reason, Mr Haslam," returned Grant, grimly, "but, since you have not given me your whole confidence, I cannot possibly give you mine."

"Very good. That's level. Are you going to follow me again to Wynton?"

"I may do so. I may do all sorts of things."

"Good! So long as I'm warned! But, before I go to see Miss Holland, what about an interview with her brother?"

"I was going to suggest it," answered Grant, rising. "We will go to him now."

They left the library. George Holland had been locked away in a room at the top of the house. Grant took the key out of his pocket as they neared the door, and then inserted it. A sudden exclamation escaped from him.

"What's the matter?" asked Haslam.

"The door's already unlocked," replied Grant.

CHAPTER 27

Grant swung the door open, glanced rapidly round the room, and set his teeth a shade more firmly. The bird had flown.

"Now, perhaps, you begin to see some of my difficulties," he observed to Haslam. "I am asked to clear up a mystery, yet I cannot count upon the whole-hearted assistance of anyone around me—not even of those in whose interests I am supposed to be working! You frankly deny me your entire confidence, and here before us lies proof that someone else has acted behind my back, without my authority."

"I don't quite understand you," answered Haslam, crossing the room to the window. "If Holland has been clever enough to escape——"

"He must have had someone to assist him," the detective pointed out, shortly. "Look out of the window. A sheer drop. One glance was evidently enough for Holland, since you will notice that the window is still locked on the inside. No, obviously, he escaped through the door. The door has not been broken open. The inference is, therefore, that someone with a duplicate key—mine has never left my pocket—has let him out. That suggests rather unpleasant things, doesn't it?"

"It does," admitted Haslam, solemnly, as he came away from the window. "I suppose you're quite sure you *did* lock the door after leaving Holland here?"

"I could only have failed to do so through carelessness or design," answered Grant. "It is not likely that a detective of my standing would be careless. That only leaves the other alternative, on which you naturally must be allowed to form your own opinion."

"Right," said Haslam. "Then, having formed my opinion, the choice of an accomplice within these walls is narrowed down to Mr Blythe, Rose, and the cook. I confess, I don't think any of them let George Holland out."

"Then your theory is narrowed down to—what?"

"Frankly, to nothing."

"Which is the least likely theory of all," remarked Grant. "But there are two other possibilities you have not considered. The first is that another accomplice is, or was, hiding in the house, and set Holland free."

"Good Lord!" murmured Haslam. "If a Census man came to the Brambles, he'd get into difficulties!"

"The second is that Pike himself may have let Holland out."

"I say, stop that, old chap!" exclaimed Haslam, aware of a sudden dampness on his forehead. "Pike's as dead as a doornail, isn't he?"

"It might be as well to verify that," answered Grant. "Will you please wait here for me?"

Haslam nodded, and then, noting Grant's expression, added, "On my honour."

"That's good enough," said Grant, and left him.

Grant was only away a few minutes, but to Haslam it seemed considerably longer. The disappearance of George Holland added one more mystery to the bewildering series, and he felt that his mind was incapable of grappling with it. Had he not been on parole, he would have descended to the library for a dose of consoling whiskey, but he decided that to break his word would snap the bond that was being forged between him and the detective, to the advantage of neither party. So he stayed, and wandered round the room vaguely, while the light of the new day grew.

What would the new day bring? He decided that, whatever the next twenty-four hours were destined to hold, they could not be more crowded than the twenty-four hours that had just passed. And somewhere in that unknown region where our destinies are spun, one of the spinners paused to smile.

"The devil of a time you've been!" he exclaimed, as the detective's form reappeared in the passage. "And why did you walk so softly? Trying to make me think you were Pike's ghost? Or trying to surprise me in the middle of some incriminating pursuit?"

"Neither," answered Grant. "I'm trusting you. I've told you so."

"Of course—so you have! I keep on forgetting!"

"You wouldn't, perhaps, if you also trusted *me?*"

"But I do trust you, man! It's only—oh, well, never mind. What about Pike? Did you find him?"

"Pike didn't let George Holland out of this room," replied Grant.

"Well, all I can say is, thank God for that!" said Haslam, fervently. "By the way, what have you done with Pike?"

"I carried him back into his room."

"The amount you get through, Grant, is positively astounding! But, I say, oughtn't you to have left him in the passage? Don't the police like to have a look at a dead body before it's moved?"

"For practical purposes," answered Grant, "you may regard me as the police."

"True," murmured Haslam. "I recognise the atmosphere."

"It may also interest you to know," pursued Grant, "that I have been on the telephone to certain quarters, and that I have been given full authority to conduct this matter in my own way and —for the moment—with the utmost secrecy. I am developing a theory which, if it is the right theory, can only be proved if the murder of Pike is kept an absolute secret for the next twenty-four hours. I want you to understand that very clearly. Not a single soul must know of it outside ourselves."

"But you said I could tell Miss Holland," objected Haslam.

"Yes—she is the one exception," responded Grant. "And I only make that concession because she is the least likely of all to talk about what she knows. You see—and you will tell her this from me—silence is the one thing that may save her brother from being hanged."

"Yes, I'll tell her that. You think you will find her brother, then?"

"It will be surprising if we don't. His flight was natural, but it hasn't helped his case in the least."

"Ah, his flight. Let's get back to that! Pike's ghost is exonerated of complicity. Who's the next suspect? It couldn't have been you or I. Personally, I'm convinced it couldn't have been Mr Blythe, Rose, or the cook, either. If Holland didn't manage to open the door himself, I'll wager it *was* one of his friends who managed it while you and I were chatting in the library."

"The young lady of the mill, perhaps?"

"Good Lord! I never thought of that!"

"I don't consider it's worth thinking of. What about his sister?"

"Oh, nonsense!"

"Agreed. And I don't think it was Rose. And I don't think it was the cook. Let's go and have a chat with Mr Blythe."

"I say, Grant! Be sensible! You surely aren't going to suggest ——"

"Sh!" replied the detective, catching hold of his arm.

A creak resounded from below. Suddenly Grant leapt to the door, closed it softly, and retreated back into the room dragging Haslam with him. Their light, a candle, was quickly extinguished, and, obeying the detective's whispered command, Haslam crouched in a dark corner of the room, and waited.

Another creak sounded through the closed door. Then, the faint tread of slow and cautious steps came along the passage. The steps drew nearer, and, when they paused outside the door, a faint streak of yellow light was pencilled along the floor, illuminating the slender crack.

Haslam felt his heart thumping. Now, one mystery at least was about to be cleared up. He was immensely comforted to note the gleaming nozzle of the detective's revolver. It was directed straight at the door.

A hand was placed upon the door-knob, the door-knob was

turned, and the door slowly opened. But only a little way. The unseen person behind the door had paused, and seemed to be listening. Then, abruptly, the door closed again, a key was turned, and the footsteps began to hurry away.

"By Jove!" muttered Haslam. "We're trapped!"

He was about to dart forward, but felt Grant's detaining hand on his shoulder.

"Wait!" whispered Grant.

"But, man, we're locked in," exclaimed Haslam, "and God knows what may happen——"

"Don't worry," came Grant's even voice. "You forget, that was the duplicate key. I have the original in my pocket. I know what I'm doing."

He slipped to the window, unfastened it, and opened it. Leaning out, he stood motionless for a full minute after the retreating footsteps had ceased to sound. Then he softly closed the window again, and refastened it.

"Now, then," he said, and walked to the door. Producing his key from his pocket, he unlocked it, and stepped out into the passage while Haslam was relighting the candle. The candle light was hardly necessary now, however, for every moment the greyness was becoming more dissipated, and through an east window on the landing a brilliant streak of gold heralded another conquest of day over night.

Haslam's impulse was to dash after the individual who had locked them in, but he paused as he noted that Grant seemed in no such hurry, and was studying the door-knob.

"What are you doing?" demanded Haslam.

"Finger-prints," replied Grant, laconically. "That door-knob will supply me with the proof I need as to the identity of our visitor."

"Who do you think it was?" asked Haslam.

"Mr Blythe," said Grant. "His bedroom is under this, and I heard him enter it when I had my head out of the window. Also, I saw the glow of his light. The finger-print test is hardly necessary."

"But have you got an impression of his finger-print, to compare it with?" asked Haslam, curiously.

"Of course, I have," responded Grant. "I've got yours, too."

Suddenly Haslam laughed.

"Well, you are a cheerful little fellow!" he exclaimed, and glanced out of the passage window. The streak of gold was widening to a thick bar. "Thank God for the day, Grant. I'm for the bathroom. Do you mind? I shall be of no use to you or to anybody until I've had a cold tub."

"Of course, I don't mind," answered Grant. "I want you to get as fresh and alert as you can. You and I will need our wits today, and we're working together, or pretty nearly. Go where you want to, and do what you like. Only, remember, silence concerning Pike is absolutely imperative. That's the only instruction I have to give you."

"Do you really mean that you're going to let me run about loose?" asked Haslam. "I'm surprised and charmed!"

"I want you to run about loose," returned the detective, smiling. "You may hit upon something useful. All I ask is that I may count upon your presence here tonight. I'll probably need you, then, if ever a man did."

"I won't desert you," Haslam assured him. "My plan is to go and see Miss Holland immediately after breakfast, and I'll probably be back to lunch. But, anyway, you can count on me for tea. Maybe I'll be engaged on a little clue-hunting myself in the interim."

"I hope you will be," remarked Grant.

They began to descend the stairs.

"Oh, by the way," said Haslam, dropping his voice, "am I to keep silent, also, about Holland's escape?"

"Not to Miss Holland. Take my advice, and go and see her early."

"I mean to. But what about—Mr Blythe?"

"Leave him to me, please. I'd rather interview him alone, if you don't mind. I'll be paying him a call quite shortly."

The bathroom door, with the power of revival that lay behind it, beckoned to Haslam from the end of a corridor, but he paused for a moment to study the detective's face earnestly.

"I say, Grant," he said. "You know old Blythe's straight, don't you?"

"I think he's as straight as you are," responded Grant, as he walked away, "and just as liable to err."

"Upon my soul," thought Haslam, as he hurried towards the bathroom, "it's positively annoying, the way I like that fellow!"

CHAPTER 28

Sometimes, when we are over-tired, we take joy in the simplest and absurdest things. A financier, after an arduous day in which he has made or lost a hundred thousand, may find enormous relief in telling a small child a fairy story. Cabinet ministers and severe judges, we know, will poke small balls into little holes, and smile with almost miraculous pleasure as the balls disappear into the nooks prepared for them. And a soldier, temporarily freed from the smell of blood, may spend a delicious hour with a kitten and a reel of cotton.

Haslam, after the most wearing night within his experience, felt this queer, irresponsible sensation as soon as the bathroom door was locked and the tap began to run. The night was over. Another night would come, but that was not yet! A beam of sunlight slanted, with its eternal optimism, right into the polished white tub, dancing on the water and making it illogically precious. As the sunlight drove away the night, so the illuminated water would drive away the night's staleness, making Haslam's blood tingle again, and his mind work.

"I suppose all these things have really happened," pondered Haslam, as he threw off his clothes. "Or is the whole affair some glorified nightmare? Has poor old Pike really been murdered? Surely I shall see him about the place today! Did Mr Blythe really lock Grant and me in a room only a few minutes ago? And have I really ridden over twenty miles since midnight?"

He glanced at his trousers, hanging now over a chair. The dust on them looked very genuine. Grime on his hands, too, testified to the fact that he had lately mended a puncture on the outskirts of an eerie village. He jumped into the bath, and as the warm water purred about him, destroying his oppressions and instilling into him a sense of security and dominance, his heart was full of gratitude for the individual who had invented coke boilers and had rendered possible a hot bath at five o'clock in the morning.

But Haslam was wise, and knew the scurvy tricks which hot water can play on one! Before he left the bath, he submitted to the less immediately appealing virtues of the cold tap. Then, as he applied the towel vigorously, he began to feel his sluggish blood coursing through his veins again, and his strength received new birth. By the time he was dressed, he felt as though he had had a normal night's sleep.

He had dawdled luxuriously over his dressing, and had shaved as carefully as though he had been about to attend an important first night at a London theatre. It was six before he finally emerged, his toilette complete. Now, abruptly, he found himself faced with the question—what should he do next? Only one definite thing occurred to him. It was to go and see Miss Holland. He could not do that, however, for at least two hours. How on earth should he fill up the meantime?

His desire to see Mary Holland again increased every moment. He had a tremendous amount to tell her, but that was not his sole motive in desiring the interview. He wanted to look at her again, to hear her voice, and to encourage bright smiles into her too sad face. Two hours? How could he wait two hours!

Something else was also making him restless, and he soon realised that this was a desire for breakfast. He wondered what the day's programme would be, and whether Cook would be in any condition to fry bacon. Then his mind switched on to Mr Blythe and the detective. Had they had their interview yet? Or were they both tucked back in bed, sleeping while he was fretting?

Curiosity took him to Mr Blythe's door. He listened, and heard nothing. Then he listened at Grant's door, with the same result. Wandering vaguely about the house, half-impatiently, yet half delighting in an odd sense of independence, he presently bumped into Rose, coming out of her room. She started slightly on seeing him, but soon recovered herself.

"Good morning, Rose," Haslam greeted her, cheerfully.

"Good morning, sir," she replied.

"Did you get any sleep?"

"Yes, thank you, sir. I made myself."

"Sensible girl!"

"Well, one isn't good for anything, if one doesn't, is one? That's what I told Cook. What's the use?"

Haslam smiled at her, and paid an inward tribute to her spirit.

"That's the right idea," he nodded. "Is Cook getting up, too?"

"Gracious, no! *She* won't be up all day, I shouldn't think, not from the look of her. Can I do anything for you, sir?"

"No—I don't think so." It was pleasant, talking to this cheerful, practical maid. Pessimists hate optimists, but one optimist can always entertain another. "What will you do, Rose, if Cook stays in bed all day?"

"Oh, manage somehow. But I expect she'll get up presently."

"And, meanwhile, you'll have plenty to do." A sudden thought flashed through his mind. "Look here, Rose, I'll give you one less to cook for. I'm going out to breakfast. Yes, I feel like a walk. I'll have breakfast at the inn."

Rose looked at him, with a slight frown.

"Hadn't you better stay and have some breakfast here first?" she asked. "I'll get it early for you, if you like."

"That's very nice of you, but it's not necessary," responded Haslam. "You can tell Mr Grant and Mr Blythe what I've done—Mr Grant will understand. I may be able to pick up something in the village. Information, you know, as well as breakfast. Oh, by the way, Rose, we're not saying anything about poor Pike just yet. You understand?"

"Yes, sir. Are they Mr Grant's orders?"

"They are. You might drop a hint to Cook, also, though I don't expect either you or she will be seeing anyone outside the Brambles today."

184

"No, sir. We're not to leave without Mr Grant's permission, so he said."

"That's right. Now, don't look at me like that, Rose! I've got his permission."

"I'm glad for that, sir," answered the maid, flushing slightly. "I —I——"

"Go on, Rose. I like you to be frank."

"Well, I was going to say, sir, that I know you wouldn't do anything you thought wrong, but I think we've all got to obey the detective now, sir, haven't we?"

"Yes, we have. He's boss. And he's given me leave of absence till tea."

A faint shadow flitted across Rose's face. Haslam's presence at the Brambles was wonderfully comforting to her. He was always ready with a kind word or a genial smile, and she knew in her heart that she would be able to face the ensuing hours much more bravely if he were about the place. But after all, she told herself, one couldn't always have it all one's own way, and it was silly of her to feel like that. Probably Cook would soon buck up a bit, and Pike—How easily one's mind runs back to its old grooves! With a sudden chill, Rose remembered that she would get no companionship that day from Pike. Something rose to her throat, and she tried to move on. But she found Haslam's hand detaining her.

"What's the matter, Rose?" he asked, gently.

"Nothing, sir," she replied. "It all just came over me again, sudden, that's all. Will you just let me make you one cup of tea, before you go? I'll bring it to you in the library at once."

"It's what I'd like more than anything else in the world, Rose," exclaimed Haslam. "You think of everything!"

She disappeared, with rather ominous promptness; but when, five minutes later, she brought Haslam his cup of tea, with a bit of crustless toast added, she showed no trace of any drooping spirit, and appeared her old solid self again.

"There, sir," she exclaimed, briskly, as she laid the tray down. "You want to take something before you go out, I always think.

Particularly after a night like what we've had."

"Thank you, Rose," answered Haslam. "Yes, it was a night, wasn't it?"

"Yes, sir. I hope I never spend another like it. What do you think Mr Grant will do to that poor young man who was caught? I listened at the room he's locked up in just now, but I didn't hear a sound. I expect he was asleep."

"Very likely," murmured Haslam.

She hesitated for a moment, then asked, "Do you think—he did it, sir?"

Haslam also hesitated for an instant before replying, "No, Rose, I don't."

"I'm glad for that! Poor young man! But, then, what was he here for? Who else could it have been?"

"Oh, I believe Mr Grant is following up certain ideas of his," said Haslam, lightly. "You know, for a moment, he thought it might be me!"

"Yes, I know that, sir," exclaimed Rose, and suddenly stopped, flushing red.

Haslam looked at her curiously, and suddenly read a truth in her eyes.

"By Jove, Rose—you knew I was out last night!" he challenged her. "You did—and you never said anything! Am I right?"

Rose did not reply in words, but her colour replied for her.

"Did you hear me?" he asked.

"I—I saw you get in through the window," she answered, very flustered.

"Then why on earth didn't you tell the detective?"

"What was the good?" Rose's voice was half-shamed, and half-indignant. "I knew you could never do anything wrong, sir, but there, you never know what a detective will think! They're so funny."

"You know, you're rather a trump, Rose," remarked Haslam. "Yes, upon my soul, you are! But everything's in such a tangle that I advise you in future to tell Grant every single thing you know. If you don't, he'll worm it out of you in the end."

"Well, he didn't worm it out of me this time, sir, anyway," she retorted.

"No—because he knew he could worm it out of me! I can't tell you why I went out last night, Rose, but Grant knows, and he's quite satisfied about it. He suspects me no more than he suspects you." He drained his cup, and rose. "Well, now I'm off. I hope everything will go smoothly till I return. I say—look after Mr Blythe, won't you?"

"I always try to, sir."

"Yes, I know you do. But he may need a little extra help today. He's an old man, and this affair is getting so much on his nerves that he may make mistakes and do something foolish. Keep him smiling all you can. And, above all, obey Mr Grant."

So saying, he nodded cheerfully, took his hat, and went out into the grounds. Rose looked after him, feeling that a little of the sunshine had gone out with him. Then, as though to make the balance even, she suddenly started polishing things.

CHAPTER 29

One man's meat is another man's poison, and one maid's loss may be another maid's gain. While Rose was bustling about the seemingly deserted house, with not a soul to help her (for Cook might have been as dead as Pike for all the appearance she put in), and not a soul to talk to, Jane, at the Heysham inn, became suddenly a little less limp. To become less limp was, with Jane, the giddy height of sensational existence.

She was doing vague things which in due course would partially materialise into vague achievements. Her achievements always had certain ghost-like qualities. She produced effects without the substance. Her pictures showed undeniable streaks of cleanliness, and were prolific in little lanes through the dust, but the substance of cleanliness was lacking. Her breakfast-tables appeared to be set, but when you came to use them, you missed the salt. Her conversation was frequently pregnant with meaning, but, when you tried to discover what she meant, you could not; or, if you could, you gathered up your loins and ran away from it.

"Well, I never," passed through her morning-muddy mind, as Haslam's figure came swinging along the road on a bicycle. "Here's that nice gentleman again."

The reflection took a lot out of her, and she paused in her occupation of rubbing the front door knob, which she rubbed every morning at seven o'clock to prove that it could never be bright again. But you cannot rub a door knob and watch a nice gentleman approach at the same time. One of them has got to go. So Jane let the door knob go, and opened her mouth in illustration of its shape.

"Now, will 'e stop, I wonner?" was her next thought. She could not see why he should, but she hoped very much that he would. And her mouth opened a shade wider when he actually did. The door knob, now, could have entered the aperture without trouble.

"Good morning," said Haslam, pleasantly, as he dismounted. "Can I get some breakfast here?"

This request reduced Jane's limpness several degrees. Mere existence became tinged with the magic touch of life. Nevertheless, one could not be unseemly. The idea must be gently combatted for a while.

"Breakfast?" answered Jane, ponderously guarding the interests of both chastity and the inn. "Well, zur, 'tis early for breakfust."

"I'm in no immediate hurry," replied Haslam. "Perhaps you could manage it by half-past seven?"

"Arf-pas seven," pondered Jane. "Well, there's another gent hordered 'is for eight."

Haslam, too, pondered. He was burning with impatience to see Mary Holland, but he could not well call upon her before nine, and Wynton was barely three miles away. He could cycle the distance in twenty minutes. Yes, eight o'clock would do. He told Jane so.

The concession granted, reaction set in, and Jane became penitent.

"I dessay I could manage arf-pas-seven, if you wanted," she remarked, doubtfully.

"No, don't trouble. I'll take a stroll."

It occurred to Jane that that would be rather a pity.

"You can zit in the garden, if you like," she suggested, almost archly. "There's a lovely garden round the back."

"Thank you—maybe I will," nodded Haslam. "But I'll take a stroll first."

The "other gent," hearing voices below, pulled the curtain a little aside, and watched Haslam go. He became thoughtful for a few moments, then walked to his door, and dropped a pair of boots outside with a thud.

"Jane!" he called.

He only had to call three times. After the third summons, Jane decided that it wasn't a dream and she really had been called, and poked her head up the stairs.

"I forgot to put my boots out last night, my dear," said the other gent. "Let 'em have a brush up, will ye?"

"Yezzer," answered Jane, slithering up. She looked at the other gent's tousled head, and giggled. Something in the expression of the tousled head admitted this gentle familiarity. The mere fact that the tousled head had not been modestly withdrawn seemed, to Jane, to imply a pleasing sense of comradeship. Not that she liked "conmercials," she told herself. Particularly fat ones. They were too fresh! Still, there were few rare flowers in Jane's humble garden, and buttercups and dandelions had to do.

"You be in early, don't you, my dear?" remarked the fat commercial.

"Wotcher mean?" demanded Jane, as she picked up the boots. "Sorce!"

"Who's your sweetheart?"

"Me wot?"

"Your sweetheart? I heard ye talking below!"

"Go hon, now!" retorted Jane, as maidenly flushes mingled with her smuts. Jane could still flush, but whether this was due to her own chastity or to others' forbearance may be debatable.

"Come on! Confess!" persisted the fat commercial. "Who was he?"

"You ain't 'arf fresh, aincher?" said Jane, as she prepared to depart with the boots. "'E was jest a gentleman." She emphasised the word slightly; then added, with a touch of pride, "'E's comin' to breakfust."

"Oh, is he?" exclaimed the fat commercial. The information appeared to interest him.

"Yes. There'll be two of yer," snorted Jane.

"Your arithmetic is marvellous!" observed the fat commercial, and withdrew his tousled head.

Jane lumped down the stairs, dropping one boot ahead of her, and stopping to watch how far it would fall. She hoped vaguely that it would not hit a tray with some crockery on it, which she had placed on the floor over-night; but she decided that fate must take its course, and fate was kind. The boot stopped obligingly on the last stair but one, and its toe made love to a milk-jug.

Upstairs, the fat commercial sat on his bed, staring reflectively at the wall opposite, and he did not move for five full minutes.

Meanwhile, Haslam was strolling through the pretty lanes, rejoicing in the miracle of contrast. No wonder people worshipped the sun, he reflected. At its magic touch, haunted lanes became things of sheer delight, and terror was sent flying. The illusion of eternal perfection lay over the land. Yet—was it illusion? Haslam held out his hand, allowing the warm amber light to play upon it. He looked at the glowing hills, inhaled the fragrance of the wakening air, and listened to a lark's blithe note, that seemed like a liquid jewel set in the midst of blue ether, beyond the reach and knowledge of oppression.

But this small, gay bird was afraid of larger birds, and was itself an ogre to the insect world. The air, fragrant now, had power to chill or stifle. In each glowing hill dwelt a million miniature cities of death, each entity imagining itself, at chosen moments, supreme. And even the sun itself, which had this strange power to make our blind souls rejoice, was a colossal fire-ball of fierce and terrible destruction!

"It is because of our secret fears," thought Haslam, "that we seek our little human havens, and hug them to us, while we can."

And, even as he had thus thought, he smiled to realise that his own steps were leading him towards the little green plateau on which he had first seen Mary Holland, and over which her warm memory would always hover.

"Companionship—that is our great need," he reflected. "The only truly terrible thing in life is to rejoice or suffer singly!"

He was back at the inn by a quarter to eight, and spent the remaining minutes before breakfast in the garden, watched intermittently by Jane and the fat commercial, each with a different emotion. At five minutes past eight, with an approximation to promptitude betokening special effort, Jane summoned him into the coffee room, and watched him take his seat with the interest of a parent watching its child's first sight of a Christmas Tree. The Christmas Tree, in this case, was the fat commercial, a slight disappointment to Jane, who had hoped it would be the eggs and bacon. Still, the eggs and bacon received their due of attention.

"Morning, Sir," nodded the fat commercial.

"Good morning," replied Haslam. "We are going to have another wonderful day."

"It looks like it," agreed the fat commercial, "but you never know." A remark which proved to be prophetic.

After a short silence, during which Jane noted that she had forgotten the pepper and went to fetch it, the commercial made another remark.

"Pretty country about here, ain't it?" he said. "Do you know these parts, sir?"

"Not very well," answered Haslam. "Have some toast?"

"Thank you," said the commercial. "Ah, then you're a stranger, I see."

"Practically. And you?"

"Same. I'm only here on business. Not much of a place to do business in, though, eh?"

"I shouldn't think so," agreed Haslam. "May I trouble you for the sugar?"

"I beg your pardon, sir," exclaimed the fat commercial. "Ah—here comes the pepper! That's right, my dear." He took the pot from Jane, ignoring the fact that she had held it out to Haslam. "I always say, life's no good without pepper. Eh?" He laughed, a little coarsely. Then he turned to Haslam again. "Yes, sir. This is a quiet spot, as I dare say you've found out. Been here long, may I ask?"

"A few days."

"Staying here?"

"At the inn? No. A little way off."

"Ah."

"Have some salt?"

The fat commercial took salt.

"Now, I'm willing to wager," he pronounced, "that nothing much ever happens in these parts. Go through your days, go to bed, get up again—that's right, my dear, isn't it?" he broke off, turning to Jane again.

"Nothin' 'appens," assented Jane, depressed.

"There you are, you see! In London, you get traffic noises, and fires—" he winked at Haslam "—and, oh, all sorts of things. Never pass an undisturbed night, for one reason or another!" He winked at Haslam again. "Now, have *you* ever been disturbed in the night at Heysham, my dear? I'll wager you haven't."

"No, never," replied Jane, more and more depressed.

"There you are again! And has *this* gentleman ever been disturbed since he's been here? Well, now—have you?"

Haslam began to dislike the fat commercial.

"It would take a cannon to wake me," he replied. "Pass the marmalade, will you?"

Conversation languished. The innkeeper, bustling down late, and pretending that he had been up for hours, entered the room briskly, shooed Jane out, rubbed his hands together, and then shooed himself out. Alone with the fat commercial, Haslam found himself peculiarly disinclined to talk, or to give any information whatever regarding his movements. The fat commercial was not in the least offended, if indeed he noticed Haslam's attitude. He behaved with perfect good humour throughout the meal, and, when he found that his companion was not in the communicative mood, he accepted the situation, and only broke the business of eating and drinking with occasional remarks.

But when, after breakfast, Haslam mounted his bicycle and began his journey to Wynton, the fat commercial stood in the inn porch and watched him till he was out of sight, and then dawdled away quite half-an-hour in casual enquiries regarding his breakfast companion. Neither Jane nor the innkeeper could tell him a quarter as much as he wanted to know.

Haslam, as he sped along the road, soon forgot the commercial traveller. He had only parted from Mary Holland about nine hours earlier, but those nine hours had been so crowded that they seemed more like nine days, and nine days, to a man fast falling in love, is an eternity.

"I suppose I am in love with Mary Holland?" he asked himself, soberly. And soberly he replied, "I am," and decided to inform her definitely of the fact at the earliest opportunity.

Life sparkled; yet Haslam was not as entirely free from oppressions as he tried to make out. He passed a tramp, and eyed the perfectly innocent man with vague suspicion. A cyclist behind him suddenly turned up a narrow by-way. The cyclist was as innocent as the tramp, but Haslam wondered whether he were again being shadowed by Grant. As he reached Wynton, however, he did not care whether he were being followed or not, or whether the tramp were some deep-dyed villain or a harmless knave. Sentiment captured him entirely, lending wings to his pedals, and all but killing a hesitating hen in the middle of the road.

He reached the humble house in which Mary Holland lived, and rang the bell. A window was thrown open above him.

"Please come up," called Mary's voice. "The door is open."

Leaning the bicycle against the wall, he entered quickly, and ran up the stairs.

CHAPTER 30

Miss Holland's landlady, watching Haslam ascend from one of those dim recesses which appear to have been especially designed by architects for the benefit of the curious, nodded appreciatively to herself. If her thought could have been translated into words, it would have run something like this: "Well, thank goodness, up goes a bit of pleasantness at last!" The only outward indication of that glowing thought, however, was a temporary period of suspended animation (the animation never being very excessive), and a gentle uplift of the eyes.

Her next thought was more definite.

"I'll give 'em ten minutes," she reflected, "and then I'll just go in and clear the breakfast things away."

Curiosity would not tolerate more than ten minutes; and, perhaps if she forgot to knock, no great harm would be done.

Meanwhile, quite unconscious of the landlady's attitude or existence, Haslam knocked on Mary Holland's door, and entered in response to her invitation.

"Good morning, Miss Holland!" he exclaimed, cheerily, as he closed the door behind him and shut out the landlady's hope. "How are you?"

"We've more important people to talk about than me," she replied, fighting against personal temptations. "What has happened?"

"I'll tell you in a minute," retorted Haslam, "but I insist upon inquiring about you first. Did you get any sleep?"

"Yes. But I was anxious and restless, naturally. Please don't keep me in suspense any longer, Mr Haslam. Did you see my brother?"

That question answered one of Haslam's. Clearly, George Holland, when he fled from the Brambles, had not sought sanctuary here. Miss Holland evidently knew nothing.

"Yes, I have seen your brother," answered Haslam, slowly, "and I'll tell you the whole story. But first I want to ask you something." He looked at her earnestly, and she flushed a little, though she did not drop her eyes. "I want to ask you if you have ever wondered why I am taking such an interest in your affairs?"

She flushed a little more deeply, and faltered, "It's—it's because you're awfully good."

"No, it isn't," said Haslam. "You know it isn't! Don't you suppose there's any other reason? Of course, there is! It's because ____"

"No! Please!" she interposed. "Not just yet!"

And again, unconsciously, she answered another of Haslam's questions. When a girl definitely postpones hearing a proposal of marriage or a declaration of love, and does not slay the tendency at sight, a future sanction is implied; and although this may not imply much at a dance, it implies considerable among the unromantic elements of a just concluded breakfast.

"All right," nodded Haslam. "We'll leave that till later. But, don't forget, it's got to come. And now for my story."

He gave her a detailed description of all that had occurred, dwelling on every point which he thought would interest or affect her, and leaving out nothing. It was a relief to be able to talk without restraint, to know that his listener was appreciating every word he said and had no cause to suspect him. With Grant, despite the better understanding that was growing up between them, Haslam had to weigh and consider every word. With Mary Holland, there were no obstacles, for they were united by an absolutely common purpose, and knew each other to be guilty only of an attempt to shield a third party.

Only once was Haslam interrupted. This was precisely ten minutes after he had entered the room. The landlady possessed among her rare virtues the virtue of punctuality, and began to

196

clear away the breakfast things exactly 9.13.

"Dear me, I beg your pardon for not knocking, I'm sure," she breathed, secretly regretful that there had been no more definite reason why she should have knocked; for Miss Holland and Peter Haslam were sitting on two separate chairs quite eighteen inches apart.

"That's all right," replied Miss Holland.

And Haslam added, adroitly apologetic, "I really oughtn't to have come so early to talk business, but that view I want you to paint, Miss Holland, is some little way off." He turned to the landlady. "I suppose there's a garage here? One can hire a car?"

"'Arriss's," said the landlady. "But it don't seem as if it's necessary to 'ire nothing 'ere." She frowned and lowered her voice slightly. "Someone's gone off with my boy's bike. There now! In the night!"

It occurred to her, vaguely, that a little more surprise might have been evinced.

After her welcome departure, Haslam continued with his story, and it was well on the way to ten before he came to the end of it. When he had concluded, there was a short silence. Suddenly Miss Holland shot out,

"Mr Haslam—you don't think——"

"No, I don't," he answered, rising and walking to the window. "Your brother seems to be a fool, but I'm sure he's not a murderer."

"If he were, would you still protect him?"

"Would you?"

"I don't know."

"Nor do I. I'd want to know the motive. And that's the whole trouble of it, Miss Holland. Motives baffle us. Do you realise, Miss Holland, what a tremendous amount has happened during the past twenty-four hours, and yet we're no nearer a solution of the mystery than we were? We don't know why the Brambles is visited. We don't know what part your brother has in it. We don't know who murdered Pike, or why. We don't know anything!"

"But Mr Grant thinks he knows, you say?" answered Miss Holland.

"He's got some theory he's working on, and I'd give a lot to get a glimpse inside his mind. But he's a Sphinx. He won't let out more than he wants to. And, of course, I'm only partially in his confidence."

"Because of me."

"Yes, because of you. And I'd rather have your confidence than his, so that's that!" He thought for a few moments. "Grant has got some big game on, that I'm sure of. It's going to be played tonight, and I can't leave him in the lurch. But, meanwhile, I'm free to help you all I can, and it seems to me that our plan is to go to that old mill again and see what we can discover. That was why I threw out the hint of a motor trip to your landlady. We may find your brother there, or the girl, or else get some clue of them. What do you think?"

"Yes, please, let's go," she replied. "We can't sit still and do nothing!"

Haslam nodded. "Right, then. That's our plan. Since your brother didn't come here to you, as I should have thought he would have done, he probably went straight back to the mill to meet the strange girl I found there—on his bicycle, or on your landlady's son's—whichever one was left for him by the supposed murderer of Pike. By Jove, it is a jig-saw, isn't it? By the way, I wonder *why* your brother didn't come straight to you?"

"What could I have done for him?" she pointed out.

"Well, he looked to you for financial help, you know. Perhaps someone prevented him. Perhaps someone's prevented him from returning to the mill. You see, there are so many people mixed up in the affair. Why, even a fat commercial traveller I bumped into at the inn at Heysham seems to have some interest in it! He——"

Suddenly he came away from the window.

"What's the matter?" asked Miss Holland.

"Talk of the devil!" muttered Haslam. "The brute's in the road, outside!"

They stared at each other. Then Haslam cautiously returned to the window, and took up a position behind the curtain, from which he could see but not be seen.

"Keep back!" he whispered, as Mary Holland made a movement to join him. "He mustn't see us. There's something mighty queer about that fellow!"

"What's he doing?" she whispered back.

"Looking at this house. He appears mighty interested. Now he's looking away. Good Lord!" A low exclamation escaped him. "He's vanished!" Haslam came away from the window again, wearing a puzzled look. "Now, why in heaven's name did he do that? I never saw a fellow disappear more quickly!"

"Suppose—suppose he's looking for George?" faltered Miss Holland.

"More likely someone's looking for *him*," frowned Haslam. "Confound the brute. Anyway, Miss Holland, we'll decide not to let him worry us. We mustn't begin jumping at shadows. What about getting across to that garage now? Are you ready?"

"Yes. Let's. I'll just put on my hat."

She ran into the next room, and Haslam spent the short interval before her return by the window. He saw no more, however, of the fat commercial.

A few minutes later, they were out in the road, walking towards Harriss's Garage. They did not need any directions, for Harriss's Garage blazoned out its presence and its petrol pump in hues of unmistakable yellow, forming the first claw of a civilization that would presently make Wynton a less picturesque and more profitable place to live in.

As they walked up the road, a man slipped out of the shadows, and crossed rapidly to the house they had just left. He knocked on the door.

"Do you let rooms here?" he asked, when the landlady appeared.

"I do, sir," replied the landlady. "But I don't know as I 'as any just now."

"That's a pity. But perhaps I could see them for some future time? How many rooms have you?" he asked.

"Two bed, one sittin'," breathed the landlady.

"Are they occupied at this moment?"

"Yes, sir. Leastways, no. The lady's just gone out."

"The lady? Oh, then you only have one lodger. Is the other bedroom vacant?"

"No, there's two, you see—but the lady's brother, well, I've not seen 'im lately, 'e's got the room but 'e's gone away."

"For good?"

"That I don't know."

"I see." The man paused. "Then, I understand, no one is in any of the rooms at this moment?"

"No, sir."

"I wonder if you'd let me have a look at them?" he asked.

"Well, I don't see why not," replied the landlady. "They ain't at their tidiest, of course, it bein' early, but if there's one thing I do insist on, it's being clean. That I must 'ave." She looked at her visitor in a sort of virtuous indignation against the policy of Dirt. "One must be clean."

"An excellent principle," agreed the man.

They ascended the stairs, and, this time, the landlady knocked on the sitting-room door. There was no object in not knocking, for she knew the room to be empty. The door was thrown open for the visitor's benefit, and she stood aside, to watch the effect. The effect was gratifying.

"This is a delightful room," exclaimed the man, enthusiastically.

"Well, it's comfortable, I'll say that for it," nodded the landlady. "*And* clean."

"May I go in?" asked the man.

"You're welcome, I'm sure."

He entered, and gazed around.

"You're well supplied with cupboards, I see," he commented, and looked in them all. This thoroughness vaguely surprised the landlady, but she did not interfere. She allowed him to make a complete investigation of the premises.

The situation became a little more delicate when the bed-rooms were reached, but her faint protests died on her lips, and she allowed the bedrooms to be similarly investigated. To tell the truth, there was something about the man that rather awed her, and her attitude was guided by a perfectly accurate instinct that, in a division of opinion, she would come off second best. When the three rooms had been toured, the visitor expressed himself as charmed with the place, and ventured to wonder whether she would consider an offer for the whole house.

"Well, that'd depend on 'ow much, wouldn't it?" she replied.

"Naturally," nodded the man. "But it would be a good offer, if it were made at all. I have a rich friend in mind. He'd probably give a thousand or two, if the place happened to suit him. May I have a peep at the garden, and poke round a bit?"

"Yes, sir," gasped the landlady. A thousand or two! Her ample bosom fluttered.

Thus, Detective Grant completed his examination of the house, satisfied himself that George Holland was not in it, and came out into the sunlit road again just as a little two-seater emerged into the same road a hundred yards farther up from the yellow glory of Harriss's Garage. The occupants of the little two-seater were Mary Holland and Peter Haslam, with Haslam at the wheel.

But Grant did not follow them. He was more interested in a fat commercial traveller he had spied, and who had disappeared somewhat precipitally a little while earlier.

CHAPTER 31

The life of Old Jim—he had another name, but no one ever troubled about it, and he had almost forgotten what it was himself—had not been an eventful one, and if you had asked him to give you an account of his seventy odd years, he would have wagged his head and replied, "Breakin' stones, mostly." But you are not to imagine that Old Jim broke stones as a penance for wrong-doing. He broke stones because he had no brain for anything else. He was not clever enough to do anything that could send him to prison. He was not mad enough to do anything that could send him to a lunatic asylum. He could just break stones, and so, whenever there were any stones to break in his vicinity, he was given the job of breaking them. He developed a passion for the occupation.

No one troubled much about Old Jim, and Old Jim never troubled about anybody. He wanted to be let alone. His sense of achievement was satisfied when he had converted a pile of big stones into a pile of smaller ones, and the big stones were his enemies, and the smaller stones were his friends. It was rumoured that a one-time Chairman of the local council was responsible for Old Jim's existence, and had made special provisions that Old Jim—or Young Jim, as he then was—should never lack any stones to break. Certainly, there seemed to be an inexhaustible supply. But there was no definite proof of this story, and another theory inclined to the view that Old Jim broke stones to pieces all day, and slipped out and stuck the pieces together again at night.

The one certain thing was that his life was uneventful until

a certain summer morning, when several eventful things occurred to make him pause in his stone-breaking and open his
mouth. (He was too experienced a workman ever to break
stones and open his mouth at the same time.) He had started
his labours very early that day, for he had an enormous number
of stones to break—almost enough to rebuild the old ruin of a
mill that frowned upon him a little way off—and he felt in good
trim.

For a while he worked uninterrupted. Occasionally he paused
to gaze abstractedly at the ruined mill, or to listen vaguely to
a lark, but the work proceeded steadily, and the antagonistic
stones were splintered into friends. Presently, however, he saw a
figure approaching on a bicycle, and he decided to pause a little
longer, and have a pull at a bottle of cold tea.

The figure was that of a young man, and he seemed in the
deuce of a hurry. This interested Old Jim, who could not understand why anybody should ever hurry, particularly on a pleasant morning like this. His interest grew, and the bottle of cold
tea paused in the air, when the young man jumped off his bicycle
and, after a rapid glance at the stone-breaker, wheeled the machine across a space of stubble and went into the mill.

"Well, I never, now!" thought Old Jim, and took a pull.

A minute later, the young man came out of the mill, hesitated, and approached Old Jim. Old Jim knew the way to five
different places, and wondered which one it would be. But it
was none of them.

"I wonder—have you seen anybody about here?" asked the
young man.

"Seen anybody?" repeated Old Jim. He knew he had not, but he
thought hard, to satisfy the young man that his answer would
be no careless one. "No," he said then. "I ain't aseen nobody."

The young man frowned, and looked worried.

"How long have you been here?" he asked.

"Over seventy year, sir," replied Old Jim. "Man and boy."

"No, no! I mean—how long have you been working here? Just
now? This morning?"

"Oh, I see. Ah! Mebbe hower. Mebbe more."

"And you've seen nobody all that time? Nobody at all?"

"Nobody, sir. There ain't been nobody." He looked along the road, and suddenly his eye lightened. "Ah, now—there 'e be! You was fust, ye see. There 'e be!"

The young man swung round, and started violently. Another cyclist was approaching at a great speed—a cyclist with a lean, narrow face, burning eyes, and a lantern jaw.

Suddenly, Old Jim found himself alone. The young man had sprung away, and was standing now beside his bicycle, which he had leaned against a bush a little way off. The second cyclist slowed down quickly, and dismounted.

"Now then, young man, I want a word with you," he panted.

The young man hesitated, then appeared to make up his mind, and nodded.

"I'm not sure that I wouldn't like a word with you, too," he replied, and jerked his head towards the mill. "Shall we go in there?"

"Why not here?" demanded the second cyclist.

The young man jerked his head now towards Old Jim, whom the lantern-jawed one did not appear to have noticed.

"Oh, all right," he answered; and, a minute later, they had both disappeared into the blackened, ruined structure.

"Well, I never, now!" thought Old Jim.

A big stone before him became invested with the personality of the second cyclist, and Old Jim brought his pick-axe down upon it with peculiar vim. He paused, and regarded the destruction with smiling satisfaction. The satisfaction was so pleasant that he treated four other large stones in a similarly lusty fashion. Then, his emotion spent, he forgot all about the two cyclists, and resumed his work in a more lethargic and amiable spirit.

He could not have said how long a time elapsed, for time meant little to Old Jim, when suddenly he became aware that something curious was happening. He looked up. The young man had left the mill, and was leaping on his bicycle, and the lantern-jawed man was rushing after him.

The attitude of the lantern-jawed man did not please Old Jim at all. He represented a danger zone, and the danger zone might involve himself as well as the young cyclist. Hardly realising what he did, Old Jim scrambled to his feet, and held his pick-axe ready. He let the young cyclist go by, but when the pursuer attempted to follow, he swung his implement around, and brought the lantern-jawed one to the ground.

There were some moments of confusion. Old Jim heard himself being shouted at. He didn't like it, and he continued to swing his pick-axe about him. He did not stop until the savage pursuer had ceased shouting and shaking his fist, and had resumed the chase. Then Old Jim stood at ease, watched them disappear, the you man well in advance, wiped his moist forehead, and murmured,

"Golly!"

It took him some time before he was able to settle down to work again. He did not mind being mildly interested in things, but he did dislike being rudely disturbed. Not until he had had another drink of cold tea and a bite of bread and cheese did the world resume its normal aspect. Then, throwing himself once more into his labours, he chipped steadily and doggedly, while the lark still sang above him, and the wind rustled in the grass.

His next interruption was of a different character, and came, perhaps, half-an-hour later. Who could say? Looking up, he noticed a girl walking towards the mill.

"Well, I never, now!" thought Old Jim. "What's she want?"

Whatever she wanted, she did not receive, for she had hardly disappeared into the mill before she reappeared out of it, and came across to the stone-breaker.

Something about her made Old Jim feel queer. He did not know what it was. He only knew he felt uncomfortable, and he pulled out his bottle of cold tea, as though imagining it might help to ease the situation. The girl's eyes were terribly sad, and cold tea was a great comfort.

The girl drew close, and then asked, in a scarcely audible

voice,

"Has a young man passed this way lately?"

Old Jim did not answer at once. Something warned him to go slow.

"Young man," he said, reflectively. "Well, let me think, now."

"Yes, please—please try and think!" exclaimed the girl.

Old Jim thought. No alternative occurred to him other than to confess. Yes, he admitted, he had seen a young man, but, of course, he couldn't say if it was the young man she was looking for. When the girl gave him a description of the young man, however, further hedging was impossible, and Old Jim decided to tell the truth, the whole truth, and nothing but the truth.

"'E sed 'e was lookin' fer someone, too," observed Old Jim, "so 'twould be the same, I reckon."

"He asked for me?" cried the girl. "Yes—and then?"

"Well, I 'adn't seen you then," retorted Old Jim. "'Ad I? So I sed I 'adn't. And then up comes another feller, and—well, there, I don't know nothing about it."

"About what?" asked the girl, fear creeping into her eyes. "What do you mean? What happened?"

Old Jim rubbed his nose, and gave up any further attempt at finesse.

"Well, 'twas queer, miss. They went into that old mill, and when they come out agin' they was quarrellin'. The young feller, 'e jumps on 'is bicycle, and the other feller, 'e goes to make arter 'im, but I trips 'im up, and that gives the young feller a good start, see? That's all I knows. I don't know nothin' more. But the young feller 'ad a good start, I sees to that!"

The girl swayed, and looked as though she were about to fall. Old Jim rose suddenly to his feet, and took hold of her.

"Now, then, don't you worry, my dear," he mumbled. "You go 'ome, and don't you worry. That's the best place fer you, miss ——"

"Which way did they go?" asked the girl, faintly.

"That way, but it's no good your tryin' to catch 'em up. Sit down a minute, and 'ave a drink o' this——"

But she slipped out of his grasp, and ran off in the direction he had pointed out to her. Old Jim looked perplexed and disappointed. He decided, however, that he had as much chance of catching her as she had of catching the others.

"She ought ter be 'ome, that's where she ought ter be," he thought, gloomily, and, finishing the bottle of cold tea, prepared to continue with his work. But he changed his mind, and hobbled across the road to the old mill instead. He spent five minutes poking about, then emerged again and hobbled back to his stones, and, squatting down beside them, made up for lost time.

His next—and last—interruption occurred at about a quarter-to-eleven. It took the form of a two-seater, in which were seated a man and a lady.

"Now, if they stops and asks me any questions," decided Old Jim, "I ain't agoin' ter say *nothin'*."

He was becoming a little indignant with Fate, and he also had an uneasy feeling that he was becoming involved in unpleasant matters which were no concern of his. He remembered how young Jones, the baker's assistant, had been dragged into the witness box, and what a rough time he had had, and through no fault of his own, either. Yes, much better decide not to answer any more questions. Much better.

The two-seater slowed up, and the man hailed him from the car.

"Have you seen anybody about here lately?" he asked.

"No," bawled Old Jim, without stopping his work.

"Are you sure?" persisted the man.

"I tell 'e no!" shouted Jim. "I ain't seen nobody. I bin 'ere a long time, and there ain't bin nobody."

His denial was so vehement that it aroused more interest than he had intended.

"I don't believe you," remarked the man, shortly, and got out of the car.

"Well, I never, now!" mumbled Old Jim to himself. "Wot's the good o' lyin'? They won't believe yer!"

But the next moment, the world grew dazzlingly bright. He found a ten-shilling note under his nose.

"If you've seen any of the people we're looking for," said the man, "you can have that."

"'Oo are yer lookin' for?" cackled Old Jim, deciding to have seen them, whoever they were.

"No—you first," replied the man.

Jim told his tale, and, as soon as he began, he knew that the ten shillings would be his. Such interest as shone in the two motorists' faces could not have been evinced for strangers. Obviously, the people he had seen were the people who were wanted.

When he had finished, the ten-shilling note was handed to him. It was wonderful luck. But even greater luck followed. Suddenly the man put his hand in his pocket, and drew out a second ten-shilling note.

"The first is for your information, and the second is for tripping a blackguard up," said the man.

And, gasping, Old Jim drops out of our story.

CHAPTER 32

"We'll go slowly," said Haslam, as he slipped in the clutch and the car began to glide away. "It's not likely that we can overtake your brother, but the girl can't have got very far. Of course, it's a thin chance, but we may come upon her."

"I hope we will," answered Miss Holland, so fervently that Haslam glanced at her.

"You think she is worth saving, then?"

"Aren't all people worth saving?"

"Why, in one sense, yes. But, what I meant was, you are very charitable towards her after all the trouble she has caused."

"So are you," she retorted.

Haslam smiled.

"Touché. But isn't my case a bit different? I'm outside all this. And she seems to have ruined your brother's life."

"Perhaps it is he who has ruined hers, Mr Haslam," replied Mary Holland. "It is because of that fear that I feel I must do all I can for the poor girl. A man can get out of a scrape. A girl has hardly any chance."

Haslam nodded. He agreed with her. Life was by no means impartial in its attitude towards the sexes.

They crawled along for two or three miles. Then, as they had no luck, they turned into other roads, scouring the land on either side. It was, as Haslam had said, a very thin chance, but they hated the idea of giving up. After an hour, their efforts were rewarded. They had just reached the top of a hill, and down in a valley, where a little river ran, they saw a figure. It was the figure of a girl, and she was standing on the banks of the river. Haslam's instinct told him that this was the girl they were looking for, and he suddenly began racing the car down the hill.

"I don't like the look of her," he murmured, in explanation.

"Nor do I," replied Mary Holland.

At the bottom of the hill he slowed up, and brought the car to a standstill by a gate. He was out of the car and through the gate in an instant, and, as he ran across the meadow through which the river ran, the girl started, and turned.

There was a look of dull despair on her face, a despair into which confusion suddenly shot. Turning round again, she took a few hesitating steps forward, but Haslam was too quick for her, and gripping her unceremoniously, pulled her swiftly away from the bank.

"You mustn't do that!" he cried, in her ear. "Things may not be as bad as you think!"

His voice was purposely loud, for he wished to pierce her dazed comprehension. She did not hear him, however. Suddenly he felt her whole weight in his arms, and realised that she had fainted.

"Poor child!" he thought; and, lifting her, he began to carry her back to the car.

Mary Holland met them half-way to the gate. She had a brandy flask already open. Haslam set the girl down, and, in a few minutes, she came out of her faint.

"Don't speak for a little while," said Mary Holland. "Just remember that we are your friends. Presently you can talk."

"Who are you?" whispered the girl.

"I am George Holland's sister," answered Mary. "And this is Mr Haslam, whom you have already met at the mill."

The girl shrank, but Mary patted her sleeve, and presently they helped her towards the car.

"Where are you taking me?" asked the girl.

"To Wynton, I think," replied Mary, with an enquiring glance at Haslam.

"Yes, that will be best," nodded Haslam. "Unless you can tell us where George Holland is?"

She shook her head wearily.

"Is there anywhere else you would like to go?"

"I have nowhere to go," she answered, almost listlessly.

"I'm afraid you must take the dicky seat, Miss Holland," Haslam whispered to Mary. "She may go off into another faint any minute, and wants someone beside her."

"Why, of course," responded Mary. "I was going to suggest it."

They got in the car, Haslam started the engine, and the return journey was commenced. It was a strange, silent journey. The girl they had rescued seemed too fatigued to talk, and they did not think it wise to worry her with questions until they were safely home. Haslam divided his attention between driving the car, watching the girl at his side, and keeping an eye open for any signs of friends or foes along the road. He chose a circuitous way back, thinking this would reduce their chances of being detected, and it was obviously important to attract no attention while getting into Wynton.

Fortune seemed to favour them for once. They saw no suspicious signs, and all was quiet at Wynton when they glided into the little town. Quickly and deftly, the girl was conveyed up to Mary Holland's rooms, while Haslam took the car back to the garage, paid for it, and received his deposit money back from the somewhat anxious Mr Harriss.

When Haslam got back from the garage, he found a pleasant surprise waiting for him. The landlady was laying the table for lunch, and she was laying for two. Since the girl from the mill had been successfully smuggled into Mary's room without the landlady's knowledge, the second place was obviously intended for Haslam.

Mary put her finger to her lips, and Haslam offered no comment. Then she slipped into her room, which adjoined the sitting-room and was only accessible from it, and he had no opportunity to thank her till the landlady had disappeared and the meal had started.

"I told her that you were commissioning some pictures, and that it was politic to be nice to you," Mary explained. "You don't mind staying to lunch, do you?"

"Fearfully," laughed Haslam. "Of course, the landlady believed you?"

"Of course."

"Then she must be an extraordinarily obliging creature, Miss Holland. Most landladies would have put a different interpretation on it. We should be food for kitchen gossip!"

"But you *have* commissioned some pictures," she objected.

"That's quite true. My interest in you is purely impersonal. All the same, kitchens, as a rule, don't admit that relationship. Why, at this very moment, your landlady *ought* to be thinking, 'Pictures! Fiddlesticks. *I* believe he's her young man!'"

"You're forgetting to eat," Mary reminded him.

"The term, 'young man,' has a plebeian aroma which does not exactly appeal to a snobbish author," Haslam continued, ruthlessly, "but I would forgive your landlady that, because in all other respects she would be quite right."

"*Do* have a potato!" sighed Mary.

"I will, on the one condition that you will regard my acceptance of it as incriminating."

"You *are* funny!"

"And you are adorable. I love you, Miss Holland. Now I feel much better, and I'll have a potato."

Mary flushed, and suddenly cast a guilty look towards the next room.

"Do you think we ought to talk like this, just now?" she asked.

"Had a man any right to crack a joke or press a girl's hand during the War?" retorted Haslam. "My dear, you and I are going through a war, and so far, it seems to me, we haven't done so badly. We are putting our whole energies into it—for the sake of a small nation. I insist that we not only have a right to talk like this, but that we need to talk like this. And I intend to go on talking like this till the meal is over."

He kept his word, and, under his buoyant spirit, Mary Holland regained her courage and hope. It seemed impossible, during these moments, that tragedy still existed, just as it seemed impossible in a theatre or a quiet garden, during the War, that across a thin strip of water men were slaying each other in thousands. But here, too, the tragedy lay close at hand, and twice during the meal Mary went into her bedroom to interview the frightened girl who lay there, still too dazed or too suspicious to respond.

After lunch, Haslam threw off his light mood, and suggested that Mary should make a serious attempt to rouse the girl. She had refused to eat, as she had refused to speak, and, while her obstinacy lasted, there seemed nothing to do for her. Moreover, this girl might be able to tell them much that they wanted to know. Mary spent a fruitless hour with her, however, while Haslam smoked in the sitting-room and pleasantly absorbed the feminine touches which Mary's tenancy had imparted to it.

At three o'clock, Haslam rose to go.

"You won't stay to tea?" asked Mary, sudden depression descending upon her.

"I wish I could," answered Haslam, "but I'm more or less pledged to be back at the Brambles by four. You see, all sorts of things may have happened—I've been away eight hours."

She nodded. "Yes, you must go back. But, please promise me one thing. Please!"

"It is already promised," he responded, taking her band. "What is it?"

"Be careful," she said, turning her head away slightly. "If anything should happen to you now, I don't know what I'd do."

"I promise you that I will be as careful as you would want me to be, if you were by my side," answered Haslam, gravely. "And will you make me the same promise?"

"Yes," she whispered.

"I will return at the first possible moment," he said, pressing her hand warmly. "Meanwhile, if we want each other, we'll know where to find each other."

She smiled, and watched him go; then, rather abruptly, went back to her bedroom and sat down beside the strange and silent guest.

Haslam walked rapidly back to the Brambles, but broke his journey at the inn, where Jane, thinly disguised as a barmaid, was doing her depressing best to add the lure of smiles and wit to the lure of the tankard. Beer was beer, wherever it was served; but, from other points of view, the Heysham bar was singularly lacking in temptations, and the morality of the local swains stood high.

Haslam had a drink, and noted that the fat commercial traveller was still on the premises. They exchanged nods over their glasses, but did not converse. Just before he left, Jane leaned forward across the stained counter which, like the world, was three-quarters sea and one-quarter dry land, and asked, archly,

"Are you comin' to breakfust agin to-morrer?"

"I don't think so," answered Haslam, smiling.

"Oh, but you better! I'll get one of the 'ens to lay a speshul hegg for you!"

This was Jane's brightest remark of the day. But it did not conquer. Haslam resumed his way without committing himself to any assignation.

"Friendly with that chap, aren't you?" observed the fat commercial, sidling up to Jane a few moments later.

"Go hon," giggled Jane.

"What had he got to say for himself this time, eh?" asked the commercial.

"Well, ain't you a one?" retorted Jane. "'Sif I'd tell you!"

It did not take Haslam long to cover the last lap of the journey. He reached the shaded lane that led to Mr Blythe's house, saw the gate's distorted shadow stretching out into a little patch of sunlight permitted by the clearing of the drive, arrived at the gate, and opened it. In a few more seconds, as he swung round the curve, the smooth green lawn came into view. No one was on the lawn, but the little tea-table stood ready on the grass, so evidently the place was not entirely deserted.

Haslam glanced towards the house, and, as he did so, received the biggest shock he had ever received in his life. He pulled up, stunned.

Approaching, with a tea tray, was Pike.

CHAPTER 33

The apparent resuscitation of Pike went as near to undermining Peter Haslam's sanity as anything had done since he first visited the Brambles. In fact, as Haslam stared at the butler, who seemed quite oblivious of the fact that he was a glaring anachronism, an entirely new theory came to him which aimed directly at his sanity.

"Am I, perhaps, really mad, after all?" wondered Haslam. "A madman does not know his condition. Has Life played some extraordinary trick upon me, and am I truly the lunatic for whom the lantern-jawed man was looking when I first met him?"

Haslam did not ask these questions frivolously. He put them to himself seriously. It occurred to him that, if he were insane, the whole series of events through which he had lately passed might be either twisted truths or sheer illusions; certainly, from the angle of insanity, it appeared ridiculous waste of time to worry about logical explanations. A man was killed. Next day, he appeared in a garden, carrying a tea-tray. Madness which could produce that could produce anything!

"The difficulty is," reflected Haslam, soberly, "I have never been mad before. If I had been, I should be a little clearer about the signs."

Then another alternative occurred to him—hardly less uncanny, but more complimentary. Sane people often swore they had seen ghosts. Maybe, this was Pike's ghost.

"I will act Horatio," thought Haslam, "and challenge it."

He coughed. The ghost of Pike stopped. Suddenly Haslam felt

very hot and foolish.

"Good afternoon, Pike," he said.

"Good afternoon, sir," replied Pike. And resumed his way.

Clearly, it was not a ghost. But this threw Haslam back upon his uncomfortable theory of insanity; and, had he been gifted with second-sight and gained a vision of Mr Blythe at that moment, having his hair shampooed by the Heysham barber and dilating on Pike's virtues, he would have asked for the address of the nearest lunatic asylum without more ado, and would have gone there.

"Best servant I ever had," Mr Blythe was saying. "I hope I never lose him."

"Yes, sir, good servants ain't too many these days," answered the barber.

"Indeed they are not," nodded Mr Blythe vigorously, while the barber respectfully suspended operations until the nod had finished. "Why, only this morning, I lost the address of a man I wanted to write to. I'd written it out on a bit of paper—hi! don't pull my head quite off, please!—and must have thrown it away by mistake. Pike told it to me at once. There, what d'ye think of that? He'd heard me read it out or something, had stored it up, and there it was, ready when wanted. Upon my soul, I feel like doubling his wages, so I do. Brilliantine? God bless me, man, when are you going to stop asking me that? You know perfectly well I detest the wretched stuff!"

Meanwhile, the admirable Pike, unconscious that his master was thinking of doubling his wages, placed the tea-pot on the table, turned, and waited for Haslam to approach.

A feeling of resentment was growing up in Haslam which he decided to use all his efforts to restrain. "I shall see red in a minute," he thought, "and then I'll be really dangerous. And the fact that Pike has already been murdered once may make it appear reasonable to me, in my frenzy, that we may go on murdering him as much as we like. Yes, Peter Haslam, you'd better go slow for a bit."

He walked to the table on the lawn, and sat down.

"Mr Grant and Mr Blythe are both out, sir," said Pike, "but orders was left that, if you returned in time for tea, it was to be served on the lawn."

"That's all right, Pike," replied Haslam, struggling to speak naturally. "Suit me admirably."

"I've just got to bring the toast, sir," said Pike, and, with a slight bend of his somewhat angular body, he departed.

Haslam took out his handkerchief, and wiped his brow. He touched the tea-pot. It remained. This occurred to him as odd. It ought to have disappeared. He stared hard at a vacant space on the table. It remained vacant. This occurred to him as extraordinary. Something ought to have appeared.

"I do wish," he muttered, irritably, "that madness were consistent! But there are cases, of course, in which one becomes mad on one subject, and remains perfectly sane on all others. Pike evidently is my subject. I am a monomaniac on Pike. Good God, here he comes again!"

Pike approached placidly with the toast. As he drew near, Haslam suddenly shifted his chair, so that he might come into physical contact with Pike's person. But Pike, a perfect servant, avoided the collision, and Haslam was forced to adopt a more obvious ruse. He leaned forward, and tapped Pike upon the sleeve, as though about to say something important. The sleeve was quite solid, and this discovery interested Haslam so much that he forgot what he was going to say.

"Is there anything else I can do for you, sir?" asked Pike, politely.

"Now, by Jove, I *am* mad!" thought Haslam. "I am behaving like an idiot, and Pike pretends not to notice it. Perhaps he's my keeper?" It suddenly occurred to him that Pike had asked him a question. "Can you do anything else for me?" he exclaimed hastily. "No—I don't think so. Yes, you can, though. Tell me how you're feeling?"

Pike's eyebrows went up slightly.

"Very well, thank you, sir," he answered.

"Are you quite sure?"

"Yes, sir."

"You mean, you feel absolutely and perfectly fit?"

"Absolutely and perfectly fit, sir," answered Pike.

Haslam banged his fist on the table, and burst into laughter. Pike's eyebrows went a shade higher. Haslam stopped laughing, and frowned.

"It's very 'ot sir," remarked Pike, with a shade of concern in his voice. "Would you rather 'ave your tea in the library, sir? It's cooler there."

"No!" barked Haslam. He felt furious. A little more of this, and Pike would certainly be murdered for the second time in twenty-four hours.

Just as Pike was about to leave, a new thought rushed into Haslam's mind, and, despite the heat, for Pike had not exaggerated, a cold chill passed up his spine.

"Good Lord!" thought Haslam. "I wonder whether Grant and Blythe are *really* out? Suppose the rascals about here have turned the tables? Pike's not dead. The man who we thought had murdered him got away. George Holland also got away—let out by Mr Blythe. Mr Blythe! Whew! Is Mr Blythe in it, after all? If so, what the devil has happened to poor Grant? I don't like this at all."

Pike was waiting, in response to Haslam's request, but Haslam let him wait while his mind continued to race.

"Grant knew something this morning that he didn't speak to me about," he reflected. "He'd got some game on. Perhaps he's played it, and failed—because he had to tackle it single-handed. Well, either I am mad, or else I'm in for a hot time. I must get to the bottom of this as quickly as possible."

He spoke aloud:

"What time will the others be back, Pike?" he asked, casually.

"I can't say, sir," replied Pike.

"Didn't they leave any message for me?"

"No, sir."

"Where are they?"

"Mr Blythe's gone to the village, sir, I believe."

"What for?"

Pike eyed Haslam patiently, paused for a moment, and then answered, "To get 'is 'ead shampooed, so 'e said, sir."

"Ah. Nice and cooling for a hot day," commented Haslam, and made up his mind that he was not mad. The cross-examination reacted on him like a tonic, and he felt his strength and vigour returning to him. "Is that all Mr Blythe went to the village for?"

"I believe 'e was going to buy something, sir."

"What?"

"I beg your pardon, sir?"

"Granted, Pike. I said, what?"

Pike smiled very faintly. A gradual transition appeared to be coming over him, and Haslam watched him shrewdly, feeling that he himself was being equally shrewdly watched.

"I don't know what Mr Blythe's going to buy, sir," said Pike, slowly, "but it must be something too 'eavy for 'im to carry, because I'm to call for it later on at the inn."

"Oh! You're to call for it, eh," frowned Haslam. "Rather an odd idea, isn't it?"

"Mr Blythe 'as odd ideas, sir," returned Pike.

"All right. That's that. Now, what about Mr Grant? Where's *he* gone?"

Haslam noted the slight hesitation, and decided that he was going to be told a lie.

"Mr Grant's gone back to London, sir," replied Pike, again with his quiet smile.

Haslam thought: "That means, he hasn't." Aloud, he said, "Any idea why?"

"No, sir."

"Coming back tonight?"

"I believe not, sir."

"Why? Did he say he wasn't?"

"Mr Grant 'asn't made a confidant of me, sir," responded Pike.

Something in the man's attitude angered Haslam. He felt they were reaching a crisis.

"Don't be impertinent, Pike," said Haslam, quietly. "I have my

220

reasons for asking these questions, as you'll doubtless guess. And, I may say, it will be in your own interests to answer them. I haven't been idle myself all this morning, you know." This was a mere attempt to intimidate Pike, but Pike did not appear in the least ruffled. He answered that he begged Mr Haslam's pardon, but that he didn't quite follow.

"Well, you soon will follow," retorted Haslam. "What's happened here while I've been away?"

"Nothing, sir."

"Don't be a fool!" cried Haslam, his anger rising. "Think again!"

"Well, nothing out of the ordinary, sir," said Pike. "Everything's gone on as usual."

Haslam rose from his chair, and faced Pike squarely.

"Your answers are thoroughly unsatisfactory," he said, with a fierce note in his voice. "Let's end this tomfoolery! Are you aware that there is something wrong with this place?"

"Why, yes, sir," answered Pike.

"Are you aware that there was a disturbance last night?"

"Yes, sir."

"Perhaps you, yourself, were not disturbed?"

"I was, sir."

"You were attacked?"

"Yes, sir."

"Brutally attacked?"

"Most certainly, sir."

"Damn it, man! You were murdered!"

"Without a doubt, sir," admitted Pike. "My body is lying in a cellar at this moment, sir."

"Heavens above!" shouted Haslam, clenching his fist, and shaking it in Pike's face. "Then who the devil——"

"My name is Grant, sir," replied the other, "and I am deeply relieved that it has taken you so long to discover the fact."

CHAPTER 34

Once more, the world swayed and turned topsy-turvy; or, rather, it turned back from topsy-turvy to the right way up. Haslam sat down weakly, and fought a strong inclination to cry.

"It was rather a mean trick to play on you," he heard Grant saying, "but I couldn't resist the opportunity to test my disguise. You see, my life itself will probably depend upon my disguise in a few hours' time."

"I don't complain," murmured Haslam. "But please don't expect anything useful from me for at least five minutes. I'm all to pieces. I could sob, like a child!"

Grant put his hand for an instant on Haslam's shoulder. It was a half-sympathetic, half-apologetic action.

"What about getting on with your tea, then?" he suggested. "Then we'll chat."

"Yes—that's the idea," said Haslam. "I think a dash of something in it wouldn't matter."

Grant took the hint, and, producing a flask from his pocket, poured a few drops of brandy into Haslam's cup.

"Brandy is not a habit of mine," observed the detective, "but I include it in my first-aid kit."

"Neither is it a habit of mine," retorted Haslam, "but, you must admit, you've put me through it. I suppose you carry that flask about with you to revive your victims with afterwards. Well, it's the least you can do." He drained the cup, and began to feel better. "I say, why don't you get a cup for yourself, and sit down?"

"I've had my tea, thank you," answered Grant, "and I prefer to remain standing, in case we are being observed through field-glasses from distant hills."

"Here! Shut up!" exclaimed Haslam. "Or I'll have to come upon you for a second dose. By the way, you haven't actually proved that you're not Pike yet! Suppose you give me some sign?"

"You ought to have demanded that before," returned Grant, smiling. "If I had been Pike, I might have poured poison in your tea instead of brandy. Well, here's my proof. Did you find Miss Holland's brother at the Old Mill? That was quite a trim little two-seater you set out in. A Standard, wasn't it?"

"How the deuce did you know?" exclaimed Haslam. "I suppose you *haven't* got more than two eyes, by any chance?"

"No; two eyes are enough for anybody who will use them. I reached Wynton before you did this morning, looking for Master George. After you and Miss Holland left, I called at her house, went over every room, and drew a blank. Did *you* find him?"

"No. I'm surprised you have to ask the question. Why didn't you follow us all the way?"

"I had other work to do. And, you must remember, although you doggedly refuse to tell me everything you know, I am relying on you to a certain extent. I've got to. I can't be everywhere. Well, you didn't find Master George. Did you find anybody else?"

Haslam hesitated.

"Thank you," said Grant. "And exactly where was she?"

"She wasn't at the old Mill, Sherlock Holmes," retorted Haslam. "We got on the track of her through an old stone-breaker. He'd seen both her and George Holland, but at different times. The last I know of George, whom we didn't unearth, is that he was being chased by that confounded lantern-jawed fellow. They met at the old mill, had a row or something, and George ran away. The girl we found, some time later, on the verge of throwing herself into a river. This is a fearful business, Grant. I believe, if we'd been two minutes later, she'd have drowned herself."

Grant looked very grave, and thought for a few moments.

"You're right, Haslam. It is a fearful business. Where is the girl now?"

"At Miss Holland's. We brought her back. Don't ask me anything about her, Grant. We could get absolutely nothing out of her. She was almost in a state of coma."

Grant nodded. "Then all you know is that, in some way, she is mixed up with George Holland?" he asked.

"That's the idea."

"You don't know in what way?"

"I don't. I've got a theory, that's all."

"And I am not to learn your theory?"

Haslam hesitated again. Then he asked, bluntly,

"Have *you* any theory?"

"None—regarding her—that I can act upon," admitted Grant.

"Well, I don't feel justified in acting upon mine just yet," said Haslam. "At the present moment, the girl is with Miss Holland, and can't get away. Until George Holland turns up, she's evidently got nowhere to go to. Oh, those two are tangled up all right, but I've an idea Miss Holland will soon prove or disprove our theories regarding her, and then we can act accordingly."

"I hardly regard Miss Holland as an impartial personage," remarked Grant, a little dryly, "but we'll drop this matter for the moment, if you want to. Anyhow, I have my hands too full to think of her just now."

"Yes, what was that 'other work' you spoke of? And why are you rigged out like Pike? Let me hear you talk, for a bit."

"I saw a man at Wynton who interested me," said Grant. "A fat commercial traveller——"

"By Jove! I know the man!" cried Haslam. "Forgive me for interrupting you, Grant, but I was going to tell you about him. He's staying at the inn at Heysham, and he asked me all sorts of questions."

"Did he? What were the questions?"

Haslam related all that he could remember of the conversation, and Grant listened attentively.

"Thank you," said the detective, when Haslam had finished. "Despite your troublesome attitude, you are helping me quite a good deal. Your story confirms my own impression of that fat commercial, and definitely decides me on my plan."

"Which is?"

"To go and see him at the inn."

"Disguised as Pike?"

"Oh, yes. I should get nothing out of him in any other guise."

"But do you mean to tell me," exclaimed Haslam, "that the fact of Pike's murder has been kept secret all this time?"

"I have made it my special business to see that it has been kept secret, and to kill any rumours that may have got abroad. The only person who knows of Pike's death outside Miss Holland and those immediately associated with last night's incidents, is a certain person at Scotland Yard with whom I have been in communication, and by whose authority I am acting. I have not even informed the local police yet."

"They won't thank you for that!" commented Haslam. "I should have thought they ought to have been informed at once."

"In ordinary circumstances, of course, they would have been informed, and in due course they will be informed. But this is not an ordinary case, Haslam. It is a most extraordinary case, and its solution depends upon the most water-tight secrecy. Mr Blythe, at this moment, is making amends for his past misdemeanours, and is in the village talking about Pike as though he were still alive. As I mentioned before I revealed myself to you, he is leaving a parcel at the inn for Pike—that is, myself—to call for. When I call, I hope to have a chat with our stout commercial."

"I'm glad to learn that you think Mr Blythe trustworthy," said Haslam. "Personally, I always believed in him, but last night—or, early this morning, rather—you were under the impression that he locked you and me up in a room!"

"He did," answered Grant, grimly. "My impression was correct. Mr Blythe is as innocent as a new-born babe—and as irresponsible. It was he who allowed George Holland to escape.

No—not by design, by accident. He knew of another key that would unlock the door, and went, on his own initiative, to interview the boy. The boy wouldn't tell him anything, and he left after a fruitless errand. It wasn't till some time after that he wondered whether he had relocked the door, and slipped back to find out. He found the door unlocked, opened it slightly, heard someone breathing, and then locked the door."

"Well, I'm dashed!" exclaimed Haslam. "There's one little mystery cleared up, anyway! Mr Blythe locked us up instead of George Holland! Was that it?"

"It was. And George Holland, of course, had already escaped. That is the one weakness in our armour, Haslam—George Holland! I would give anything to have him under lock and key again, and I wish you'd brought him back to Wynton instead of the girl. You see, *he* knows, and if the truth leaks out through him to a certain quarter, my whole plan is upset—and I stand a pretty good chance of sharing Pike's fate."

Haslam looked serious. "I wish you'd tell me what your plan is," he muttered. "Can you let me know, at any rate, why you want the fiction spread that Pike is still alive? Whoever killed him must know it!"

"That's true," answered Grant, slowly, "but I am yet to be convinced that the person who killed Pike is the chief person in this drama. We have to deal with more than one uninvited guest, you know."

"Yes, and now that Pike is removed, they will imagine they have a better chance of getting into direct touch with Mr Blythe ——"

"No, that is where our theories conflict," interposed Grant. "You and Mr Blythe believe that the uninvited guests come to see Mr Blythe. My theory is that they don't care a rap about Mr Blythe, and that they come to see Pike. Had Mr Blythe gone to London without taking Pike with him, they would not have stopped coming."

"It's possible," admitted Haslam.

"I'm sure of it," said Grant. "We have to account for two attacks on Pike, on two separate nights. The first was not successful, the second was."

"But he might have been looking after Mr Blythe's interests," Haslam pointed out.

"He might. But do you think it? Don't you believe that Pike had some secret of his own? Then, here's another thing, Haslam. You remember that, early last evening, I was shot at? I would be willing to wager a hundred to one that Pike fired that shot. He was behind me at the time. I had told him to go back to the house, and he had disobeyed me. Everything points to it—besides, it fits exactly into my theory."

"Let me get this straight," said Haslam. "You suggest that Pike fired at you. If that's so, he was in league with these confounded callers—despite the fact, remember, that he was always quarrelling with them, and was eventually murdered by one of them."

"Thieves fall out, as well as friends," observed Grant.

"True. And, of course, if he were in league with the rascals, nothing would have pleased him more than to have you out of the way."

"Exactly. The assumption is that, when he fired at me, I was chasing one of his own pals." He paused, while Haslam pondered over the suggestion. "But I haven't told you quite all," Grant went on. "I'm coming now to a particularly curious fact, and, to me, a very significant one. I found a number of keys in Pike's pocket. I made it my business to find the door or cupboard to which each belonged. I fitted every key to a door or a cupboard or a box but one. There is one key over—one that baffles me." He took it out of his pocket as he spoke, and regarded it contemplatively. "It's not rusty, you note. It appears to be in use. I believe that it is the key to our mystery, and that, when we can find the lock it fits into, we shall have solved our puzzle."

"I admit that's interesting," said Haslam, "though I'd hesitate to put so much value on it myself. Have you shown it to Mr Blythe?"

"Of course. He knows nothing about it, and doesn't recall ever to have seen it. The servants are equally ignorant. We've all tried our luck with it, and you can, too, if you like. I'd present you cheerfully with fifty pounds if you were successful."

"Done!" cried Haslam. "It shall go to a hospital!"

He took the key, and spent half-an-hour indoors searching for key-holes. It was a fascinating occupation, though a fruitless one. In the end, he had to admit himself beaten.

"Hopeless," he commented, handing the key back.

"No, not quite hopeless," replied Grant. "There is one man from whom I expect to learn the secret of this key."

"Oh! And who is that?" demanded Haslam.

"Our fat commercial," said the detective.

CHAPTER 35

The shadows were winning again. Already they had conquered the lawn save for a few thin bright streaks, and were licking across the wide gravel drive towards the porch. Haslam and Mr Blythe watched them frowningly as they sat and waited for the detective's return.

"Think I'd have been wise to let sleeping dogs lie?" jerked out Mr Blythe, suddenly.

"No, I don't," replied Haslam. "I believe I'm a bit of a fatalist; what will be, will be! We can't stop it."

"Maybe we can't," nodded the old man, "but we can be in too great a devil of a hurry, eh? You're going to die, my boy! You ain't going to stop *that*. But why jump over a precipice?"

Haslam smiled. "You waited a great many months before jumping over *your* precipice," he remarked.

"Yes, yes, that's true," mumbled Mr Blythe. "I let 'em go on calling, and calling, and calling. I suppose I had to do something at last, eh? But, you know—" He paused, and rubbed his nose. "Damme. I can't help wondering whether, if I'd acted differently, I might have saved poor old Pike. You know what I mean, eh? Might not have started the particular train of events that led to his death, anyway. Bless my soul, Haslam, I almost feel as if I'd killed the poor fellow myself, so I do!"

"That's nonsense," replied Haslam. "If we take that point of view, we're always killing people, and saving people. The fact that I jump on a 'bus at Trafalgar Square at a certain time, and prevent someone else from jumping on the 'bus, may cause him to get killed in an accident to the next 'bus. Or, by forgetting to shave one morning, I may cause a man to stop in the act of crossing a road to stare at my beard, while the motor-car that would have run over him flies harmlessly by. Every big thing that happens can be traced back to some small thing, but you mustn't blame the small thing. Big things would happen, anyway, and we can't prevent them or arrange them."

"Hark to the author spouting!" exclaimed Mr Blythe, with a wink. "I've read all that, word for word, in your last book!"

"We must repeat ourselves sometimes," laughed Haslam. "Anyway, I don't think it's necessary to waste any sympathy over 'poor old Pike.' Has Grant told you that he believes it was Pike who fired at him?"

"Ay, he did. But Grant thinks nasty things about everybody. When this wretched business is over, I'm going to pay him five pounds a week to keep away!"

"I hope you don't propose to do the same with me," laughed Haslam. "In spite of its queer associations, I'm getting a sort of affection for this place."

"Glad to hear it, my boy!" exclaimed the old man. "I'll pay *you* five pounds a week to come!"

"Done!" cried Haslam. "Then I shall give up my career and subsist, at a profit, on your hospitality. Tell me, did you bump into the commercial traveller at the inn?"

"I did. We had quite an interesting discussion about the weather. I thought it was going to be fine, but he thought it was going to rain. We also discussed politics. I was for Protection, and he was for Free Trade. Or t'other way round, I forget which. We got along finely."

"Sounds like it! And what about Jane?"

"Jane? Who's she?"

"The fair barmaid. Surely you didn't miss *her*?"

"Oh, is that her name?" chuckled Mr Blythe. "Well, I didn't progress as fast as you, that's evident. I gave her the parcel Pike was to call for, and she breathed on me, and that was as far as we got." He jerked his head towards Rose, who was emerging from the house. "Now, if they set up a girl like *her* in the bar, they'd double their trade. They wanted her once, you know."

"What did you do?"

"Raised her wages."

Rose approached, respectfully but firmly.

"Don't you think you ought to come in now, sir?" she said. "It's getting quite cool, and you've no hat."

"Quite right, my dear, quite right. I'm coming right in," answered the old man. Turning back to Haslam, he remarked, "Worth her weight in gold, she is! Bless my soul, she's been after me and mothering me all day long. She's like an old hen looking after her chick. Me, a chick! That's good, eh? Ha, ha!" He chuckled, as they made their way towards the house. Then, suddenly, he grew grave again, and stopped before the porch. "Wonder what'll happen inside these walls, Haslam, before I come out again! Grant said he was psychic. Believe I'm getting a bit that way myself. If we've got a quiet night in front of us, I'm a bad prophet!"

Haslam nodded, gravely.

"Yes, I expect there'll be more happenings tonight," he said. "But Grant seems to think he's got the game in hand, so we won't worry."

"Worry? Worry? Dear me, no!" cried the old man. "We'll all sleep like little children, I'm sure, with all the windows wide open and all the doors unlocked! All the same, Haslam," he added, "if anyone else gets killed tonight in my house, I shall feel like giving myself up to the police as an accessory. You see——"

"If you *will* stop and talk on the doorstep, sir," interposed Rose, suddenly appearing again, "may I get you your hat?"

"Cluck, cluck!" retorted Mr Blythe, as they went in.

For half-an-hour they sat in the library. Haslam suggested a game of chess, but the old man shook his head, saying he was quite sure he could not give his mind to it, and that he had been beaten too much lately for his vanity; so they smoked and chatted intermittently, casting many glances towards the French windows, and listening. Once Haslam challenged the old man, whose ear had been cocked for two solid minutes.

"What are you listening for?" he asked.

"God bless me, how do I know?" answered Mr Blythe. "A shriek, a footstep, a ring at the bell, a muffled gasp——"

"Whoa! Steady! Steady!" interposed Haslam, warningly. "You don't need me to teach you how to write a shilling shocker!" But he found himself listening, too. "All I can hear," he observed, "is the ticking of your old grandfather clock in the hall."

"That's all I can hear, too," said the old man. "But d'ye notice how loud it's ticking? When life goes on normally, you never hear the thing at all. But when normal life stops—eh?—and there are rum things abroad, then you hear the old grandfather clock. Just listen to it, Haslam! Tick, tock—tick, tock—look, out—tick, tock! Whirr, click—six o'clock—here's the shock—tick, tock——"

The door flew open, and Rose burst into the room. "Come quickly!" she cried. "There's someone in the summer-house."

Mr Blythe collapsed, but Haslam received the news with a fierce, unreasoning joy. Nothing could be worse than this nervous inactivity, this grasping at shadows, and he rushed out into the garden like a thwarted hunter. The thought of risk did not occur to him. Indeed, it seemed much more dangerous waiting in the library than racing across the lawn to meet a definite antagonist. "I'll have him this time, whoever he is!" he thought, and reached the summer-house almost before he knew it.

The door was open. The summer-house was empty. But, a little way off, something was moving in the shadow-cloaked bushes.

Haslam paused only for a moment, but it was a moment too long. He felt himself suddenly seized around the leg.

"By God!" he shouted, hoarsely, and wheeled round. His raised fist dropped limply by his side. Rose was clinging to him, flushed and panting.

"Let me go, you fool!" cried Haslam, suddenly.

But the fool clung to his leg, and before he could disengage it, the movement among the bushes had ceased.

"Well, that's that!" growled Haslam, savagely. "What the devil

—Wait a second!"

Free now, he dived into the bushes, but he found nothing. Then he returned to Rose, and regarded her grimly. She was sobbing quietly to herself.

"Why did you do that?" asked Haslam, trying to be stern, but finding it annoyingly difficult.

He had to repeat the question before she answered him. Then she said, in a trembling, half-choked voice,

"There was something bright in the bushes! I saw it!"

"Well?"

"It—it was a pistol!"

"Very possibly."

"If you'd gone on," she murmured, with a shiver, "you'd have been shot."

Haslam looked at her, smiling gravely.

"You may be right, Rose, but—Hallo! What's that?"

A fox suddenly darted out of the undergrowth, and flashed away. An idea occurred to Haslam.

"Do you think that was the cause of the trouble?" he asked. "Do you think that might have been the thing that caused the movement among the bushes?"

"Foxes don't carry pistols, sir," answered Rose, a little hysterically.

"No. But they have wonderfully bright eyes when they are watching you. A fox's eye might gleam like the end of a revolver, eh?"

But Rose shook her head.

"I'm sure it wasn't a fox," she whispered, pointing to the summer-house door. "That was closed when I called you into the house a little while ago."

"Yes, I know it was," nodded Haslam, thoughtfully. "It wasn't a fox. To you and me, at least, Rose. But it might be a fox, perhaps, to Mr Blythe? What do you think?"

They began to walk back, while the fox, also, was returning to the security of its burrow. But neither earth nor bricks form security for man or beast while greed, oppression, and enmity stalk in our midst! Rose glanced at Haslam furtively once or twice, and Haslam, sensing her frame of mind, smiled back. It occurred to him as very probable that Rose's protective impulse, and the strength of her firm young fingers, had saved his life—that, but for her, he might at this moment have been lying stretched out by the summer-house, instead of walking back towards a cosy, comfortable library, with all his life and hopes still before him. Yet, so blind are we—happily—to what might have been, and what will be, that he could not dwell on that other inanimate conception of himself as a real thing. As Butler remarks, we are all immortal to ourselves, since we never know the moment when we are dead.

"Still—it doesn't do to think too much," reflected Haslam, and then Rose broke in upon his thoughts.

"Are you angry with me sir?" she asked, appealingly.

"I am quite sure I could never be angry with you, Rose," answered Haslam, with a very gentle note in his voice. "All the same—have you heard the story of the man who was awakened by his wife when there were burglars in the house?"

"No, sir."

"She woke him up, and cried, 'Burglars!' He bounded out of bed, and rushed to the door. Just as he reached it, she cried, 'Don't go! Don't go! They'll kill you!' So he got back to bed again, and told her not to wake him up again next time."

Rose smiled faintly.

"But I had to tell you, sir, didn't I?" she asked.

"Of course, you did. But—if there is another time—perhaps you'd better let me get on with it, eh?"

But Rose, too, had her views.

"That I won't, not if someone's pointing a pistol at you!" she retorted. "Wait till Mr Grant comes back. He's a detective."

"Oh! And doesn't it matter if a detective gets killed?"

"It's their job," she insisted, stoutly. "Same as mine's washing up."

Mr Blythe was standing in the porch.

"Well, what was it?" he asked, half-sheepishly.

234

"Foxes," answered Haslam.

"Rats," retorted Mr Blythe. "Why don't you say pink elephants?"

A shadowy form appeared silently in the drive.

"Hands up!" shrieked Mr Blythe, bringing his stick to his shoulder. "Who's that?"

"Grant," came the curt reply. "What are you all doing there? Get inside, the lot of you. You're asking for it. And see, from this moment, that not a single window or door remains unlocked."

"God bless my soul!" muttered Mr Blythe, weakly. "If that's not really Pike come to life again, I'll eat my hat! What's happened, Grant?"

"We won't worry just now about what's happened," returned Grant, shortly. "What we've got to think of is what's going to happen."

"Well, I know one thing that's going to happen," snapped Mr Blythe. "I'm going back to the library, and I'm going to take it neat!"

CHAPTER 36

About an hour before Mr Blythe went into the library to "take it neat," a little scene was enacted in the bar parlour of the inn at Heysham; and since this scene was the prologue to the drama that was later on acted at the Brambles, it will be well to relate it.

A smart but rather bored-looking butler entered the inn, walked up to the counter, and asked whether a parcel had been left there for him.

"Ah, you're from the Brambles, ain't you?" replied mine host.

"That's right," nodded the butler. "And glad enough to be out of it for a bit."

"Why's that?" demanded the innkeeper. "Here, Jane—bring along that parcel Mr Blythe left this arternoon, will you?"

"Oh, I don't know," responded the butler moodily. "Gets on my nerves a bit."

Jane appeared with the parcel, and handed it across the counter.

"You oughter come 'ere more often, Mr Pike," she said, with a heavy simper. "That'd cheer you up."

"What you ought to do isn't always what you can do," answered the butler. "For instance, *you* ought to be walkin' out on a nice arternoon like this. But you ain't."

"'Ark at 'im!" giggled Jane. "Fancy, now! Oo'd I go walkin' with?"

"Now, you ain't goin' to tell me you'd 'ave any trouble there," retorted the butler, as he took out a coin and tossed it on the counter. "'Arf a pint, if you please."

"Ay, I expeck you find it a bit lonesome at the Brambles," commented the innkeeper. "But you've got a good master, any 'ow, by all accounts."

"Well," said the butler, slowly, "'e *used* to be all right. Odd, of course. And getting old. But we used to live a nice quiet life, and that just suited a man like me. I never went in much for company."

"What's wrong now, then?" asked the innkeeper. The butler tapped his forehead lightly. "Never! That a fack?"

"Just a bit, you know," nodded the butler. "All the same, it's not 'im I've worried about lately. No, it's 'is two friends."

"Oh, then he *does* like company," came a voice from a stout man, sitting in a corner.

The butler turned round, stared at the stout man, and then turned back to the innkeeper.

"'Oo's 'e?" he asked.

"Commercial. Stayin' 'ere," replied the innkeeper, in a low voice. "Nice sort o' feller."

"Ah," said the butler, and drained his glass.

The drink seemed to brighten him up a little, and he ordered another.

"Yes, it's them guests of 'is that are upsettin' things," he continued. "When you've got used to one way of livin', you don't like alterin' to another. P'r'aps I'm pertick'ler, but there you are. First, along comes this writer chap, the boss cottons on to 'im, and makes 'im stay——"

"That's right," nodded mine host. "'E come 'ere first, and took a room for a week."

"And then shifted over to us," assented the butler. "Well, that was a dirty trick to begin with, wasn't it?"

The innkeeper considered the point. He wanted to agree with his customer, for conversation was always pleasant and he wished to keep him talking. Moreover, he might order a third drink. But a certain sense of justice existed in the simple man's breast, and he could not let the statement stand unqualified.

"We-ell, I dunno about that, azackly," he said. "'Course, I was sorry to lose 'im, but 'e paid 'is week's rent like a gentleman, I'll say that."

"Oh, I expeck 'e's all right," growled the butler. "'E's 'armless, anyway. Thinks 'e's a bit clever, but ain't."

"That's orl *you* know!" exclaimed Jane, tossing her head. "Jealousy, I expeck!"

"No, it ain't! 'E's simple. Smart at 'is writing, I dare say, and at making up detective stories—but, when it comes to *acting* in a detective story—well, I reckon anyone could deceive 'im."

"You seem to have studied him," remarked the stout commercial traveller, genially.

"I 'ave. P'r'aps I've 'ad my reasons." He glanced at the stout commercial, and an eyelid flickered.

"A student of human nature, I see," observed the commercial. "And what about the other visitor? Have you studied him, too?"

"Yes, I 'ave. 'E was a bit deeper. But 'e's gone back to London, I'm glad to say."

The commercial appeared to be interested in this news.

"Back to London, eh?" he repeated. "Are you sure of that?"

"What do you mean, am I sure of it?" exclaimed the butler. "'Course I'm sure of it! 'E went up this mornin'. Ask the porter. 'Course, 'e's gone—and good riddance!"

"That's right," corroborated the innkeeper. "I saw 'im go by. Why, 'e come in 'ere to ask about the trains."

The butler looked at his empty glass, and the commercial suggested that he should have it refilled.

"It's on me," he added. "We'll drink to the confusion of the departed guest! I'll have one with you."

"Thank you, I'm sure," murmured the butler, and shoved his glass across.

There was a short silence. The glasses were filled and emptied. The butler's tongue became more and more unloosened.

"And 'ere's 'oping the other feller will soon follow suit and go back to where 'e belongs to, too," exclaimed the butler, as the last half went down.

"And that will end your troubles, eh," responded the fat commercial, "and allow you to return to the simple life!"

"Yes, that's right. All the same, the writer—'Aslam, 'is name is —p'r'aps you've 'eard of 'im?—'e's not such a bother. A quiet, uninquisitive sort of a chap. No, I don't really mind 'im. It was the other chap I was glad to see the back of. Now, you see, all's clear sailing."

"All clear sailing, eh?" queried the commercial traveller.

"Yes, all clear sailing," repeated the butler, and again an eyelid flickered.

"Well, in that case, Mr Pike," interrupted the innkeeper, "what was you worryin' about? Or is it the good stuff you've put inside you that's makin' you think dif'rent?" He winked at the commercial, and the commercial winked solemnly back. "A glass or two do make a dif'rence!" He chuckled at his little joke.

The butler suddenly became querulous and worried again, as though in self-defence of his original attitude.

"Ah, but there's other things to bother one," he said, frowning. "The 'ouse is fallin' to bits. All out o' repair. Things always goin' wrong. I reckon you want a plumber on the premises."

"Ah! Plumbers' jobs goin' around, eh?" said the commercial, carelessly. All the same, he seemed to be showing quite a good deal of interest.

"You better apply for one," suggested Jane.

"What? Me!" laughed the fat commercial.

"Yes. I should think you'd make a nice plumber, now," sniggered Jane, and suddenly burst into shrieks of laughter. No one knew exactly why her laughter was so voluble, and even she could not say how the sudden vision of the fat commercial stuck in a drain-pipe had got there. The innkeeper looked rather annoyed, but the commercial himself remained perfectly unruffled.

"Well, you never know," he remarked. "P'r'aps I may apply for that plumber's job yet!"

"I'm afraid you're too late, sir," said the butler. "We've got a tap leaking now. In the pantry. I couldn't stop it, however much I tried. So we've got the plumber turning up this evening, if you please——"

"This evening, eh?" queried the commercial.

"Yes, with 'is little bag——"

"Sure it'll be a little 'un?"

"Maybe it'll be a big 'un, but I reckon a little 'un would do. And what time d'you suppose 'e's coming?"

"Couldn't guess! Eight?"

"No—ten. The plumber's coming at ten o'clock tonight, with 'is little bag, because 'e couldn't come no earlier. And I've got to let 'im in, of course, while the other servants 'ave gone up to bed, and Mr Blythe and Mr 'Aslam's probably enjoyin' themselves playin' chess, or snoozin'."

"Rather late, isn't it?" queried the innkeeper.

"Ah, that's what I think!" exclaimed the butler, in an injured tone. "Maybe 'e'll get there later still. Any'ow, I've got to wait up for 'im, even if 'e don't turn up till *everybody's* gone up to bed, and I've got to wait till 'e's through with 'is job, too—to see that 'e don't go out with more in 'is little bag than 'e brings in with 'im."

The butler eyed the commercial traveller hard as he uttered these words, and the commercial traveller eyed the butler.

"Ten o'clock, eh?" said the commercial, softly.

"Yes, ten o'clock," repeated the butler. "At ten o'clock I've got to let that plumber in."

The door opened, and another customer entered. The commercial traveller walked back to his corner, and the butler followed him a little way.

"Suppose that plumber doesn't turn up?" asked the commercial traveller, as he sat down.

"Well, in that case," responded the butler, "I'd 'ave to sit up all night, wouldn't I?"

"It looks like it."

The butler leaned forward slightly, and fixed the commercial traveller with a searching gaze.

"What's your opinion," he asked. "Do you think the plumber will turn up?"

"I feel sure he will, Mr Pike," replied the commercial. "I feel sure he will. But, perhaps, he may not turn up till half-past ten, you know. These plumbers are most undependable fellows."

"If 'e turns up at 'arf-past ten, sir," said the butler, solemnly, "I'll be there to let 'im in."

"By the back door?"

"By the back door."

A sudden exclamation from the innkeeper made them both turn swiftly. They caught a fleeting glimpse of the new customer, flashing out of the doorway, and of the innkeeper lumbering after him.

"What's that?" cried the commercial.

"Think the young feller's 'ad a fit!" gasped Jane, wide-eyed.

"Gone off with anything?"

"No, zur. 'E jest stood there like, an' stared, and I thort 'e was goin' to faint, zo I did——"

The innkeeper returned.

"Did you catch him?" asked the commercial.

"No, sir, I didn't try," panted the innkeeper, mopping his face. "'E was too quick for me. But what 'e runs off for like that beats me. Seemed like as 'e'd seen a ghost!"

"Perhaps he had," remarked the commercial, smiling.

"Yes—p'r'aps 'e 'ad," nodded the butler, also smiling.

They both walked to the door, and looked up and down the road. A dog flew up and barked at them. There was no vestige of the young man.

"Well, that's a rum thing," observed the commercial, "but it's not our business."

"No, it ain't our business," agreed the butler, as, with a nod, he departed.

All the same, as Detective Grant walked back to the Brambles, he would have wagered very confidently that it was their business.

And equally their business, he considered, were some faint footprints in the road-dust which he examined very closely, and which he decided were not the footprints of himself, or Mr

Haslam, or Mr Blythe, or the commercial, or the young fugitive.

"There will be many travellers on the highroad tonight," he reflected grimly, as he turned in at the gate, "who will not need sign-posts to direct them to the Brambles!"

CHAPTER 37

"Grant," said Mr Blythe, at ten minutes to ten that evening, "I want ye to tell me something."

They were seated once more in the library, and the hour for which they were waiting was fast approaching. The grandfather clock was ticking very loudly.

"Fire ahead," replied Grant, puffing calmly at a cigarette. "What is it?"

"It's this," answered Mr Blythe. "I think ye'll admit I've not done so badly for an old man, but unless ye answer this question to my satisfaction, I'll hand in my notice, and quit first thing tomorrow morning. This library used to be a comfortable, congenial haven, but its turned into a mere ante-room for a Chamber of Horrors. Now, then. Is this thing going to be settled tonight, or is it not?"

"It is going to be settled tonight," responded the detective.

"Good!" exclaimed the old man. "But how d'ye know?"

Grant considered for a moment. Then he said, thoughtfully,

"I'll tell you. There are two reasons. The first is that, by the way the scene is set, it is impossible to avoid a culmination. One way or other—whether we succeed or fail—the mystery of the Brambles and of your uninvited guests will be solved."

"Ah! And the second reason?"

"An even more certain one, Mr Blythe." He paused, and looked moodily into the fireplace. "I know it."

"So you've just said!"

"I mean, I know it with some other part of me," explained the detective. "I know it with that part of me which is not logical

—at least, not consciously so. The fate of many people will be decided tonight—inside the next hour or two. There will be deserved or undeserved sorrow, holy or unholy rejoicing. New chapters will begin, for better or worse. For better, we will hope. It almost seems as if——"

He paused, and did not finish his sentence. Haslam, suddenly caught up in the invisible waves which surrounded the detective, playing upon his sensitive nature and whispering things without the reasons for them, looked at Grant strangely.

"As if—what?" he asked.

Grant shook himself out of his trance.

"Nothing," he said, shortly. "Nothing, at least, that is within the interest of anyone here aside from myself."

"Are you quite sure of that?" demanded Haslam. "We're all human—and we know you are!"

Grant turned and looked at his questioner. Perhaps their souls met in that instant. When Grant rose and walked to the door, Haslam felt as though a curtain had been lifted slightly and had dropped again.

Grant opened the door softly. The grandfather clock in the hall immediately became more audible.

"Tick, tock—tick, tock—look, out—tick, tock!"

"Firewood, tomorrow, I think," murmured Mr Blythe, almost venomously. "What are ye doing, Grant? Heard anything?"

"I thought so," he replied. "But I wasn't sure." He raised his voice a little, and called, "Rose!"

"Yes, sir," came Rose's voice back.

"Everything all right?"

"Y-yes, sir," she answered.

"Good. I'm going to leave the library door open now. If you're frightened staying there alone, come in to us."

"Thank you, sir," chattered Rose. "I'm not frightened."

"That's a plucky girl, that maid is," commented Haslam, as Grant returned into the room. "What's your idea, Grant, in wanting her to stay in the kitchen till our transformed commercial traveller calls?"

244

"If our transformed commercial traveller gets the slightest suspicion that all is not as he imagines it to be," replied Grant, "the whole game's up. Rose's presence in the kitchen will help to keep up the illusion, if he calls before ten. But, after ten, it will be natural for her to have gone to bed."

"But she's not to go to bed," interposed Mr Blythe.

"No. She will come and wait here, with the rest of you. That is, after she has collected Cook."

The cook had stubbornly remained in her room all day, but was due in the library at ten. Grant had insisted on this, and when he had given her his reasons, she had readily consented.

"What's that whistle of yours sound like?" asked Mr Blythe, suddenly.

Grant took a whistle from his pocket, and, drawing close, blew it very softly.

"When—or if—I blow that," said Grant, "it's my S.O.S."

"Thank 'ee," murmured Mr Blythe. "I hope ye won't need to blow it. But, after all, a whistle's a whistle."

"Still, it's just as well to know mine. There may be others about, you know."

"I see," answered the old man, acidly. "If we hear any of the others, we're to stay here like good little boys and go on playing Kiss-in-the-Ring!"

Haslam laughed, and Grant smiled—quite broadly, for him.

"Touché, Mr Blythe," said the detective. "That's certainly one to you."

"Whirr-click!" said the grandfather clock in the hall, and struck ten.

Rose appeared in the doorway, with wonderful promptitude. A look of relief was on her face. She seemed almost happy. Her lonely vigil was over.

"May I go and fetch Cook now?" she asked.

"Yes, please," answered Grant. "The sooner the better."

Five more minutes went by. The plumber was not expected till half-past ten, but every moment might bring his arrival, and the plumber was not the only man abroad that night. The entrance of the cook provided a diversion; despite her arresting appearance, however, she was soon forgotten again, and was tucked away in a corner with injunctions not to make a sound or a movement if she valued her life. Her frozen obedience to these injunctions showed, with painful clearness, that she valued her life very considerably, although, as Haslam oddly reflected, one could not exactly see why.

The grandfather clock wheezed the quarter. At twenty-past, Grant suddenly crossed to Haslam, and sat down beside him.

"Haslam," he said, quietly, "in a very few minutes now I shall have my hands full. I shall be pitting my wits against those of one of the sinister characters who have put a curse upon this house—The most sinister character of them all, if my theories prove correct. It is likely to be a whole-time job, but, unless I am forced into a corner, no one can help me at it. What is going to be your attitude, in the meantime, if any of the other sinister characters have to be dealt with?"

"You think there will be others?" asked Haslam.

"I am almost sure of it."

"You mean—they will arrive with the plumber?"

Grant shook his head. "No, they will not arrive with the plumber. I cannot say when, or where, or how they will arrive. Their interests are not identical with those of the plumber."

Haslam thought hard. Then he said, "You keep me rather in the dark, Grant."

"That is only because, even now, I am not sure how far I can count on you. I don't want to keep you in the dark. I'd like to put you in charge of this room. Suppose I do that?"

"I shall continue to act according to my discretion, of course."

"But not according to mine?"

"There's not a wide difference between us, Grant," muttered Haslam. "I know what you're driving at. You mean, if George Holland comes poking around—which isn't likely, is it?—" He broke off suddenly, and looked at the detective sharply. "Have you any reason for thinking that George Holland *will* be coming here again tonight?"

Grant had not told Haslam of the meteoric visit of the scared young man to the Heysham inn. He decided, now, not to.

"If you mean I believe it was George Holland who drew you out to the summer-house, you're wrong," the detective replied, a trifle coldly.

Haslam noticed the tone, and was momentarily irritated by it—an irritation which he immediately afterwards repented. But his nerves were in a bad jangle.

"You talk of putting me in charge of this room while you are away," he exclaimed. "Well, the responsibility will fall on me anyway, won't it?"

"Yes—it will, now," nodded Grant. "But if you had been willing to throw your lot whole-heartedly and unreservedly with mine, and to act as my assistant at this crisis, I should have accepted the full responsibility myself."

"One man can never be responsible for another man's actions," Haslam remarked.

"I was speaking officially," responded Grant. "Morally, I know, each of us is responsible only to himself and to God. There is no mediator. All the same, Haslam," he added, frowning heavily, "I should leave this room more confidently if I felt that your belief in rigid principles and faith in their ultimate sanity were as great as mine."

"Ha!" jerked Mr Blythe, nearly jumping out of his chair.

It was twenty-eight minutes past ten, and the back door bell was jangling.

"Grant!" exclaimed Haslam.

But Grant had gone.

For a few moments, the inmates of the library waited in breathless silence. Then Haslam slipped swiftly to the library door, which the detective had closed behind him, and opened it a crack. He heard the back door opened, and the faint sound of voices. But he could distinguish nothing definite. Then, silence fell again.

Suddenly it occurred to Haslam that one of Grant's strict injunctions was that the study door should be closed, and kept closed. He shut it quickly, with a wretched, impotent sensation.

"No—not the lights!" he whispered, as Mr Blythe put lower the lamp. "Grant wanted them to remain."

"Eh?" quavered the old man, and put forth his hand to turn the lamp up again.

But, at an exclamation from Haslam, he stopped. From the darkened room, the lawn was faintly visible, and a figure was slinking by.

"Wait—wait!" muttered Haslam, hoarsely.

He ran to the French windows, and peered out. The figure outside was now standing stock still. It was not looking towards the house, but towards a clump of bushes, and it seemed to be listening. It was the figure of George Holland.

Hardly realising what he was doing, Haslam slowly and softly unfastened the window-catch, and pushed the window open. George Holland was so intent upon whatever engrossed him at the moment that he did not move. A sudden dart across the little strip of grass, and Haslam knew that he could secure the boy. But he hesitated.

"Grant's discretion, or mine?" he reflected. "Grant would have me catch him. But what shall I do with him when I've got him? Keep him here—to be imprisoned, while a poor girl commits suicide at the first opportunity she's given?"

"Capture him," whispered the cold principles of Grant.

"Let the poor boy go," whispered his own warm humanity. "He's not taken a life—only some useless coloured stones, for which God is surely giving him enough punishment as it is!"

"Capture him!" repeated the voice of Grant. "The community must have him. Am I not risking my own life for the community at this very moment?"

Almost with a groan, Haslam slipped silently out on to the lawn. Ten yards of velvety grass separated them, now five, now

———

Where was the boy? Haslam reached the spot to find him vanished. Yet he could have sworn his approach had not been detected. He paused a moment, hesitating what to do next, and as he hesitated a hand suddenly descended on his shoulder.

"Now, by God!" shouted Haslam, swinging round fiercely.

The grip loosened. The owner of the hand melted away. Haslam found himself staring into blank darkness.

He remained staring for two or for twenty seconds; he could not have told you which. Then, in a sudden panic, he thought,

"Good Lord—suppose Grant is whistling!"

He raced back to the window.

CHAPTER 38

When Detective Grant unlatched and opened the back door, he saw the dim outline of a typical workman standing before him. For a second, the two men looked at each other; then Grant said,

"Are you the plumber?"

"'Oo else?" asked the plumber's gruff voice.

"Well, come in. But you're late."

"Better late than never. I mightn't 'ave come at all, see? Where's the tap?"

"This way," said Grant. "In the scullery."

He closed and refastened the back door, and then silently led the plumber through the kitchen into the scullery. The plumber's eyes were very busy. They noted that the kitchen was empty, and that the man who had let him in appeared to be in sole charge.

"Servants gorn ter bed?" he asked, carelessly.

"Yes," replied Grant. "I tried to get one of 'em to wait up for you instead o' me, but there was nothin' doing."

He grinned suddenly at the plumber, and the plumber grinned back.

"So they're up in their rooms, eh?" enquired the plumber.

"That's right," nodded Grant. "Went up 'arf-an-hour ago."

"I see." The plumber paused. "And what abart the others? They gorn ter bed, too?"

"What—Mr Blythe and Mr 'Aslam?"

"That their names?"

"Yes. No, they ain't gone to bed. They're in the library, where they'll stay till midnight. They're playin' chess. Wonderful 'old, chess seems to 'ave," reflected Pike. "When they start playin' chess, they never think of anything else. Reg'lar absorbs 'em, chess does."

"Ah," observed the plumber. "Then they won't come disturbin' us, eh?"

"Not they. Why, you could mend taps all over the 'ouse, if you wanted to, and they'd be none the wiser. 'Check,' ses one. 'Damn it,' ses the other. And then they starts another game, as I said, till midnight."

"But if I started mendin' taps all over the 'ouse," remarked the plumber, "the servants might 'ear me?"

"Oh, I expeck they're asleep by now. Sleep as 'eavy as tops, they do. Both of 'em. But, of course, I don't expeck you'd go bangin' on the taps right outside their door, would you?"

"No—I don't expeck I would," agreed the plumber. Then, suddenly, his manner changed. "Then, all's clear, Pike," he said, "and you and I can get to business."

Grant's manner changed, too.

"Right you are, boss," he said. "But, between you an' me, I'm gettin' a bit sick of business!"

"Oh, you are, are you?" exclaimed the other, frowning. "Well, the time you go out of business is for me to decide, not for you."

"Is it?"

"You know very well it is. Now, then, let's cut all this."

"P'r'aps I don't want to cut all this," grumbled Grant. "P'r'aps I'd like a little bit of a chat."

"And p'r'aps I *wouldn't*," retorted the plumber, wrathfully. "What the devil's the matter with you tonight, Pike?"

"Well, boss—things have got a bit difficult lately."

"I know that! If they hadn't, we'd have had this present little matter cleared up long ago."

"Ah, that's right. But p'r'aps you don't know jest 'ow difficult it's really been for me!"

"I'll tell you something I *do* know, Pike," snapped the other. "I know how difficult it *will* be for you if I have any nonsense from you." Grant remained sullenly silent. His suspicions that Pike had been merely an agent, that he had been in this man's power, were being confirmed. He decided to find out exactly what hold the plumber had had over Mr Blythe's butler. "Well—get a move on!" exclaimed the plumber.

"Look 'ere," returned Grant, acting like a cornered man with his fists up. "What'll you do if I throw the whole job up?"

"Confound you! Are you serious?"

"I say, what'll you do?"

"Do you mean to say, Pike," said the plumber, slowly, fixing him with his eye, "that, after all your years' of association with William Bowling, you don't know him yet?"

Grant stared back at William Bowling without altering his expression. But his mind was racing. William Bowling! The name was associated with one of his greatest professional failures and bitterest personal disappointments. He had never seen Bowling before, but he knew him as an accomplice of the arch-thief Maxley, and Maxley was the man who, through his daughter's lack of co-operation, had been allowed to slip through his fingers two years ago. Later, Maxley had been caught on the continent, but Bowling, always a shadowy figure, had evaporated. Now, here he was, in the solid flesh.

New trends of thought were springing up in the detective's mind, and while he stared back at Bowling, ready to answer all his immediate cues, his mind was also far away, conjecturing, constructing, groping.

"I'll tell you what I'll do, Pike," Bowling was saying. "I'll allow certain information to trickle to certain quarters. It shall be known that the respectable man who applied for the job of caretaker at the Brambles when it was empty, and who was afterwards taken on as the new owner's butler, wasn't always called Pike. Once he had another name, a name that was published in quite a number of newspapers. In short, Pike, if you backslide now, tomorrow you will be known as Sandy Bessington, who murdered a certain young man on a lonely beach, and who even then wasn't quick enough to get away with the spoils."

"Do you think I meant to murder him?" demanded Grant,

feigning terror.

"Privately, I know you didn't. You've not the pluck to murder anyone, or the brains to profit by any chance. You're a fool, Pike, and that's why you're so useful in your present job. The one thing you've shown sense over up till now is in knowing on which side your bread's buttered. And now then, my good man, we've had enough of this. Where is it?"

"'Arf a moment, 'arf a moment," muttered Grant. "You're in too much of a 'urry! You say, 'Where is it?' as though it was all as easy as winkin'."

"Come, come!" rasped Bowling, ominously. "So it is! You generally carry them on you, don't you?"

"Yes. But if I'd 'ad this on me, would I 'ave troubled to ask you in like this——"

"That's true," admitted Bowling, frowning. "Why the devil are you making such an elaborate job of this?"

"You call yourself clever, but it seems to me you can be a bit of a fool at times, too, William Bowling! Things ain't *right*, I tell you——"

"Damn it, man, I know that!" fumed Bowling. "We had enough trouble to get the thing here, owing to that chit of a girl turning faint and the bungling of her confounded young man. And then, when we got it here, every time I called there was some difficulty. You never had it on you, or else someone popped out of that blessed library like a jack-in-the-box, and I either had to hop off sharp or be hauled in for a trying, nerve-racking interview! You're a bungler, Pike, that's what's the matter. You've been losing your nerve! If you'd contrived to stay here while Mr Blythe went up to London, the thing would have been settled in a trice——"

"Mr 'Aslam was in the 'ouse——"

"Haslam! Bah! We could have dealt with *him!* But when that confounded fellow Grant came along, it looked to me that the game was up. Well, it's a good thing for you the game *wasn't* up, and that Grant went back to town. He'll be back again tomorrow, I expect—just a few minutes too late." Suddenly Bowling whipped out a revolver. "Pike," he said, "I don't much care for you tonight. No, I don't seem to like you a bit. And I'm rather afraid there'll be a nasty accident if you don't hurry."

"Oh, all right, curse you!" snarled Grant, and, taking the key that had baffled him out of his pocket, he threw it on the table. "There you are. Go your own way."

Bowling looked at the key, but did not immediately take it.

"Put up your hands a minute, Pike," said Bowling. "You've never given me any trouble before, but you're a bit unsteady tonight. Let's just see whether you've got anything dangerous on you?"

Grant had two things on him which would have interested Bowling. One was a revolver, which he could use as skilfully—and was as ready to use—as Bowling himself, and the other was a pair of hand-cuffs. It became rather important to Grant, therefore, that these objects should not yet be revealed. He did not want to force an issue until he knew a little more about the key on the table.

"If you come any nearer to me," he exclaimed, putting passion and indignation into his voice, "I'll shout! Yes, by God, I will! D'you think I've got no pride? I'll raise the alarm, so I will——"

"Be quiet——!"

"Be quiet yourself! And, even if you *do* shoot—well, I don't think I'd care much. As I told you, I'm fed up with this, and I wouldn't be the only one to be cooked by your shot. I reckon even chess ain't too absorbin' to hear a pistol shot! So now, then!"

"Perhaps the fool's right," muttered Bowling.

"'Course I'm right!" retorted Grant. "'Aven't we worked long enough together for you to know that? Look 'ere, William Bowling, I may be a bit nervy tonight, but you're worrying over the wrong man. *I'm* not the one you want to keep that revolver for! Why, if I'd 'ad one, I'd 'ave killed old lantern-jaw last night in this very 'ouse, so I would!"

"What? Birkett?" exclaimed Bowling, and Grant made a note of another name.

"Yes. Birkett," he replied. "'E's got in and gorn for me twice. 'E nearly did me in last night. There's your foul play for you, if you like. And now p'r'aps you'll see why I don't go carrying valuable things about with me in my pocket. I've been badgered on all sides lately, I tell you, what with Birkett, and you, and that young fool of a Holland."

Bowling lowered his pistol, and slipped it back into his pocket.

"I dare say I've been a bit hasty, Pike," he nodded, taking up the key. "It seems as if you and I'll have to carry this business on a little different in the future. We'll have to move our headquarters, for one thing. And we'll have to settle with Birkett, for another. I've had my eye on him for a long while. Someone followed me here tonight. Birkett, eh? As he couldn't get it from you, he knows I'll have better luck—I being constitutional, so to speak, and him being not! Suppose he's tracked me here tonight, Pike, and is lurking outside?"

"Wouldn't surprise me," agreed Grant, as they moved towards the kitchen door.

"On the other hand," proceeded Bowling, pausing at the door, "it may not have been Birkett. It may have been Grant."

"No, not Grant," answered the detective. "I told you. 'E went up to London today. I told you that at the inn."

"Yes, but Grant's a sly customer. There's no one I dislike more —and whose neck I'd wring more happily. But, of course, it mightn't have been Grant. It might have been that young fool of a Holland."

"Ah! That's a sillier notion still," retorted Grant, scornfully, and keeping his ears particularly wide open now. "Why'd 'e come pokin' round 'ere again?"

"Why?" exclaimed Bowling. "For the same reason that he's been poking round here ever since he first took over the job for his sweetheart of delivering the goods into your hands! Didn't you tell me yourself that the soft idiot's been trying to get the necklace back ever since he knew what it was he'd passed on to you? I tell you, Pike, I've had a pretty time of it lately, dodging and watching him, and Birkett, and you, and Grant, and the whole pack of you! Many's the time I've wished I could slice myself up into quarters, so that I could be in four places at once! And now—silence! Not a word while we're going upstairs!"

They slipped out into the passage. Grant lingered behind, and allowed Bowling to lead. Clearly, Bowling knew his way about.

Bit by bit, the detective's theories were being proved and substantiated, and the full strange story of the Brambles was being unravelled. Preceding him up the stairs was the genius of the affair, the glorified receiver of stolen goods who, acting as an agent of the criminal underworld, used the Brambles as his headquarters and built up a connection there which, for a while, even the advent of Mr Blythe had not disturbed. Locked in a cellar lay the body of Pike, alias Sandy Bessington, murderer by design or accident, and, through pressure and self-interest, the brainless go-between who took in the tainted prizes that were handed to him by the mysterious, uninvited guests, passing them on in due course to the master organiser when he called for them. Bowling, doubtless, had many ways of disposing of the prizes on the continent, and, with equal doubt, took a large share of the profit in return for the risks he ran and the brains he used on the behalf of other less ingenious sinners. Outside in the grounds lurked Birkett, the black sheep who had strayed from the black sheeps' fold, still waiting for his chance to obtain the necklace which he knew to be somewhere in the Brambles —yet the exact location of which was known, at that moment, to only one man in the world—William Bowling. And outside, also, lurked George Holland, who had unknowingly assisted his misguided sweetheart to convey the necklace from Mrs Eltham Smith's house at Arundel to Mr Ambrose Blythe's house at Heysham, and who was now desperately trying to regain the necklace. For what purpose? Probably, to restore it, in order that he might clear his conscience as far as was possible before starting life afresh with a worthless girl.

Grant wondered whether Bowling had himself put pressure upon the girl, and whether he had organised the theft from a distance, as appeared to be his habit. Bowling had been behind many of Maxley's schemes, and Maxley himself might have been associated with the girl in some way . . .

"Now, then! Now, then!" whispered Bowling. "What are you stopping for?"

"Jest came over a bit faint," muttered Grant. "Get on."

"I am getting on," returned the other. "I wish you'd keep steady!"

"Don't worry," said Grant, with a grim light in his eyes. "I'm going to keep steady."

CHAPTER 39

They mounted the back stairs until they reached the upper landing. Grant raised his finger warningly as they passed the room in which the maids were assumed to be sleeping, and he had a nasty moment when Bowling paused outside the door and listened. If for any reason he chose to peep into the room, or if the necklace were hidden somewhere there, he would discover that Grant had lied to him and that the servants had not retired. But Bowling only paused for a moment. Proceeding, he did not stop again until they reached the unoccupied room in which George Holland had been locked up, and near which Pike's body had been found. Then he stopped, and, opening the door, walked in.

Grant followed him. Bowling strode rapidly across the room to a cupboard, and, entering it, threw his flashlight upon one of the darkest recesses. He loosened a brick, took it out, and pressed the wall behind. Immediately, on the other side of the cupboard, a little panel slid aside, revealing a small door with a keyhole. The key was fitted into it, and the door was opened.

"Ah!" exclaimed Bowling, with a satisfied grunt, as he thrust his hand through. "Here she is!"

When his hand was withdrawn, it held a case, which he promptly opened. The Arundel necklace reclined inside.

"Wonderful, what a lot of trouble these simple little things can cause, eh?" murmured Bowling, sardonically. "All this bother, over just a few coloured stones! I can never understand myself what folks see in 'em!"

He chuckled, and slipped the case into his pocket.

"What's it worth?" asked Grant.

"About £10,000, I should say. But you'll know when I've got rid of it. Amsterdam, I think, for this little beauty. What's five per cent of £10,000, Pike?"

"£500," blinked Grant.

"Exactly. So, if I sell it for £10,000, that's what you'll get. And you talk of quitting!"

"And what'll the other party get—the party that stole it?"

"Well, that's rather a puzzle," frowned Bowling. "They'd be entitled to the usual fifty per cent, in the ordinary way, but don't you think George Holland has lost his claim by his attitude? I can see very clearly, Pike, that our biggest scoop at the dear old Brambles is going to be our last scoop there. You must give notice, and quit. We'll get a new pitch, you and I—start afresh, eh? And—look here, Pike. Others are turning against *us*. What about our turning against *them*, and keeping the lot?"

"Can't make out why you've not turned against *me* long ago," mumbled Grant, wondering whether the moment were arriving to produce the hand-cuffs.

"You're too useful, my lad," returned the other. "You know the game upside down. You can separate the meal from the chaff. And, at any moment, I can have you hanged."

"Yes, you know 'ow to apply the pressure all right," muttered Grant, edging closer. "I expect you 'ad something up your sleeve against the girl, and used pressure there, too?"

"I did," smiled the unpleasant fellow. "She'd got into some mess with Holland, and I threatened to tell him that it wasn't the first time she'd made a fool of herself over a man. Remember Maxley?" The eyes of the man he was addressing narrowed; clearly, he had heard of Maxley. "Well, she was head over heels in love with him. A regular ladies' man was Maxley. That was what undid him at the end."

Grant's fingers gripped the revolver in his pocket. Suddenly, however, he changed his mind, and strolled to the window.

"'Ow far did things go between 'er and Maxley?" he asked, looking out.

"Oh, not far, I don't believe," answered Bowling. "She was just silly about him and helped him get out of London once when he was identified by a picture in the papers, and Grant nearly had the cuffs on him. He threw her off soon afterwards. But it was a good enough story to have queered her with young Holland, or so she thought; and it's brought us the little case in my pocket, Pike. Now, then, I'll be quitting. I won't be coming to the Brambles again. It's getting too hot here. You'll get a code letter from me in about a week, and it'll contain your instructions. Till then, lie low, and watch out for Grant if he comes poking back here, as I've no doubt he will."

"Didn't Grant once swear 'e'd lay you low?" asked Grant, still staring out of the window.

"He did," answered Bowling, as he moved towards the door. "It was one of his little mistakes. If he's hanging around the garden outside, I'll lay *him* low!"

Grant saw something that interested him among the bushes.

"I don't think you need worry about 'im," he said. "No, nor about anybody. It's clear out there."

"Good—then I'll clear, too." He turned at the door. "Coming?"

"No, thanks. You can let yourself out."

"As you like. But suppose I meet somebody?"

"You won't, if you go down by the back way. Any'ow, I'm goin' to make sure that you *don't* meet anybody. I'm goin' into the library, to keep my eye on 'em till you're clear."

"Good idea," nodded Bowling.

"'Course it's a good idea," returned Grant. "You ain't got 'em all." Suddenly he darted to Bowling's side, and gripped his sleeve. "Sh!" he whispered, hoarsely. "Wait a bit! Someone's coming! Switch off yer light, for God's sake!"

Bowling whipped out his revolver, and for a few moments they strained their ears in the darkness.

"Must 'ave been mistaken," muttered Grant. "Nerves all gone to bits."

Bowling looked at him angrily.

"You're not safe tonight, Pike, that's a fact," he rapped out.

"I've had about enough of you, and I'm going to quit before you do any real damage."

He swung swiftly out of the room. Grant darted to the window. Then, as Bowling began to descend the back stairs, he slipped out of the room, turned in the opposite direction, and flew down the main staircase.

Haslam heard him coming, and was on his feet in an instant.

"Quick!" whispered Grant, as he entered the room. "Out on to the lawn with me, Haslam. The rest of you, lock the door and windows after us, and stay here till we return."

"Right," replied Haslam, already at the windows. "I'm yours this time, Grant."

In two seconds, they were out on the lawn. They made their way round to a clump of bushes from which they could see the back door of the house. Here, they hid, and Haslam felt a revolver slipped into his hand.

"Cover the man who comes out of the back door," whispered Grant, "but don't shoot unless I give the word."

The moon, lately risen, began to emerge from a thick bank of clouds, and, just as a streak of pale light touched the house, the door opened slowly. A figure came out.

It stood still for a few moments, in a listening attitude. Then, satisfied, it began to move forward, but before it had advanced more than two steps, another figure darted out from the concealed angle of a wall on the near side of the house, and had seized it from behind by the neck.

"Devils!" gasped the first figure, struggling violently.

"Cheat!" snarled the second. "I'll have the lion's share this time, Bowling, for a change!"

But Bowling was a powerful man, far more powerful than his assailant, and, although he was being attacked from the back, he gradually began to work his big frame round.

"You will, will you?" he panted. "We'll see, Birkett!"

It was a short, terrific struggle. Haslam felt the sweat on his brow as he watched the wrestlers and waited for some command from Grant. But Grant never moved, and neither of the wrestlers knew that they were both covered by revolvers.

Suddenly Birkett gave a cry. Bowling had wriggled almost free, and was pressing on his throat. Then Birkett knew he had only one more chance, and he took it. A knife flashed in the air, and Bowling's grasp relaxed as he slipped, without a sound, to the ground.

For a moment, Birkett stared at his dead opponent, dazed. He had sunk so low during the last few days that his sense of relative values was hopelessly warped, his brain was muddy, and he was practically a lunatic; but an expression crept into his eyes as he stared at the fallen figure that suggested a momentary realisation of the enormity of his acts, and a terrifying wonder as to their wisdom. Then, however, victorious greed swept over him again, and in a blind frenzy he dropped beside Bowling.

Still Grant made no sign, but waited for the culmination of this tragedy. Events were working according to plan, and perhaps, even at this crisis, Grant possessed, unknown to himself, a dramatic instinct. Since there was no instant necessity to interfere with the course of events, the course of events proved too interesting to be diverted.

Birkett fumbled about Bowling's coat, and suddenly, with a low exclamation, drew a case from a pocket. Then he jumped up, and opened the case. The case, empty, dropped from his hands.

This was the moment chosen by Grant to reveal himself. He stepped quietly out of the shadow of the bushes, and stood in the full moonlight.

"Good evening, sir," he said.

It was the application of the third degree. Birkett started violently, and looked up. His eyes became frozen in his head.

"Pike!" he shrieked. "My God!"

And he swooned.

CHAPTER 40

"Mr Grant," said Ambrose Blythe when, a quarter-of-an-hour later, they were seated once more in the library and the detective had finished his narrative, "I take off my hat to ye! I suppose we mustn't grieve for the two rascals who have met their death through their rascality, and for the third who, I expect, will spend most of the rest of his life in prison. Very well, then. We won't. It's taken you less than two days to solve the mystery of this place, and I don't believe Sherlock Holmes himself could have done it in less time. And, now, is this the end?"

"Not quite," replied Grant, gravely. "There's one more thing to do."

Haslam looked at the detective sharply, and his heart sank.

"Why not let sleeping dogs lie?" he asked, gently. "Surely you're satisfied with your work?"

"One should never be satisfied with one's work, while there still remains work to do," answered Grant.

"Tut, tut!" retorted Mr Blythe, briskly. "If we did all the work there was to do, we'd died of gasping! You've cleared up the mystery, you've ended—or seen ended—the careers of three prize rascals, and you've got back Mrs What's-her-name's necklace. Bless my soul, that's a bag, now! And the necklace is thrown in, mind ye, for I didn't ask you to come down here and get that, for I couldn't, never having heard of the damned thing. If you want more than that, you're a glutton!"

"It's true, we have the necklace back," said Grant, rather wearily, "but we haven't got the thief who stole it yet."

"Why trouble about that?" asked Haslam.

"You know my views," returned Grant. "Officially, she's wanted. I can only act officially."

"H'm! She?" queried the old man. "What about the boy, then?"

"He seems to have been perfectly innocent throughout. It was the maid who stole the necklace, and it was the maid who, according to the original plan, contracted to convey the necklace to Pike, in order that he might pass it on in the usual way. She funked it, and Holland, when he gave the parcel to Pike, did not know what he was doing, and he appears to have made every effort to repair the wrong."

Mr Blythe frowned. In chivalry to the maid, he attempted to divert attention to the man.

"I don't agree with you, Grant," he said, tartly. "Drop the whole thing, or go for Holland. *He* may tell a different story, and I'm sure, if he's half a man, he'd rather go to prison than have the girl sent there. If you're so darned particular, he was a sort of an accomplice, wasn't he? He could have informed the police when he found out what he'd done, but he didn't."

"Holland will have to be questioned, of course," nodded Grant, "but he is the side issue in this case. Naturally his evidence will be taken."

"If you can find him, eh?"

"If we find the girl, we shall find George Holland, Mr Blythe. He will not desert her. That is why I do not need to concentrate upon him."

"I see your point," admitted the old man. "You might get Holland without the girl, but you won't get the girl without him." He shrugged his shoulders. "Well, well, you know your business better than I do, and I'm not going to interfere with it. By the way, wasn't it a bit risky letting Bowling march out of the house with the necklace in his pocket?"

"We were both covering him," said Haslam. "He had very little chance of getting away with it."

"But I thought detectives took no chances."

"And I did not, on this occasion," remarked Grant. "I fooled him just before we left the room upstairs, and, while he was listening for footsteps which I invented for him, I took the case out of his pocket and emptied it."

He rose, and looked at Haslam. Haslam rose, too, and returned the detective's gaze. Each read the other's thoughts.

"In a few minutes, I shall be going to Wynton," said Grant. "Do you want to come with me?"

"Of course, I do," answered Haslam.

"How shall we stand, if you come?"

"I shall be a lay figure."

"That means, though you won't help me, you won't interfere with me?"

"Exactly."

"On those terms, I'd like your company. On any other terms, I should have locked you up."

"Damme!" cried Mr Blythe. "I wouldn't let you do such a thing! He's my guest!"

"We need not discuss it," returned Grant. "The occasion hasn't arisen."

"Then why mention it?" snapped the old man. "Grant, I admire ye, and I've got a sneaking respect for ye, but, at the same time, I tell ye frankly, I positively detest ye! And, now, be off, if you're going, because I've a notion I'd like to go to bed."

Grant nodded.

"I shall probably have paid a call on the local police before I return," he said. "Meanwhile, I suppose I can trust you not to let Mr Birkett escape?"

"Funny, ain't you?" retorted Mr Blythe. "You seem to think it's a habit! If you think I can contrive the escape of a man who's hand-cuffed and foot-cuffed, who's insensible, and whose first impulse if he woke up and got free would be to stick a knife into me, you over-rate my powers, sir. I've no burning desire to pay a call on Mr Birkett, thank ye!"

"Then I'll not worry," answered the detective, smiling, and turned to Haslam. "George Holland may still be about the house, you know." We'll have a look round before we leave."

"He may be, but I doubt it," said Haslam. "Clearly, it was Birkett who scared him off when I went after him, as it was Birkett who made the mistake of catching me instead of Holland. Probably the boy ran off in terror, and never came near the place again."

"That's my opinion. We'll make sure, though. Are you ready to start now?"

"Yes. Right now."

"Good. Then we'll be going. Goodnight, Mr Blythe."

Mr Blythe put out his hand, and remarked, half-apologetically,

"Now, you're not going to take all I've said about you to heart, are you? You're my guest, just the same as Mr Haslam is—invited guests, both of ye—and I don't mean half I say."

"Don't worry," responded Grant. "I'm not."

"All the same," added Mr Blythe, "if you think better of it and let that poor girl go, I'll think none the less of ye. Goodnight, Mr Haslam."

"Goodnight, Mr Blythe," replied Haslam.

The two men slipped out into the garden.

Mr Blythe stared after them moodily. The clock struck half-past eleven. It was late, too late for an old man to be up. But he took out his pipe, and filled it contemplatively, feeling curiously indisposed to go to bed.

He struck a match, and lit his pipe. Still standing by the window, he puffed away silently, full of strange emotions which he could not describe, and queer thoughts which he could not elucidate. He felt as though something were slipping from him, yet did not know what it was. The load of oppression, perhaps. A realisation of new friendships. A glimpse, through chaos, of things beyond. Or just a trick of the moonlight.

He heard a light step behind him. To his astonishment, he did not start and turn, but went on quietly smoking.

"Is that you, Rose?" he asked.

"Yes, sir," replied a voice at his side.

"Ah! And why aren't you in bed?"

"I was coming to ask the same question, sir."

"Were you? Well, that was very nice and thoughtful of you. But then, Rose, you are a very nice and thoughtful girl, so there's nothing surprising in that."

"It's very good of you to say so, sir——"

"Tut, tut! It's true." There was a pause. Suddenly he exclaimed, "D'ye know, Rose, that—now poor Pike's gone—you're the only person I've got to look after me?"

"I'll do the best I can, sir, that I promise," answered Rose, with rather tremulous enthusiasm. "But there's Cook——"

"Cook!"

"And, I suppose, you'll get another butler."

"I'm not so sure, Rose. I don't like new people bothering around me. I—I rather think I'll do without another butler." He shivered slightly.

"Hadn't you better close the window, sir? It's getting cool."

"God bless me, if you ain't a sort of mother and daughter to me all in one," cried the old man. He closed the window, and returned into the room. "Tell me, my dear. Do you think you can stand this house, after all that's happened in it?"

"Why, of course!"

"Ye mean that?"

"Yes, sir."

"Good! Good! We'll wipe out all these nasty memories, hey, and begin things afresh. Upon my soul, I almost feel like a schoolboy again. We'll spring-clean the place—plan it all out, you and I, eh? P'r'aps I'll send you off for a holiday by the sea somewhere first, and go off somewhere myself, and then we can return to the old place—d'ye really like it, Rose, eh? Honest?"

"I love every brick of it, sir," she replied. "And—I like what's in it, too."

"Tut, tut!" He suddenly rubbed his eye with his hand. "No, I'm not a school-boy, my dear. I'm getting very old. Very old. That's why I don't want another move. I want to live and die here—and you can look after me, if you will, till some young rapscallion comes along— But, wait a minute! Has the rapscallion come along yet?"

"No, sir," answered Rose, colouring.

"Then he's a fool, but God bless him for delaying! And, till he comes, you'll look after me, eh, and help to brush away the dust, and keep off an old man's shadows. I don't expect it will be for so very long. Tell me, Rose, how old d'ye think I am, now?"

"I couldn't guess, sir!"

"Nonsense!"

She reflected. "Fifty-seven?"

"No, twenty-three," retorted Mr Blythe, chuckling. "And we'll reserve a room for Mr Haslam for whenever he wants to come here—and, maybe, one day he'll bring someone with him. A certain person who paints pictures, eh? Who paints the most delightful pictures. A certain person——"

He trailed off. Rose looked at him anxiously. He was staring into the empty grate, and her simple mind could not realise that he had suddenly forgotten fifty years, and was thinking of another certain person whom once he had known. He had only known her for a short time. Life had singled him out for solitude. But it had been a very wonderful time, while it had lasted, and there was a way she had of smiling...

"Mr Blythe! Mr Blythe!"

"Eh?" jerked Mr Blythe.

"What's the matter, sir? Are you ill?"

"Ill? Bless my soul, no! I was—I don't know! Ill? Bless my soul!"

"You're tired, sir," said Rose, gently, taking his arm. "You really must go to bed."

"Yes, a little tired, perhaps," he nodded. "You're right, Rose. I must go to bed. I can see, I'll have to mind my p's and q's when you're around!"

They walked out into the hall. Suddenly Mr Blythe stopped.

"Listen, Rose!" he cried. "Listen."

"Come to bed, sir," she urged.

He pointed to the grandfather clock.

"Listen, my girl. Tick, tock—tick, tock—tick, tock—tick, tock! Do you hear?"

"Yes, sir."

268

"Just that. Tick, tock. Nothing else! You don't hear anything else, do you, Rose?"

"Why, no, sir."

"Nor do I," nodded the old man, peacefully. "Nor do I." And he allowed her to lead him up to his room.

CHAPTER 41

The walk to Wynton was a silent one. Grant and Haslam seemed to be the only people on the road, and neither of them was in a mood for conversation. Occasionally, they exchanged a few words, but, for the most part, the scrunching of their footsteps was the only sound that broke the stillness of the lanes.

Towards the end of the journey, Grant suddenly became a little more communicative.

"There's not much more to do now," he said, shortly. "How do you and I stand?"

"Square, I think," replied Haslam.

"Yes, I think so, too," nodded Grant. "Still—you'd like me to turn back?"

"I would! The prospect of seeing you arrest that girl isn't a happy one."

"You still believe there are extenuating circumstances, then?"

"How can I say?" retorted Haslam. "Life's too big a tangle altogether. If we can't straighten out our own tangles, how can we expect to straighten out other people's?"

"We can't," admitted Grant. "I don't try to. I am merely a servant of the community, joining in the necessary work of protecting the community. I am interested in results, not judgments, and I try to obtain results. Perhaps—in my heart—I do not relish the prospect of arresting that girl any more than you do. Perhaps I relish it less."

Haslam glanced at him curiously.

"I think you'll always be a bit of an enigma to me, Grant," he said, "but I like you." He paused. "I wonder whether, at rock-bottom, you and I disagree so much, after all?"

He waited for a reply, but received none. The journey was completed in silence.

They reached Wynton close on midnight. Of the few lights that still twinkled in the village, Mary's was one. The yellow blind glowed faintly.

"Will you knock?" asked Haslam, as they paused, "or shall I call?"

"You call," replied Grant, and slipped back a little into the shadow.

Haslam stood under the window, and called softly,

"Miss Holland."

A shadow appeared on the yellow blind almost immediately, and a faint voice replied,

"Who is it?"

"Haslam," he answered. "Detective Grant is with me. Can we come in?"

"Yes," came Mary's voice, more clearly now, as she opened the window a little. "I'll be down in a moment to let you in. I must just put on something."

They waited a couple of minutes. Then the door opened, and Mary appeared in the doorway. She wore a dressing-gown, and her hair was slightly disordered.

"Come in," she said. "Tell me—what's happened?"

Grant stepped forward, and took command.

"We have come to enquire whether your brother and the girl are here?" he asked, brusquely. Mary looked at the detective, and shook her head. He went on, "You need have no fear for your brother, Miss Holland. I have sufficient evidence to prove that he was merely an innocent accomplice, and all I shall require of him is to be a witness. The law will probably assume that he has merely acted foolishly."

"You mean that?" cried Mary, with relief in her voice.

"With the girl, however, matters are on a different footing," proceeded Grant. "She is a directly guilty party, and I have come to arrest her."

Mary studied the detective for an instant, and then replied, "I am afraid you will find that difficult, as she is not here."

"I understand from Mr Haslam that she was brought here today?"

"That's quite true. But she went away again. Won't you come in? It's cool talking out here."

They followed her up the narrow flight of stairs, and continued their conversation in Mary's sitting-room.

"When did the girl leave?" asked Grant. "And under what circumstances?"

"They left about two hours ago."

"They?" said the detective, sharply. Haslam, also, raised his head quickly at the word.

"Yes. My brother went with her."

"You did not tell me that your brother had been here."

"You did not ask. I should have told you."

"I wonder if I am to believe that?"

"You can believe it or not. I don't really mind much. I should have told you because you would probably have guessed it, in any case, and it's too late now, anyway, for you to catch them."

"That's open to opinion," grunted Grant. "But why should you object to their being caught? I have told you, your brother is safe."

"Do you really mean, Mr Grant," flashed Mary, "that you would expect me to help you bring back my brother, so that he can give evidence against the girl he loves?"

"And is going to marry?" queried Grant.

It seemed a curious, almost irrelevant question, and Haslam glanced at the detective.

"Yes—and is going to marry," answered Mary, in a low voice. "I have no illusions about my brother. He is weak, and he is foolish. More than foolish, if you will. But he is not a criminal, Mr Grant. And he has some sense of honour."

Grant's face remained inscrutable.

"It would, of course, be difficult for him to give evidence

against the girl," he said. "But his mind might be relieved by knowing that his evidence would not be the only evidence. I have no doubt I could formulate my case against the girl without him. Where have they gone?" Mary remained silent.

"You refuse to answer?"

"Yes."

Grant looked at her, then turned his gaze to the window.

"Have we any right," he asked, "to expect protection from the community to which we belong, while refusing to aid the machine that protects us?"

Haslam, keenly sensitive to the subtleties of the situation, missed the expected note of sternness in the detective's voice. He glanced at Mary, and found her appealing eyes upon him.

"Am I to say where they have gone?" she asked, tremulously.

"You must do as you like," answered Haslam. "Whatever you do, I know you will be doing for the best. And I'll wager Mr Grant will know it, too, in his heart."

"Speak for yourself," snapped Grant, as though something had burst within him.

For the first time, Haslam reflected, Grant was showing signs of wear and tear; and small wonder. Forty arduous hours, without a wink of sleep, were beginning to tell upon him.

"What has the girl done?" demanded Mary, suddenly, in the middle of her hesitation.

"I can hardly think you don't know that," replied Grant. "She has stolen a very valuable necklace. Are we to condone that offence?"

"What did my brother have to do with it?"

"He passed the necklace on to another party, without knowing what he was doing. When he knew, he tried to get the necklace back."

"Then—he was quite guiltless?"

"Of the theft, yes. I have said so."

Mary and Haslam exchanged glances. Then Mary faltered,

"He—he didn't get the necklace back, did he? I mean—he hasn't—they haven't——"

"Your brother did not get the necklace back," Grant answered. "That was left to me." He read Mary's expression, and frowned. "The fact that stolen property is recovered does not imply that society is protected from the thief."

"You're right, Mr Grant," said Mary, after a short pause. "If I expect protection, I must do my bit towards protecting, even if the way seems strange, and hurts me. But shouldn't one ever be influenced by personal reasons, detective?"

"One should not be," replied Grant, "though—sometimes— one is."

"Nearly always," corrected Haslam.

"Very well, then," exclaimed Mary, shrugging her shoulders wearily. "I'll give way—but very likely I only give way because I think my information will not make any difference in the end. When my brother came back here, he seemed very excited, and I could get very little out of him. He said they would have to get away at once. But I insisted on finding out something of their plans, and the chief thing I found out satisfied me."

"What was that?" asked Grant.

"I found out that my brother was going to deal honourably by the girl. That he was going to stick to her, as a man should."

Grant nodded. "That was good work. And what else did you find out?"

"That they were going to—am I really and truly to tell you?"

"Please," muttered Grant, and his voice shook a little. Not, Haslam thought, with impatience.

"They went to Ingate station," said Mary, flushing. "Their plan was to catch the 10.15 north-bound train."

"Would they have had time?"

"I don't think so. In that case—if they missed it—they were going by the 12.40. There are no evening expresses from Wynton."

Grant took out his watch and glanced at it.

"I shall just be able to do it," he said. "But, of course, if they caught the first train, they will be well on their journey by now. Did they tell you any more of their plans?"

"No. That was all."

"Then, in that case, Miss Holland, I'll not waste any more of your time. I am obliged to you for your information."

He turned enquiringly to Haslam, but Haslam shook his head.

"If you'll excuse me, Grant," he said, "I'll not go with you. I haven't got quite your stamina."

"As you like," nodded Grant. "I expect you're tired."

"Dead beat," answered Haslam. "But I'll see you off."

Mary interposed, with a note of disappointed anxiety in her voice.

"But you won't go just yet, will you, Mr Haslam?" she begged. "I've not been told much yet. Come back, won't you, for just a few minutes?"

"Why, of course," exclaimed Haslam. "I had intended to."

"Goodnight, Miss Holland," said Grant, now at the door. "If I have pressed you rather hard tonight, you must forgive me."

"There is nothing whatever to forgive," she returned. "Good-night, Mr Grant." '

The two men left, and went down the narrow stairs. Outside, they shook hands.

"Do you want me to go to Ingate with you, Grant?" asked Haslam, impulsively.

"No, I'd rather you didn't," replied Grant. "Your work is done. The end is in my hands."

"And the end will be a capture at Ingate station?"

"Perhaps," said the detective. "But who can say?"

He turned, and walked away. Soon, the darkness swallowed him up, but Haslam remained in the street, staring after him and pondering over his last words for several seconds after he had disappeared.

Then he turned, and re-entered the house. He climbed up the stairs, and found Mary waiting for him on the landing.

"Has he gone?" she asked.

"Yes," he nodded.

"Are you sure?"

"Why, of course. I watched him disappear up the road."

She put her finger to her lips, and led him back into the sitting room. Beyond lay her bedroom door.

"Perhaps I have been very wicked," she whispered, "but I couldn't help it—particularly after I learned that the necklace had been recovered. I deceived Mr Grant." She pointed to her bedroom. "They haven't gone to Ingate. They are in there!"

CHAPTER 42

Haslam heard Mary's confession with mixed emotions. Mingled with his pleasure that the two fugitives would now be afforded their best opportunity of shaking off the detective, was an uncomfortable sensation of guilt. The fugitives were guilty, in his opinion, of no crime greater than that of blind foolishness and weakness, but he was disturbed by a vivid vision of Grant making his way to Ingate while he, Haslam, stared passively at a bedroom door behind which were the two people Grant was seeking. Mary quickly read Haslam's thoughts, and shook her head, almost petulantly.

"The blame isn't yours," she exclaimed. "It's mine!"

"I haven't said that anyone was to blame," answered Haslam. "But, if there is any, it's ours."

"Why? I don't see it! I lied to Grant, not you."

"I'm not talking of what *has* happened, but of what *is* happening," responded Haslam. "Don't you see, dear? I didn't know before, but I know now. I could even overtake him, I dare say, and tell him he was on a fruitless journey."

She laid her hand upon his arm, as though to detain him, though he had made no movement to act upon his words.

"Don't do that, please," she whispered. "It wouldn't—it wouldn't be as kind to Mr Grant as you think."

"What do you mean?"

"I mean that I know a little more than you do. The poor girl in there has told me everything. She is Mr Grant's daughter."

"Good God!" murmured Haslam, staring at her in astonishment. "How can that be?"

"She is. She's told me. She used to help her father, but two years ago she fell in love with one of the scoundrels he was trying to track, and actually ran away with the man. He must have been a fearful bounder! After that, she got mixed up in one or two bad affairs, and then tried to break loose and earn an honest living as a domestic servant. But some of the beasts she was trying to shake off got after her again, and used her as a tool. I'm not defending her, you know. She's got a bad streak in her somewhere. All the same, I can't help feeling sorry for her—and her life is bound up with George's, now."

"Grant's daughter!" repeated Haslam. "And he had no knowledge of it?"

"How could he have? He hasn't seen her. But she has seen *him*. She saw him at the old mill that evening—do you remember?—when she suddenly ran away from you. She believed, then, that the whole thing was a trap, and that you were a party to it."

"Naturally," murmured Haslam. "She would have thought that. I would have, in her place." Suddenly he straightened himself, and walked towards the door.

"What are you going to do?" she demanded.

"Don't worry. I'm on your side—as I always have been, Mary, from the start." She flushed, but he did not retract. "But I'm on Grant's side, too. Even against his own conception of duty, I am going to act for him, and prevent him from arresting his own child."

"Oh, I'm so glad you feel that way about it!" exclaimed Mary. "Surely we wouldn't be human if we felt any other way!"

"You're right," Haslam smiled. "Grant spends his whole life trying to protect other people. We'll turn the tables on him, and protect *him*. And we must act quickly, for they'll need all the time they can get."

He opened the door a little, and called through.

"Come out, both of you," he said. "The coast is clear. Make the most of it."

The frightened couple appeared almost immediately. As Haslam looked at them, reading the fear and the strain in their eyes, they seemed to him like two helpless children who had been caught by one of life's relentless tides and had been overcome by it. A wave of pity passed through him. Life is a poor matter if one has not schooled oneself to swim through its cross-currents.

The boy had hold of the girl's hand. He did not let it go, but gripped it tightly as he stared round the room, and then addressed Haslam. A faint smile, half of shame and half of recognition, was on his face as he spoke.

"I don't quite understand all that's happened," he said, huskily, "but it seems I've got to thank you——"

"We'll leave the thanks for our next and happier meeting," interposed Haslam, hastily. Time was short, and sentiment was dangerous. "You know the necklace has been recovered?"

"No! Has it?" cried the boy, and a great relief glowed in his eyes.

Haslam nodded. "And I've further good news for you. Neither Birkett nor Bowling will trouble you any more. Grant has accounted for both of them, and is himself the only person you now have to fear. At the present moment, however, he thinks you've gone north, so if you go south you'll get a good start."

"We'll go at once," muttered the boy. "Come along, Florence. We mustn't lose a moment."

But the girl, crying softly to herself, hung back.

"Do you know now who I am?" she asked, turning to Haslam.

"Yes. Miss Holland told me."

"What do you think I ought to do? Give myself up—to my father?"

"The least you can do for him," retorted Haslam, "is to spare him that!"

He patted her shoulder, and, saying that he would see all was clear, left the room and descended the stairs. In two minutes, George Holland and Florence Grant joined him, and he let them out.

"Mr Grant turned to the right, and you therefore turn to the left," he advised. "No—don't tell me where you propose going.

The less we know of your whereabouts during the next few days, the better. It will be easier than to answer questions." Suddenly, he fished in his pocket, and brought out some notes. "Add these to your little pile," he said. "You'll probably need them."

"I oughtn't to take them," muttered the boy, "but you know why I'm doing it." And he glanced towards his pale companion.

"Yes, I know, old chap," replied Haslam. "They make us do all sorts of rum things, don't they?"

"But why are *you* helping us?" asked the boy. "How do you come into it all?"

"Oh, my case is very similar to yours," answered Haslam. "If your sister wanted me to steal the crown of England for the Emperor of Japan, I believe I'd do it!"

George Holland's hand shot out and gripped his. "I say, Mr Haslam! Do you mean—are you going to look after my sister?"

"That's just what I do mean," nodded Haslam. "And I'm going up right now to tell her so!"

This time, he did not find Mary waiting for him on the landing. Reaction had set in, and she was sitting limply in an armchair in the sitting room.

"You poor child!" he murmured, crossing to her quickly. "You've been through a terrible strain!"

"It has been rather stiff," she answered. "But I oughtn't to crack up like this. I feel as weak as a kitten."

"Then I order you back to bed immediately!"

"That's impossible. You see, I haven't been to bed once, yet. This dressing-gown is only camouflage. I had to *pretend* I'd been to bed, didn't I, to deceive Mr Grant?"

Haslam laughed. His own reaction took the form of an almost exaggerated gaiety. He realised its incongruity, yet could not stem it.

"You seem pretty well up in art of deception," he remarked. "The very first time I met you, you deceived me about your pictures, and told me they were bad."

"So they were!"

"Nonsense! And then you told me all sorts of other queer stories, every time I met you, until at last, in sheer self-defence, I had to come over to your side and learn the truth."

"Was that why you came over to my side?" she asked.

"Of course, it was. Strangers may lie to us, but we must have the truth from those we are in love with."

"Don't, please!" she murmured.

"But I do please!" he retorted. "I promised your brother that I would always look after you, and I'm going to!"

The next moment, she found herself in his arms.

"You see, Mary!" he cried. "You can't deceive me any more. I know that you love me, as I love you!"

"I don't love you," she sobbed. "But I'm just too tired and happy to resist."

*

Haslam walked through the night like a man in a trance. It was many hours since he had left Mary Holland, but he could still feel the warmth of her smile and hear the wonder of her voice. Perhaps there was not more warmth in her smile or wonder in her voice than are to be found in thousands of other smiles and voices, but love weaves its eternal illusions, and life demands that it shall.

The dark lanes through which Haslam walked were no longer sinister. They were generous and kindly, and whispered the most magical nonsense. He passed, with a cheery "Goodnight," a disreputable old tramp whom, a few hours earlier, he would have regarded with the utmost suspicion. Thus, what we are to others is frequently not what we are to ourselves, but what they make of us out of their own joy or sorrow.

Haslam kept on walking because he could not face the confinement of a room. He wanted movement, and space. He wanted darkness, too, for in that medium he could paint his pictures undisturbed. But presently the darkness began to fail him. A faint light filtered through it, and, from a low tree he was walking by, a sleepy chirp sounded.

Then Haslam gradually woke out of his dream. He became conscious of a terrific fatigue. "I must be getting back," he thought; and discovered that his feet, unconsciously guided, had already brought him to within a hundred yards of the gate.

He heard steps behind him. Again, he did not start and turn. The next moment, he found Grant walking by his side.

"Hello, Grant," he said, dully. "What happened?"

Grant did not reply. Haslam glanced at him suddenly, and noted that the detective's features were tired and drawn.

"You look about done up, old chap," said Haslam.

"Yes—I'm tired," answered Grant.

They walked a few paces in silence. It occurred to Haslam that Grant had not answered his question, and a queer thought flitted into his mind. Grant had fallen easily into Mary's little trap. Had he, perhaps, mistrusted them after all, and been a hidden witness of all that followed his assumed departure. And had he, in this case, found himself beaten by the occasion and unable, even in the cause of justice, to bring his own daughter to shame—the shame of imprisonment and all the sordid business it entailed?

That might account for the detective's haggard look. Perhaps, like Haslam, Grant had been striding through the night, living with some overwhelming emotion. . . .

Suddenly Haslam slipped his arm into that of his companion, and together, in silence, they turned in at the gate, while the light of the east, with its strange message of hope, began to flood the sky.

J. JEFFERSON FARJEON'S CRIME NOVELS & SELECTED OTHER WORKS

1. *The Master Criminal* (London, Brentano's, 1924). Spitfire Publishing Ltd, 2020.
2. *The Confusing Friendship* (London, Brentano's, 1924).
3. *Little Things That Happen* (London, Methuen, 1925).
4. *Uninvited Guests* (London, Brentano's, 1925). Spitfire Publishing Ltd, 2021.
5. *Number 17* (London, Hodder and Stoughton, 1926. A 'Ben the Tramp' Mystery).
6. *At the Green Dragon* (London, Harrap, 1926. US title: *The Green Dragon*).
7. *The Crook's Shadow* (London, Harrap, 1927).
8. *More Little Happenings* (London, Methuen, 1928).
9. *The House of Disappearance* (New York, A.L. Burt, 1928).
10. *Underground* (New York, A.L. Burt, 1928. Alternative title: *Mystery Underground*, 1932).
11. *Shadows by the Sea* (London, Harrap, 1928).
12. *The Appointed Date* (New York, A.L. Burt, 1929).
13. *The 5.18 Mystery* (London, Collins, 1929).
14. *The Person Called 'Z'* (London, Collins, 1929).
15. *Following Footsteps* (New York, Lincoln MacVeigh 1930).
16. *The Mystery on the Moor* (London, Collins, 1930).

17. *The House Opposite* (London, Collins, 1931. A 'Ben the Tramp' Mystery).

18. *Murderer's Trail* (London, Collins, 1931. US title: *Phantom Fingers*. A 'Ben the Tramp' Mystery).

19. *The 'Z' Murders* (London, Collins, 1932).

20. *Trunk Call* (London, Collins, 1932. US title: *The Trunk Call Mystery*).

21. *Ben Sees It Through* (London, Collins, 1932. A 'Ben the Tramp' Mystery).

22. *Sometimes Life's Funny* (London, Collins, 1933).

23. *The Mystery of the Creek* (London, Collins, 1933. US title: *The House on the Marsh*).

24. *Dead Man's Heath* (London, Collins, 1933. US title: *The Mystery of Dead Man's Heath*).

25. *Old Man Mystery* (London, Collins, 1933).

26. *Fancy Dress Ball* (London, Collins, 1934. US title: *Death in Fancy Dress*).

27. *The Windmill Mystery* (London, Collins, 1934).

28. *Sinister Inn* (London, Collins, 1934).

29. *The Golden Singer* (London, Wright & Brown, 1935).

30. *His Lady Secretary* (London, Wright & Brown, 1935).

31. *Mountain Mystery* (London, Collins, 1935).

32. *Little God Ben* (London, Collins, 1935. A 'Ben the Tramp' Mystery).

33. *Holiday Express* (London, Collins, 1935).

34. *The Adventure of Edward: A Light-Hearted Romance* (London, Wright & Brown, 1936).

35. *Thirteen Guests* (London, Collins, 1936).

35. *Detective Ben* (London, Collins, 1936. A 'Ben the Tramp' Mystery).

37. *Dangerous Beauty* (London, Collins, 1936).

38. *Yellow Devil* (London, Collins, 1937).

39. *Holiday at Half Mast* (London, Collins, 1937).

40. *Mystery in White* (London, Collins, 1937).

41. *The Compleat Smuggler* (London, George G. Harrap and Co

1938).

42. *Dark Lady* (London, Collins, 1938).

43. *End of An Author* (London, Collins, 1938. US title: *Death in the Inkwell*, 1942).

44. *Seven Dead* (London, Collins, 1939).

45. *Exit John Horton* (London, Collins, 1939. US title: *Friday the 13th*, 1942).

46. *Facing Death: Tales Told on a Sinking Raft* (London, Quality Press, 1940).

47. *Aunt Sunday Sees It Through* (London, Collins, 1940. US title: *Aunt Sunday Takes Command*).

48. *Room Number Six* (London, Collins, 1941).

49. *The Third Victim* (London, Collins, 1941).

50. *The Judge Sums Up* (London, Collins, 1942).

51. *Murder at a Police Station* (London, Hale, 1943, under the pseudonym Anthony Swift).

52. *The House of Shadows* (London, Collins, 1943).

53. *Waiting for the Police and Other Short Stories* (London, Todd Publishing Co, 1943, a short story collection).

54. *Greenmask* (London, Collins, 1944).

55. *Black Castle* (London, Collins, 1944).

56. *November the Ninth at Kersea* (London, Hale, 1944, under the pseudonym Anthony Swift).

57. *Rona Runs Away* (London, Macdonald, 1945).

58. *Interrupted Honeymoon* (London, Hale, 1945, under the pseudonym Anthony Swift).

59. *The Oval Table* (London, Collins, 1946).

60. *Peril in the Pyrenees* (London, Collins, 1946).

61. *The Invisible Companion and Other Stories* (London, Polybooks, 1946, a short story collection).

62. *Midnight Adventure and Other Stories* (London, Polybooks, 1946, a short story collection).

63. *The Works of Smith Minor* (London, Jonathan Cape, 1947).

64. *Back to Victoria* (London, Macdonald, 1947).

65. *Benelogues* (no publishing information 1948).

66. *The Llewellyn Jewel Mystery* (London, Collins, 1948).

67. *Death of a World* (London, Collins, 1948).

68. *The Adventure at Eighty* (London, Macdonald, 1948).

69. *Prelude to Crime* (London, Collins, 1948).

70. *The Lone House Mystery* (London, Collins, 1949).

71. *The Impossible Guest* (London, Macdonald & Co, 1949).

72. *The Shadow of Thirteen* (London, Collins, 1949).

73. *The Disappearances of Uncle David* (London, Collins, 1949).

74. *Change with Me* (London, Macdonald & Co, 1950).

75. *Mother Goes Gay* (London, Macdonald, 1950).

76. *Cause Unknown* (London, Collins, 1950).

77. *Mystery on Wheels* (London, publisher not known 1951).

78. *The House Over the Tunnel* (London, Collins, 1951).

79. *Adventure for Nine* (London, Macdonald & Co, 1951).

80. *Ben on the Job* (London, Collins, 1952. A 'Ben the Tramp' Mystery).

81. *Number Nineteen* (London, Collins, 1952. A 'Ben the Tramp' Mystery).

82. *The Double Crime* (London, Collins, 1953).

83. *The Mystery of the Map* (London, Collins, 1953).

84. *Money Walks* (London, Macdonald, 1953).

85. *Castle of Fear* (London, Collins, 1954).

86. *Bob Hits the Headlines* (London, Bodley Head, 1954).

87. *The Caravan Adventure* (London, Macdonald 1955).

Serialised Short Fiction

Between June 1925 and April 1929 Farjeon's fictional reformed criminal turned private detective *Detective X Crook* appeared in over fifty issues of *Flynn's Weekly* one of the most popular, and longest running, of all the detective pulp magazines.

Plays

1. *Number 17* (1925).

2. *After Dark* (1926).

3. *Enchantment* (1927).

4. *Philomel* (1932).

Made in the USA
Las Vegas, NV
02 April 2024

88129166R00173